Miles Gibson

grew up in Christchurch, Dorset. He was educated at Somerford Junior School and Somerford Secondary Modern (now the Grange) where he failed to make an impression but finished a toast rack in woodwork.

When he left school he wanted to be a painter but joined a Bournemouth advertising agency on the advice of the careers' master who thought advertising was 'something artistic'.

He trained to be an art director by making tea and running errands until he entered a writing competition for university undergraduates organised by a large London agency. They seemed impressed by his qualifications – toast rack first class with honours – and a few months later he was offered a job as a junior copywriter at J Walter Thompson in Berkeley Square.

When he won a *Telegraph Magazine* Young Writer of the Year Award in 1969 he turned his attention to serious writing. For a time he wrote features for the *Telegraph Sunday Magazine*. His first novel *The Sandman* was published in 1984 and since that time he's written a small shelf of books, including works for children. His novel *Kingdom Swann* was adapted for BBC Television as *Gentlemen's Relish* starring Billy Connolly and Sarah Lancashire and first broadcast in 2001.

Miles Gibson is married and lives in London.

First Published in Great Britain in 2002 by
The Do-Not Press Limited
16 The Woodlands
London SE13 6TY
www.thedonotpress.co.uk
email: mr@thedonotpress.co.uk

Casebound edition: ISBN 1 899 344 89 6
C-format paperback: ISBN 1 899344 90 X

British Library Cataloguing in Publication Data. A catalogue
record for this book is available from the British Library.

1 3 5 7 9 10 8 6 4 2

Printed and bound in Great Britain by
The Guernsey Press Co Ltd.

MR ROMANCE

by

Miles Gibson

THE DO-NOT PRESS

For Geoff & Diane
Thanks for the Brooklyn Bridge

*Also by Miles Gibson
published by The Do-Not Press*

The Sandman
Dancing With Mermaids
Vinegar Soup
Kingdon Swann

'You must not mind me, madam; I
but I mean no harr
Dr Johnson

1

IT WAS LATE when he came to the house. He came with an east wind that threatened the city with bone-cracking frosts and constant rumours of snow. All day the wind had battered the windows, lifted curtains, squirted through keyholes and made the carpets levitate. At dusk the storm seemed to hesitate, inflated the shadows it found in the street and wrapped its fury in darkness.

My mother had fallen asleep in front of the television in the back parlour where she'd settled herself for the world wrestling tag-team championships. Father was locked in the cellar. I was at work in the kitchen, sitting at the table, molesting a pair of Janet's shoes. I don't remember how I first persuaded Janet to let me loose in her wardrobe, but once the custom had been established it became a weekly ritual to carry her hoard of shoes to the kitchen for an ardent evening of wax and polish.

The collection assembled for my admiration on that particular occasion contained: one pair simple black court shoes; one pair jaunty red lace-ups with rolling tongues; one pair white sling-back sandals with spiky, scuffed high heels; one pair charcoal grey stilettos; and one pair dainty suede ankle boots that, with a measure of gentle persuasion, would accept my hand as far as the wrist. This little harem of shoes could make me feel absurdly elated. I felt aroused in the knowledge of their possession, debauched by my fumbling and fondling.

I was working on one of the grey stilettos, sitting in my chair with a newspaper spread on the table to catch the tiny, oily crumbs from the sweetly scented cakes of Cherry Blossom in their flat, old-fashioned tins. I had recently inserted three fingers into the soft, leather throat of the shoe until my fingertips were nesting where her toes had left their faint but indelible impression, and had already dipped my brush in the polish when the doorbell rang. Damn! I raised the brush to the shoe and listened, waiting for someone to answer the bell. Nothing happened. I tried to ignore the intrusion, working polish into the leather. Cradle the shoe and know the woman. The weight of her body has balanced it. Her movements have stretched and fashioned it.

The bell rang again. I withdrew my fingers, set down the brush and hurried impatiently from the kitchen to unlock the heavy front door, rattle the chains and wrench at the bolt.

The stranger stepped from the shelter of the rocking privet hedge and stood blinking beneath the hall light. He was short and very pale, with a heavy, lugubrious face and a slick of grizzled hair. He wore a baggy black suit beneath his overcoat and sported a pair of cracked brown brogues.

'Marvel,' he said solemnly. He looked at me suspiciously, sniffed at the air and set down his luggage on the carpet. He was carrying a cardboard suitcase secured with a strap and a small wooden box that clattered slightly as it touched the floor.

'Can I help?' I asked, when it grew painfully obvious that he meant no further introduction.

He blinked and leaned forward, glancing from side to side as if he feared we were being observed. 'I've heard you have a room,' he said in a voice so faint that I had to strain to hear him.

'Who told you?' I whispered in return.

The stranger smiled, pressed a finger to the side of his nose and winked at me with a jaundiced eye. 'Is it true?'

I nodded. I was eighteen years old, fresh from school, and dressed to play the part of housekeeper in a long green apron with a pair of Marigolds in the pocket. We had several rooms to rent – it was a big house and we needed the money. Janet had taken a bright, sunlit room on the first floor with a little balcony to its window. Senior Franklin had a pair of rooms beneath the rafters where he cultivated his genius and scowled upon an ungrateful world from narrow windows secured with rusting iron bars. My parents slept at the back of the house and I slept above the kitchen in a room with a view of the grey backyard. And still the house seemed empty, its heavy walls and the massive floorboards absorbed our voices and muffled our footsteps, making us feel like a party of ghosts.

'I think we might have a room.'

'Is it overlooked?' the stranger inquired, frowning at me as if I intended to trap him in some diabolical snare.

'No,' I said. 'It's at the back of the house.'

'Empty?'

'Yes.'

'Warm?'

'Yes.'

He seemed reassured and settled a little deeper into the folds of his overcoat. 'Perhaps I might take a look at it,' he ventured, stooping to lift the wooden box and nursing it in his arms.

I couldn't think of a reason to stop him. I grasped the big cardboard suitcase and struggled to pull it up two flights of stairs. The room was at the end of a corridor containing nothing but a chest of drawers.

'Is this it?' He frowned at the door and looked disappointed as if he had fully expected to find a gate of beaten bronze.

'Yes.'

He took a step back as I opened the door and switched on the light. A yellow room with a green carpet. A huge eiderdown covered a narrow brass bed. There were patchwork cushions in the lap of an old armchair and plastic flowers in a vase on the table. It was modest but clean and comfortable.

The stranger leaned forward and stared about him. He looked astonished. His fat mouth trembled and his eyes filled with tears. He snuffled and sobbed and wiped his nose in his hand.

'Is it suitable?' I inquired anxiously, setting his suitcase on the carpet. His tears alarmed me.

He wagged his head and tried to speak but the tears choked him. He seemed so upset, so pathetically grateful, that I shrank back for fear that he might embrace me; and in that moment, without warning, he sprang forward as quick as a cat, and with a short kick from a cracked brown brogue, he slammed the door shut in my face!

I stood in the corridor, stunned by the violence, shocked into silence, and heard him turn the key in the lock. My scalp prickled with horror. There was something wrong. I could sense it. He might be a gangster or child molester, serial killer or human bomb. He might have a suitcase packed with cocaine or a cargo of contraband bibles. Anything. Tiger bones. An inflatable woman. The fingers and toes of his murder victims. And now he was locked in the room and I didn't know how to evict him. He might have been searching for just such a room in which to kill himself. He might have been walking the streets for days in search of this room. A quiet room at the back of a house that couldn't be overlooked. It was perfect for murder or suicide.

I retreated downstairs in time to meet father stumbling from the cellar. He groped his way along the passage towards the kitchen, clipped the doorframe, gasped in pain and surprise, spun on his heel and fell against the wall, clutching his shoulder. He was still wearing the spectacles he'd designed for the more intricate aspects of watchmaking. He had turned the cellar into a workshop and the spectacles, two magnifying lenses screwed into the frames of some old sunglasses my mother had once tried to throw away, were his first triumph at the workbench. They made him look like a startled loris.

'Did I hear the doorbell?' he asked cheerfully, wrenching the spectacles from his ears and nursing his injured shoulder.

'A visitor,' I said carelessly.

My father frowned. 'It's too late for visitors.' He was firmly of the opinion that evil stalked after sunset. He rarely answered the door and might even ignore the telephone during the hours of darkness.

'He was looking for a room.'

'What did your mother make of him?'

'She didn't see him.'

'Well, if he wants a room he can come back in the morning,' father snorted and turned towards the back parlour.

'He's already in China,' I said unhappily. My mother had insisted on giving each room a name after reading in *Homes & Gardens* that every great country house contained a Chinese Smoking Room or William Morris Library. These grand titles would make reference to some priceless collection of antique furniture or the ancient Oriental wallpaper that clung in fragments to the walls. We lived in an ugly brick house filled with the kind of furniture you find discarded on street corners. But mother was not to be discouraged. Janet was in Mexico in memory of a large potted cactus that had failed to survive on the balcony; Franklin was in Lilliput because, as he often declared, he was nothing short of a literary giant; and Marvel was now in China because of the label on the eiderdown.

Father looked concerned. He raked at his hair and hurried me into the kitchen. 'Is he all right? Did you notice anything queer about him?'

'He seemed normal,' I said innocently. It's true that he

looked like an unfrocked priest, he was shabby and fat and weeping so much that he couldn't speak; but if you ignored these details, he was perfectly fit and healthy.

'Did you discuss the rent?'

'What?

'The rent!

'No.'

'A month in advance!' father snapped impatiently. 'You know it's a month in advance!'

'There wasn't time…' I complained. I sat down and looked at the jumble of shoes on the table, but even they could offer no comfort.

'It's simple enough! You big, wet pudding!'

'He took me by surprise.'

'How did he do that? Pull silk ribbons out of his nose?'

'No. He locked himself in the room,' I said miserably.

'What?'

'He managed to lock himself in the room.'

Father stared at me for a moment or two, reluctant to believe that his only son could be so stupid. 'We'll have to sort this out,' he grumbled, and searched about him for a weapon.

'Perhaps we should talk to him in the morning,' I suggested hopelessly. A miracle might happen. If we left him overnight he might have vanished by daybreak, leaving nothing in the room but a cold white fog or the mark of Satan scorched in the carpet.

'No time!' father shouted, seizing a potato peeler from the cutlery drawer. 'It might be too late in the morning. We'll have it out with him tonight!'

I tried to reason with him but he wouldn't listen. He took the staircase in long, leaping strides, stormed along the corridor and banged on the door with his fist.

There was a startled yelp from within the room. 'Who is it?' barked the occupant.

'Wandsworth!' father shouted. 'Henry Wandsworth. You're in my house.'

There was silence.

I stood behind father and waited for the sound of exploding glass – I was quite convinced that the fat intruder would vault through the window to make his escape. We would force the lock on the door to find animal bones on the floor, a half-inflated rubber woman beckoning from the bed.

And then, to my disappointment, the door opened and the stranger appeared. He beamed and stretched out a hand to my father.

'Marvel,' he boomed. 'It's a pleasure to make your acquaintance, sir.'

We shuffled into the room and stared around. He'd already unpacked his suitcase and made himself comfortable. His overcoat had been stowed in the wardrobe and his shoes were empty beside the armchair. I looked at his feet. He was wearing a pair of red felt slippers.

'It's a privilege to be offered such charming and spacious accommodation,' he continued, slapping the bed so hard that it made the springs of the mattress sing.

'It's not bad,' father agreed, glancing about him as if he were looking at it for the first time. He had recently painted this room and I knew he was proud of the work.

His great grandfather, William Wandsworth the Chemist, had built the house. William had made a fortune from popular patent medicines and this toppling conceit of brick and stained glass served as his monument. The fortune had been squandered but the house remained. My father had inherited the impossible task of trying to keep it from falling down. He seemed to spend most of his life nailing down woodwork, tacking canvas over broken windows and scrambling among the chimney pots, repairing roof tiles and leaking gutters.

'Is this your boy?'

My father turned and stared at me as if he'd forgotten my existence. 'My son!' he exclaimed. 'The Skipper.'

I smiled weakly and stared at the floor. Skipper was the only name I'd been prepared to accept as a child. My real name was such an embarrassment that my mother alone dared use it and only then in moments of anger or great frustration. It's no fun being named after a 300 pound German wrestler. I was lean and fast, like my father, and Skipper suited me.

'He's a fine young man!' Marvel declared.

Father was flummoxed. I knew from the tilt of his chin and the way the potato peeler had been planted like a fountain pen in his shirt pocket, that he'd been prepared for a scuffle. And here he found nothing but a charming old man in a pair of carpet slippers. He loitered, shifting his weight from foot to foot, and looked distinctly flustered.

'It's a cold night,' Marvel said, trying to make conversation.

'Is it?' father said. He sounded surprised.

'Bitter,' Marvel said mournfully.

'Have you come far?' father asked, glancing at the suitcase in a corner. I saw that his precious wooden box had been pushed a little way under the bed, as if he were trying to hide it from view.

'Across town,' Marvel said, waving towards the window as the wind rattled and pulled at the frame.

Father smiled and tried again. 'How did you find us?'

'Word of mouth.'

Father nodded as he tried to think of another question. 'So tell me, what's your line of business?' he asked at last, fiddling with the folds of the curtains.

The stranger shot me a wild glance and his face turned deathly pale. 'This and that,' he said anxiously. 'I'm engaged in this and that.'

'I hope it's a living,' father grinned.

'I find myself in receipt of a modest consideration…'

'Is it regular?'

'Regular as clockwork,' he said and then, catching the drift of the conversation, he grunted, rummaged for his wallet and offered to pay for the room.

For a moment father looked ashamed but with a little encouragement he settled the business – a month in advance – and the money changed hands without complaint.

We wished Mr Marvel goodnight and crept downstairs feeling foolish.

'We'll tell your mother in the morning,' father declared, folding the bank notes into his pocket.

2

'HE'S AN ANIMAL!' mother said as we cleared the breakfast table. She clattered the cutlery on the tray and shook her head in disgust.

The Buffalo Brothers had lost their world championship tag-team belts to the combined forces of Abdullah the Turk and Boris the Butcher. It had been a bad night in the squared circle. Abdullah and Boris, fighting as the Desert Assassins, were brawlers, plain and simple. Abdullah was a sadist with a waxed moustache who liked to gouge and bite his opponents. His partner, Boris, was a swamp creature. He stood nearly seven feet tall, weighed 400 pounds on an empty stomach and always made his entrance wearing a black leather mask. Mother loathed him.

Rick and Randy Buffalo were excellent ring technicians and Randy, the younger brother, was strong enough to knock down a horse. But they were clean, tactical fighters and no match for the masters of mayhem. Mother described the final moments of the fight. Abdullah had tossed Randy from the ring, followed him down and battered him senseless with a metal chair. In the confusion Boris caught Rick – preparing to launch himself from the top turnbuckle for a flying drop kick – by blinding him with a pepper spray, brought him back to the canvas with a punishing belly-to-belly suplex and snatched the pinfall. One. Two. Three. It was terrible. A disaster.

'That's not wrestling!' mother grumbled. 'It's a mockery!' She searched the pockets of her cardigan for a short length of lavender lavatory paper and used it to pull on her nose. She was small and dark and as bright as a jackdaw. When she worked in the house she always wore the same faded summer frock printed with bundles of old-fashioned roses and any number of cardigans, depending upon the weather.

'Who was the legal man?'

'Randy was legal,' she said, as if it were obvious. 'He couldn't tag Rick while the Turk was whacking him with a chair. He was on the floor with his brains coming out through his ears.'

'Well, it should have been a count out,' I said, after weighing all the evidence.

'That's right!' mother said, triumphantly. 'Exactly. And that wouldn't lose you the belt. Everyone knows that!'

'Who was the referee?'

'Rhino Black.'

'Well, he's so stupid they have to help him tie his own shoelaces,' I said scornfully.

She shrugged. We held the same low opinion of ring officials. It was her sincere belief that the principal requirements for a referee were (1) the possession of a bow tie and (2) the total inability to grasp the fundamental rules of the sport. Any medical condition, such as fleeting blindness, random deafness or memory loss, might be considered an

advantage. A referee should be slow moving, easily distracted and given to fainting at critical moments. Randy
and the Turk had been the legal fighters and the match
should have ended with a simple count out. A true championship match can only be won on a pinfall or submission.
The Buffalo Brothers had been robbed of their belts but
remained the champions.

I brushed crumbs from the tablecloth, picked up the
tray and followed my mother into the kitchen. It was my
favourite time of day. The house was warm and still sweet
with the fragrant smoke of breakfast. There was sunlight
at the windows and music on the radio.

Father had disappeared on some urgent errand, hunting
down cabbages, meat or potatoes, and might be gone for
the rest of the morning, returning with his pockets full of
peanuts or a turkey under his arm. He never seemed to
come home with anything on the shopping lists that
mother patiently printed for him on little scraps of paper.

Janet, fortified with nothing more than a bowl of
Shreddies and a cup of strong coffee, had already gone to
work at the big department store where she stood at a glass
counter in a hall of mirrors, surrounded by lotions and
costly perfumes. She was wearing the burnished grey stilettos.

Senior Franklin, having finished two fried eggs, several
rashers and a string of sausages, had retired to the front
parlour to shout at the newspapers. He always took *The
Trumpet, The Rumour* and *Charger*, disembowelling them
in search of the arts pages, which he studied with fantastic
indignation.

Mother, despite her complaints about Boris the Butcher, remained in a buoyant mood, for she knew that justice would be done at some future tournament. The Buffalo Brothers would have their revenge. The Desert Assassins would be defeated. Wrestling is a beautiful sport. Skill and judgement, strength and cunning, count for nothing when set against the higher purposes of the game. There is destiny to be served. Poetic justice to be considered. Plot, structure and happy endings. The laws of wrestling demand that the big, bad and downright ugly shall bully and humiliate the weak until vanquished by the great and the good. Here, in the wrestling ring, order and truth are constantly threatened, attacked, overwhelmed and restored again. Mother understood these things and took comfort in them. She seemed content. She'd even received the news of Marvel occupying China with unlikely good humour.

'Why didn't he come down for breakfast?' she said, squelching across the kitchen floor. Her legs were planted in a pair of pneumatic Reeboks, making her feet look enormous.

'I didn't tell him,' I said. 'We didn't discuss the arrangements.'

'Shame! The poor man must be hungry. Make him a tray.'

'Perhaps he's asleep,' I said hopefully. 'It was late when he arrived. It seems a pity to disturb him.'

'Don't disturb him. Take him a tray,' mother said. 'He'll want to have breakfast in bed.'

'It's too late,' I argued, looking around at the smoking

wreckage. A blue haze of bacon fat hung in the air. There was coffee still boiling, as black as charcoal, on the top of the shimmering stove. Mother's cooking caused a lot of damage.

'I'm sure we can find him something,' she insisted, beginning to search the leftovers for something to salvage.

I donated a sausage from my own remains, gave it a rinse and rolled it dry in a paper towel. Mother provided a couple of bacon rashers and recovered a fried egg with a crispy brown lace petticoat found floating in the frying pan. We took a sliced tomato sprinkled with pepper, a wedge of fried potato, a grilled mushroom, and arranged these oddments on a clean plate with a pile of cold, buttered toast.

'And don't forget to ask him if he wants coffee!' she shouted as I staggered towards the stairs. 'But don't mention fruit juice – the orange is green and the grapefruit smells like lavatory cleaner.'

I crept along the corridor and nervously tapped on the door to his room.

'Who is it?' he cried out, in a voice still blurred with sleep.

'Skipper!' I shouted back at him.

I heard him creak across the floor and turn the key in the lock. He appeared in a pair of striped cotton pyjamas, buttoned to the throat, with a big blue handkerchief in the pocket. The hair stood from his scalp like feathers and his eyes seemed to bulge from their sockets.

'We thought you might like to try some breakfast,' I said, smiling, stretching out my arms to offer him the tray.

Marvel flinched as if he'd been punched in the jaw and made a strange gurgling noise in his throat. He stared down at the breakfast tray, plucked the handkerchief from his pocket and stuffed it against his nose and mouth.

'No!' he croaked feebly, wagging his head. 'No!' He staggered and clutched his stomach. He whimpered. He moaned. He toppled back into the room and the door slammed shut in my face.

I was mortified. It was the second time that he'd taken fright at the sight of me. The man was a lunatic. He was probably dangerous. I trudged downstairs to confront my mother.

'What happened?'

'He doesn't want anything!' I said, banging down the tray on the table.

'What's wrong with it?' she demanded, sniffing the plate and prodding the egg with a finger.

'I don't know. He went crazy as soon as he saw the tray. You'd have thought we were trying to poison him...'

She frowned and pulled on her apron strings.

'Where are you going?'

'I'm going upstairs to talk to him,' she said, casting the apron over the back of a chair. She pulled at her dress and closed the cardigan over her bosom as if it were battle armour.

'I think we should wait until he calms down...'

'Nonsense!' she said and disappeared.

She was gone for some time. I tried to listen out for her safety but all I could hear was Senior Franklin, honking and hissing to himself in the front parlour as he mauled the morning papers.

I ran hot water and filled the kitchen with steam. The windows turned white. The walls broke into a sweat. I had already scalded the cutlery and scoured the frying pan before mother came squelching downstairs.

'What happened?' I asked anxiously.

It was very peculiar. She wouldn't look me in the eye but made a little performance of fiddling with her hair, stroking it with her fingers and tucking loose strands behind her ears. 'He's such a gentleman!' she chuckled and blushed.

I was scandalised! The devil had charmed her like an old fox flirting with a corn-fed hen. Oh, but he was devious! 'Didn't you think he was...'

'What?'

'Queer!' I shouted, plunging both fists in the water and sloshing soapsuds over my sleeves.

'What sort of queer?'

'Strange!' I raged indignantly. Deranged. Demented. Mad as a mooncalf. Mother frowned and clucked at me in disapproval. 'He doesn't eat breakfast. That's not strange. He says he has a weak stomach.'

'So why didn't he tell me?'

'You probably didn't wait to listen,' she said, with a toss of her head. 'You're always so impatient.'

I watched her pull a delicate china teapot from the cupboard and blow dust from its spout. 'What are you doing?' I said.

'He says he quite fancies a small pot of tea.'

So there was an end to the affair. Mother had taken a fancy to the mysterious Mr Marvel and that had raised him above suspicion. Nothing I said was going to change her opinion. It was time to stifle my instincts.

I finished washing the dishes and set to work in the front parlour. Wandsworth the Chemist had built this room to impress his guests and although it wasn't especially large, it was very ornate with a high, decorated ceiling and a wealth of stained glass to the windows. The stained glass took the form of an extravagant advertisement for his infamous gland tonic, depicting men transformed into gods and gambolling with fairies. The fairies were, frankly, voluptuous and gazed down from their private paradise into a room littered with balding armchairs, a small table and a sagging sofa. Senior Franklin was sprawled in the sofa, surrounded by shredded newsprint. He clutched a scrap of paper in a brittle hand, which he waved like a flag to greet me.

'Come, my callow catamite,' he honked, 'and allow me to squander my light upon your Cimmerian darkness.' He spoke his own form of baboo English and rarely made himself understood. But he seemed to think it most amusing, threw back his head and laughed. He had teeth like an undertaker's horse.

I walked among the armchairs, slapping cushions into shape and hoping to avoid becoming entangled in conversation.

'We are told that Katie Pphart has dropped another brick into the bottomless well of exoteric literature,' he announced, wagging the scrap of paper between his finger and thumb.

I tried to assume an expression of mild surprise and interest, enough to satisfy him that I was listening, without suggesting that I cared to know more. It didn't work.

'It's called *The Cornflower Chronicle*,' Franklin continued. He held the torn paper at arm's length and squinted as he struggled to read it. He was a young man but did his best to look like an elder statesman. He was tall and gaunt and favoured old tweed jackets and hairy waistcoats with green brass buttons.

"*Satin-shouldered Harriet Harper has recently moved to the old manor house,*" he bellowed at me, "*where her employer, fresh-faced Hugo Hudson, the notorious collector of priceless Chinese porcelain, and Laurel, his crippled but strangely seductive half-sister, trick her into an evening of ritual abuse with Buttocks the butcher. A powerful tale of one woman's journey of self-discovery!*"

I began to circle the sofa, collecting newspapers from the floor and folding them into a parcel. I knew that Katie Pphart was Janet's favourite novelist and Franklin enjoyed making mischief. He despised the work of Katie Pphart. She produced an endless stream of romantic blockbusters with embossed and bejewelled covers. Her last great success, *The Sultan's Embrace*, had been Janet's bedside companion for months.

'Well, should we toss our scented bouquets or shall we lapidate the lamia?' he demanded. 'What sayeth thou, my sallow saveloy?'

'I suppose it's a romance,' I said simply, hoping that this observation was a suitable reply to his question. I nursed the bundle of wastepaper and waited for my chance to escape. The ink had turned my fingers black.

'It's ridiculous!' Franklin honked.

I shrugged. 'Romance is always ridiculous,' I said. 'Think of Shelley and Byron and Keats.'

'Sycophants and sodomites!' he shouted. 'Pedlars of high-pitched doggerel. Half-grown men who took their revenge by chewing the necks of mincing matrons in middle-class drawing rooms!'

'It couldn't be worse than Katie Pphart.'

He flared his nostrils at me, screwed the scrap of paper into a pellet and swallowed it. 'I shall need some time to digest that remark,' he said and settled down to sleep.

I worked in the house for the rest of the day, hoping to catch another glimpse of Marvel. But he stayed securely locked in his room.

Franklin went to the library in the afternoon and took supper at the Grouchers Club where he liked to preen in the company of his chums.

Father returned towards nightfall, windswept and grinning, with a box of unexplained groceries. There were lemons and household candles, biscuits and bundles of wilting spinach. Mother scolded him for failing to find the shopping list she had placed in his overcoat pocket.

Janet came home at the usual hour, brilliant and chattering, joined us for a supper of boiled ham and then went to bed with a well-thumbed Katie Pphart paperback. I thought of her curled asleep, so warm and innocent, her spangled dreams filled by cruel young men with sad and fascinating eyes. Marvel remained invisible. No one mentioned him. He might have been nothing more than a flight of my own imagination.

But that night, as I locked the house, I passed his room and heard him pacing the carpet, his movements betrayed by the creaking floorboards. I held my breath and listened. I tiptoed forward and pressed my ear to the door. He was talking to himself as he walked in circles, his voice so faint that I had to strain to catch the words.

'They must not find me!' he whispered. 'Dear God, they must not find me!'

3

THE WIND FELL, exhausted, leaving a silence over the city. It was Sunday morning. After an unusually dangerous time in the kitchen, during which mother had set fire to the frying pan and tossed blazing sausages over the floor, I retreated to the front parlour with my new copy of *Grappler*. I sat in an armchair beneath the window and flicked through a special report on Pamela Motown, the sensational, sun-kissed manager of several famous wrestling freaks, including the Cannibal and the Toad. Pamela was also the undisputed TV Cat Fight champion.

Janet was curled in the sofa with *The Best of Katie Pphar*t. She was wearing a plaid shirt and a short, grey skirt. She had neatly folded one leg beneath the pleats of the skirt but a generous length of the other leg remained on public exhibition, framed by the sofa cushions. Whenever she turned a page of her book she would pause to fondle this outstretched leg, stroking it, tracing its shape with her fingernails, flaunting its pale beauty and making it quite impossible for me to concentrate on the cat-fight goddess.

I snatched glances whenever I dared, hot and tormented by love. She was absurdly pretty with her speckled green eyes and that mane of coarse blonde hair. Her nose was small and freckled, her mouth was deliciously plump and her skin was so smooth it shone, it was luminous in the sunlight.

I think it was her prettiness and her slightly startled expression that excited Franklin to cruelty. He seemed uncomfortable in the company of women. His mother was a scholar whose specialist subject was the influence of the Chinese fleet upon the women of Madagascar, 1405-1433. She had also published an important paper on the impact of ear spools in the lives of African lake village women. But she no longer spoke to Franklin. It seemed likely that she'd forgotten him. He tried to keep track of her movements but it wasn't easy. The last he'd heard she was helping her second husband collect pollen cores from the shores of Lake Chad. Her photograph, set in a silver frame, stood on Franklin's attic writing desk. A big, untidy woman in a bleached safari jacket. Crow's-nest hair and blue eyes shrunk by a tropical sun. The picture had been taken shortly after she had buried Franklin's father in a pauper's grave near Mombasa.

His father had been an academic, a poet and an authority on the life and writings of Harriet Elizabeth Beecher Stowe (1811-1896), and it must have been love that had taken him as far as the Indian Ocean to die from dysentery in the back of a crumbling two-star hotel. Franklin had already been sent to university when the tragedy happened but he never seemed to get over the shock. His father's books and papers littered the attic, including a rare first edition of *Uncle Tom's Cabin* and autographed copies of *Old-Town Folks* and *The Minister's Wooing*. He'd also inherited a mourning brooch containing a lock of Harriet Beecher Stowe's hair and her own tear-stained copy of

Byron's poems. Franklin was surrounded by his dead father's effects. I think he sometimes wore his father's clothes. He blamed his mother for everything.

A few minutes later, when he found us together in the parlour, he lost no time in destroying our separate reveries but strode to the sofa and snatched Katie Pphart from Janet's hand. Janet gasped and snapped to attention, withdrew her lovely leg from view and tucked it beneath her skirt.

'Ah, my callipygous beauty!' he barked. 'Alas, we are spellbound yet by Pphart's azoic prose!' And he fanned the pages as if he had half-expected rose petals or a glitter of silver confetti to fall, fluttering to the floor.

'Yes, it's very sad,' Janet said, blushing and beaming at him. She adored Senior Franklin. She worshipped him. It was horrible. She understood almost nothing he said but she seemed bewitched by the sound of the words in his mouth, the way he rolled and polished them, as if each well-turned phrase that slipped from his lips were a secret declaration of love.

Franklin drew back his shoulders and held the book at arm's length, squinting along his nose. '*Whimsy Longhorn trembles and shuts her fluttering tear-stained eyes as handsome, full-throated Otis Spunkmeyer begins to unbutton her ball gown…*' He snapped shut the book in a pantomime of alarm and allowed it to fall through his fingers.

'They're supposed to be royalty,' Janet explained, very flustered. She managed to catch the book in flight and quickly buried it under the cushions.

'I stand transfixed! I am captivated! Pray give me

account of every small, precious moment. Ignore my sensibilities. Spare you no morsel!'

'Well, Whimsy Longhorn is really a princess,' Janet chattered bravely, 'but lost her memory because she was stolen by strolling players when she was only a babe in arms and then she was sold into slavery and lived with some Arab conjurers until she was captured by pirates and forced to sail the seven seas to become a gift to the Sultan of Togo who held her for ransom because of her secret royal birthmark and then she was smuggled to Austria and please don't ask me to tell you what happens next because it would spoil the ending...'

'Shocking!' Franklin sneered, pausing to peer down the front of her shirt. 'A torrent of sorry scandals! Take care, my pubescent pixie, lest it melt the glue that bindeth your mossy merkin!'

'He's teasing you!' I called out indignantly. I rattled the *Grappler* in my fist, but Janet wasn't listening.

'Ah, Mr Romance bridles!' Franklin said, glancing in my direction. He knew how I felt about Janet and calling me Mr Romance never failed to amuse him.

'Have you finished your own book yet, Mr Franklin?' Janet asked him, hoping to steer the conversation away from the perils of Katie Pphart.

'*Awake, the Jabberwocky!*' Franklin cried. This was the title of his great, unwritten novel. The book had already been hailed as a masterpiece by his old friend, Polenta Hartebeest, the literary editor of *The Trumpet*, and several glowing reviews had been prepared, anticipating its publication. The world waited with mounting impatience. 'I am scarce embarked upon the voyage,' Franklin confessed, shaking his noble head. 'Ah, morbid melancholy!'

'But you're so clever with words!' Janet gasped.

'Thank you,' Franklin said, as if he were collecting taxes. 'My tutors were known to remark on many different occasions that my humble brain was the size of Belgium...' He stopped short and turned towards the door. Mother was squelching forth with a short, fat, middle-aged man on her arm.

It was Marvel! Large as life and twice as lugubrious. Mother had worked a miracle and drawn him down from his room. He was wearing a boiled shirt, a pair of pock-marked corduroy trousers and his red felt slippers.

'Janet, I'd like you to meet Mr Marvel,' mother announced, leading him towards the sofa.

'A pleasure!' Marvel said solemnly. He gave a little nod of his head and took Janet's hand. Janet smiled and looked seductively startled.

Franklin, anxious to establish himself as the centre of attention, lurched forward to impress himself on the stranger. 'Senior Franklin!' he thundered, seizing Marvel's hand and squeezing it like a lemon. 'Harrow and Oxford. Baccalaureate. First Class. Honours. English. Grouchers and the Atlas Club.'

And then something extraordinary happened.

Marvel froze in his slippers and an expression of absolute disgust swept across his bilious face. It dragged at the corners of his mouth, pulled at his eyes and crackled up through the roots of his hair. He shivered, snatched back his hand and cradled it against his chest.

'The man is an oaf!' he shouted, falling into a chair and wiping his hand in a handkerchief.

Senior Franklin looked stunned. It was the first time in his life that his immaculate credentials had been treated with such contempt and, for the first time in his life, he was lost for words. His mouth was working but nothing happened. Whatever acid retorts, hilarious rejoins or confounding obiter dicta might have flashed through his bulging brain, he failed to voice them. He floundered. He flared his nostrils. He flounced from the room and stormed upstairs to collect his scarf and overcoat. It was outrageous. Franklin felt the need to be master of all he surveyed and he couldn't hope to master Marvel unless they played by the rules of the game. This impertinent stranger had behaved like a tourist who, presented with the pyramids or the wonders of the Taj Mahal, fails to find anything in them worth the trouble of travel. And without the blessing of pilgrims, the shrine is nothing but rubble and sand.

The front parlour fell silent. Janet looked trapped, hunched in the sofa, not wanting to stay but too shocked for flight. Mr Romance kept his smirking face behind his magazine. Mother, on the other hand, was not so easily embarrassed and continued to behave as if nothing unusual had happened.

'You'll have to excuse him,' she whispered, as we heard the front door bang shut – a signal that Franklin had taken himself away to sulk at Grouchers. 'He's rather temperamental.' Mother held the view that Franklin's unpleasant disposition was most likely the symptom of something like worms or chronic constipation. She continued to attend to our new guest, fetching him cushions and even presenting him with Franklin's abandoned Sunday papers.

'Will you take a little breakfast this morning?' she asked him.

Marvel beamed and thought for a moment. 'I think,' he said gently, 'I might manage a lightly boiled egg and perhaps a few fingers of toast.'

'You stay here and make yourself comfortable,' mother said. 'I'll call you when it's ready.'

I watched him settle down with the papers and tried to make some sense of it. Franklin was an oaf. It was true. A long and impressive education had merely lent the oaf confidence. He felt some strange and primitive urge for tribal dominance and we had learned to humour him. We had no regard for his high opinions – it was easier to tug our forelocks and smile than challenge his need for authority. Confronted with Franklin's humbuggery it was best to shrug and turn away. But Marvel would have none of it. Marvel had stood there and challenged him.

He took breakfast in the kitchen, closely watched by mother, and returned to the front parlour where he stayed for most of the afternoon, dozing beneath *The Sunday Shout*. He seemed perfectly at peace with the world, unclasped his broad leather belt for the sake of his paunch and drifted into a shallow sleep with the green and yellow lights from the window softly staining his face. But as evening approached with its threat of supper, he quietly slipped away to his room.

'That will be his stomach,' mother explained, as we gathered at the table to tackle a chicken. There were carrots and parsnips, drenched with butter, and sage and onion stuffing and her secret recipe mashed potato that stuck to the spoon and glued itself to the roof of your mouth.

'I believe he has trouble in that direction,' she added confidentially.

'He doesn't know what he's missing. There's nothing like good home cooking!' father declared, winking at mother and splashing his chin with gravy.

'Perhaps he's been unlucky in love,' Janet whispered. Despite his attack on her matinée idol, she was still prepared to weave him into her world of romance. The haunted husband. The tragic stranger.

4

FRANKLIN SULKED BY going forth on a grand tour of his favourite watering holes. We took advantage of his absence by cleaning and disinfecting the attic. It was a dismal prospect. The sagging bookshelves were loaded with crumbling leather-bound classics, bundles of letters and thousands of rotting paperbacks. We stripped the bed and wiped down the furniture but observed his strict instructions to avoid the great oak writing desk. The view on the desk remained constant. The pencils were never blunted. The notebooks had never been thumbed. The stack of fine feint paper remained undiminished. Nothing changed. The sad progress of *Awake, the Jabberwocky!* was a story that wrote itself in the dust. He made a small living scribbling savage book reviews and selling sarcastic comments to literary magazines but his greatest work refused to take shape. He had squandered so much of his energy on broadcasting his intentions to write the book, and spent so much time discussing its many merits, that he half-believed the book to be written.

I dragged the vacuum cleaner over the carpet while mother flogged the walls with a duster and squirted Springtime into the air to mask the smell of mothballs that always leaked from his wardrobe.

'I don't know how he makes such a mess!' I shouted above the noise. It puzzled me that Franklin's inertia could create such a quantity of filth. The carpet was loaded with knots of hair, cotton threads, fingernail clippings, biscuit crumbs, sugar grains, metal staples, shirt buttons, collar studs, broken teeth from a plastic comb and desiccated woodlice.

'He's a thinker!' mother shouted with a rapid burst from her aerosol. She made it sound like a clever form of self-abuse.

I switched off the motor and pulled the plug from the wall. 'Do you want me to help wash the windows?' I asked, stamping on the recoil pedal and making the flex jump across the floor. I hated cleaning the attic windows because of the rusty iron bars that scratched the skin from my knuckles as I tried to work the rag between them. They lent these attic rooms the atmosphere of a well-furnished lunatic asylum.

Mother shook her head. She didn't seem very impressed with the standard of my work. 'I'll finish here,' she said, stooping to scowl at a dust-ball that had rolled beneath the bed. 'You can go down to Mexico.'

I wasted no time but retreated thankfully downstairs to Janet's sunlit kingdom with its cosy clutter of toys and magazines. Here the air was fresh and the furniture was brightly painted, there were stuffed toy animals on the bed and a TV set on the dressing table. It was warm and simple and friendly.

I loved Janet's room. She had the disgraceful habit of leaving a trail of shoes and underwear scattered about the place whenever I went to work with my dusters. She meant no mischief. Her lack of modesty was a mark of how little she thought of me. She was only twenty-six years old but she treated me like a child, a tongue-tied skivvy, a comical playmate. It must never have occurred to her that finding these intimate morsels of cotton, satin and lace could poison my blood and drive me demented. Katie Pphart, I suppose, had never mentioned the dark allure of the fetish for the amorous animist. I'm not complaining. There were obvious advantages in playing the part of the simpleton, to be given liberty to rummage in my lady's underwear. And how dainty, how innocent, these trifles appeared in my big, clumsy hands. The lace like spun sugar and the nylon of frank transparency, the shimmering ribbons and seed pearl buttons. And the colours! Soft, blushing pink and lavender, ivory and peppermint. And her perfume – an exotic draught of flowers and spices lifting from every garment that I raised towards my face.

I was resting from my labours, sitting at her dressing table and filling a little silk bra with my fists, when I heard mother hissing at me from the landing.

'Quick! Quick!'

I dashed to the door and peered up to find her leaning dangerously over the top of the staircase.

'What?' I whispered. 'What?'

'It's Mr Marvel!' she hissed back at me. 'He's just gone downstairs. Quick! Go and talk to him.'

'Why? What do you want me to say?'

'Find out what's happening,' she demanded. 'If he's going out for a couple of hours, we can use the time to clean up his room!' She grinned, flushed with mischief, and waved me away with her apron.

I ran downstairs, swept along by her excitement, and found my quarry still loitering in the hall. He was dressed for the street but seemed reluctant to venture abroad. He held open his overcoat and stared at himself in the long hall mirror. He frowned and shook his head, refusing to trust the reflection. When he sensed me standing beside him he turned and peered at me thoughtfully, as if I might prove to be another trick of the glass.

'Tell me,' he said at last, 'what do you make of this waistcoat?' He pulled his overcoat wide to reveal a dark green waistcoat with small black buttons.

'It looks very elegant,' I said, to please him.

'You wouldn't describe it as loud?'

'No.'

He pushed out his paunch and peered down his nose. 'You don't think it makes me look a little too … conspicuous?'

I was baffled. It seemed such a tame and ordinary article that he could safely wear it anywhere without danger of ridicule. 'I suppose it would depend on the occasion,' I said, having decided upon reflection that it might be a little too formal for spending a day on the beach. 'Where are you going?'

He cocked his head suspiciously and studied me for a moment. 'I find myself called away,' he said finally and sighed in a mournful manner that spoke of some untold tragedy.

'I hope it's nothing serious.'

'A trifle,' he said, carefully closing the coat and pushing his hands in the pockets. And still he lingered, as if he needed to summon more courage before he embarked on the errand.

I stepped past him and pulled open the front door. It was a cold and sparkling day with a sky so high you could count the vapour trails in heaven.

Marvel leaned forward and sniffed at the air. He looked doubtful. 'I should return before dark,' he said, turning to look at me for the last time, and with a final shrug of his shoulders he launched himself towards the street.

I watched him disappear beyond the privet hedge before I scampered upstairs again. Mother was waiting impatiently, fully armed with her brushes and buckets.

'Has he gone?' she whispered.

'He's gone!' I said.

'Is there time?' she asked, pulling the house keys from a cardigan pocket.

'There's time!'

We unlocked his door and tiptoed forward like thieves. What did we want to find in that room? We hoped for scandal. We wanted to be thrilled by disgusting sights. But everything was in order. His shabby collection of clothes was neatly arranged in the wardrobe. A cheap alarm clock and a box of Potter's creosote cough drops had been placed beside the bed. His shaving tackle stood to attention beside a small radio on the chest of drawers.

It didn't look promising. In the interests of hygiene we ransacked the room but found nothing. The wooden box beneath the bed contained no scorpions, no shrunken heads, but merely an ancient typewriter, the ink ribbon frayed and the keys turned yellow with age. We felt disappointed and foolish.

'Poor old man,' mother said, as if by way of apology for picking through his meagre possessions.

It was five o'clock in the afternoon when Marvel returned to the house. He crashed through the front door, staggered across the hall and sank to his knees at the foot of the stairs in an attitude of prayer. He looked seasick. His skin had a ghastly waxen sheen and his eyes were bulging and bloodshot.

I ran from the kitchen to help him to his feet but he proved too heavy to lift and capsized against the wall. It was a difficult situation. I needed help but no one came to my assistance. Father was locked in the cellar. Mother was in the back parlour shouting abuse at the Beast who was trying to unscrew the head from the shoulders of Jumping Johnny Mango. It was bedlam. Mother was in a fury. I think the referee must have fainted.

I knelt down beside Marvel and did my best to comfort him. 'What happened?' I said, trying to stop him from listing to starboard and rolling onto the floor.

He raised a plump hand and let it fall against his chest, useless and dead, a glove filled with sand. 'Filth!' he moaned. 'Filth!'

At first I thought he was drunk but when I saw his distress I began to fear that he might have met with an accident or been attacked in the street.

'Are you hurt?'

He opened his mouth to speak but merely moaned and closed his eyes. I tried to check him for cuts and bruises. There was no blood. He'd burst through the buttons of his waistcoat but he didn't seem to be injured.

'What happened?' I asked him again.

Marvel belched like a bummaree and weakly clutched at my sleeve. 'The devils are trying to poison me!' he whispered breathlessly. He wagged his head and stared vacantly at the floor. He looked distinctly queasy.

'Do you need a doctor?'

'No!' he barked. The idea seemed to alarm him and he struggled vainly to escape. 'No doctor!'

'Why don't we get you to bed?' I suggested when I'd wrestled him into an upright position and propped him against the newel post. He grunted and groped for the banister, climbed the stairs on his hands and knees.

When we gained the safety of his room, he prised off his shoes, belched majestically, turned around and toppled thankfully onto the bed. The mattress farted beneath his weight. He groaned and wiped his face in his hand. His stomach churned and splashed and made a peculiar hissing sound as if he were leaking steam.

'Can I fetch you something?'

'No doctor!'

'No doctor,' I said. 'But perhaps there's something to settle your stomach…'

'Water!' he gasped. 'I need a bottle of mineral water…'

'I'll bring it,' I said, picking up his shoes and placing them in the wardrobe. He was still wearing his overcoat but he looked so comfortable that I didn't want to disturb him and by the time I'd returned with his bottle of water he had already fallen asleep.

He didn't leave his room for the rest of the night and later, when supper had been served and cleared away, I went to listen at his door and heard him snoring. Whatever demons had seized him, whatever dread phantoms had chased him back to the house, they would vanish in sleep and be forgotten.

But towards midnight, when the house was quiet and I was coming to the end of my sentry duties, I passed his room again and heard the click clack of a typewriter. It broke the silence like the call of some giant insect hidden in the riddled skirting-boards. Marvel was awake and working at his machine. He poked at the keys with two fat fingers. Slow and deliberate. Click clack. A secret message to God.

5

THE NEXT MORNING it rained. It crackled against the windows and rattled the big iron drains, flooded the porch and caused dark flowers to bloom among the pastel roses on the wall of the back parlour. The house was dark and filled with the damp, sour smell that seemed to haunt the floorboards and carpets. Mr Marvel crept through the shadows with his overcoat buttoned up to his throat and a stout manilla envelope clutched in one hand. He drifted slowly down the stairs, gliding forward, hardly daring to breathe, and found me ready and waiting for him beneath the antlers of the coat stand.

'It's raining,' I announced, strolling from the gloom of my hiding place.

He shuddered and looked at me with a pinched expression on his battered face. 'You've an eye for detail that's quite remarkable,' he said, attempting to push the envelope into an overcoat pocket.

'Are you going to the post?'

He stopped trying to stuff his pocket and stared at the envelope in surprise, as if he hadn't expected to find it about his person. He turned it around and tapped it with his fingernails.

'Can I take it for you?' I asked, reaching out to recover

it before it disappeared from view. 'You'll catch your death in this weather.'

'You're hardly dressed for it,' he argued, retaining control of the envelope by pulling it back from my snapping fingers. He sounded suspicious. I was still wearing my kitchen apron.

'It will only take a moment,' I said anxiously. I felt sure that his labours at the typewriter were concealed in that envelope and if I could only read the address I might have the key to his terrible secret. But he was cunning.

'I'd prefer to attend to it myself,' he said stubbornly. He glanced about him, impatient and nervous.

'You can trust me – if it's important.'

'No,' he said quickly. 'It's nothing.' He pushed the envelope into his pocket and gave it a gentle slap.

'I'm just trying to help,' I grumbled.

'You're a good man. And I'm much obliged,' he said, moving away and pulling open the front door. The rain punched his face, making him flinch and jerk back his head. The wind inflated his hair into a soft and trembling spire.

'I hope you're feeling better this morning,' I continued quickly, hoping to hinder his escape.

'I find myself greatly improved…' he said and wheezed as he swallowed a draught of cold air.

'Is it a weakness of some description?'

'What?' He turned and scowled at me as if I had made an obscene remark about the size of his private parts.

'When you collapsed. We were worried. We thought it might be your pipes and tubes,' I said innocently.

He grinned by grinding his teeth. 'If I might trouble you for a brolly…'

I retreated to the coat stand and rattled the bundle of sticks in their deep, brass urn. After a moment's fiddling I chose a black brolly with a bent cane handle and gave it a smack to shake out the dust.

'Thank you,' he said, taking it from me and splashing into the porch. He grunted, unfurled the brolly and battled into the rain.

I closed the front door and turned away in defeat. My curiosity burned like a rash that I couldn't scratch. I knew there was something wrong but Marvel was too clever for my clumsy attempts at detective work. For a moment I considered following him but I knew, in the time it would take me to find my shoes, he'd have disappeared in the windswept streets. So I turned, instead, and hurried down to the cellar to share my suspicions with father.

Old William Wandsworth had built the cellar to store his famous collection of wines. A door in the passage that led to the kitchen opened on a flight of wooden stairs that took you down to a large brick vault with stone shelves and a freezing, flagstone floor. The cellar had been white-washed and fitted with electric lights and a small stove but still it had the chill of a tomb. It was so cold at night that father would wrap himself in a blanket to stay a little longer at his workbench. The surrounding stone shelves were used to store the raw ingredients of his art. There were cardboard boxes filled with broken watches, coffee tins loaded with radio parts and pickle jars stuffed with screws. There were coils of wire, baskets of spanners and buckets of brushes, pencils and probes. There were also those objects that father had collected with no understanding of their true purpose – scraps of metal and plastic trimmings – stored for the day when he knew they'd reveal their identity.

I found him working at his bench. He was wearing a jacket against the cold with a knitted hat to protect his ears. He appeared to be engaged in a delicate operation on something that looked like a battleship klaxon. It was broken in half like a strange, metal fruit and while I watched he picked a loose washer from the works with a pair of long silver tweezers. He held up the washer and frowned.

'Hello! What brings you down here, Skipper?'

'It's Marvel,' I told him.

'What does he want?'

'He doesn't want anything.'

'Good!' said father, pleased with the news. 'You can tell him he's more than welcome to it.'

'He's been acting very strange again.'

'How's that?'

I described the events of the previous day: Marvel's mysterious errand, the way he'd returned home more dead than alive, and how I'd helped him back to his bed. Father wasn't impressed. He leaned back in his chair and rolled the washer in the palm of his hand.

'He probably had a few drinks,' he said, hoping to sweep away my suspicions. 'You have to understand. He's not so young. And a man his age. It's difficult. He must be lonely...'

'Do you think that's it?'

'I'm sure of it.'

'But he wasn't drunk,' I protested. 'I swear. It was something else. He was sick. He said he'd been poisoned.'

'How did he look?'

'He looked green,' I said, watching my breath uncoil like smoke. It was cold! Father was so engrossed in his work he'd forgotten to light the stove.

'Did you call the doctor?'

'No. I suggested it to him but he seemed so scared – he was struggling to get away from me – I thought he would have a heart attack!'

'At the mention of a doctor?'

'Yes.'

'Did your mother feed him yesterday?'

'No.'

'So what's your theory?'

I shrugged. There might be two possible explanations for his erratic behaviour.

(A) He was a fugitive from justice and responsible for crimes too terrible to imagine. There was no evidence to support this opinion but it gave me an opportunity for hours of salacious speculation. Missing housewife drowned in honey. Naked nympho chained to rafters. (B) He was barking mad and thought himself tormented by alien forces/ international terrorists/ government agents. I was beginning to favour this theory and, if it were true, it would help explain his hunted expression and violent changes of mood.

'I don't think he's right in the head,' I confessed.

'I like him,' said father, tossing the washer to the floor. He frowned. He already regretted having thrown it away and had to crawl around on his hands and knees, sweeping the floor to retrieve it.

'I like him,' I said. 'But I still think he's wrong in the head.'

My father grinned. 'What do you make of this?' he said, changing the subject, returning to his work on the bench. He waved his hand at a pile of rubbish, inviting my gasps of admiration. His fingers were gnarled with old adhesive.

'What is it?'

'It's a new kind of home security system,' he said proudly. 'It's a revolution in domestic intruder alarms. The sentry that never sleeps. Now children can romp in their rooms in safety. Women can sing in their showers secure. And – here's the secret – it's so simple that anyone with a screwdriver and a basic working knowledge of advanced electronics could fit one in just a few minutes.'

'How does it work?' I said, fearing that he was going to tell me.

He grinned and stared at the chaos before him. 'Well, the entire fandangle depends on a thin beam of light projected between these widgets,' he said, pointing to a pair of plastic boxes packed with wires and batteries. 'You rig the whamdoodle to shine across a doorway or window like a tripwire. Do you follow me? When you pass through the beam you break the connection and trigger the doodah that sounds the alarm in the whatsit. I've been working on it for weeks. What do you think? It looks primitive, of course, but this is only the prototype. What do you think?'

He turned to look at me, searching my face, anxious for approval.

'It's good,' I said. I didn't have the heart to tell him that you could buy a far more sophisticated version of his security system from any gizmo catalogue. The idea had fermented in his brain with no knowledge that such a gadget already existed. He was a genius, no doubt, but he seemed cursed to make discoveries that were already common knowledge. He'd achieved this remarkable handicap through years of working in isolation. In a long and undistinguished career he'd invented the nostril hair trimmer, the handy folding pocket scissors and the world's most brutal electric toothbrush. If you gave him enough time he'd invent the microwave oven and telephone answering machine.

'When it's finished you can help me install it,' he said, pleased that I seemed to be showing an interest.

'How long will it take you?'

'Oh, I just have to track down a couple of gremlins...'

'Is it safe?' I asked doubtfully. His inventions were varied and dangerous. He had once made me a pair of electrically heated gloves, wired to a bulky battery pack that I'd worn beneath my vest. The gloves had exploded on my way to school and flames had shot from my fingertips.

'Safe?' he snapped. 'How do I know if it's safe until we've tested it?'

It was too cold to argue with him. I left him tinkering with his invention and went upstairs to the kitchen to make him a flask of hot soup. I forgot my doubts about Marvel because an hour later Franklin returned, drenched to the skin and bellowing for attention.

6

HE WAS IN an ugly mood. He snapped and snarled and stalked the house like a harpy. He complained that we'd ransacked his attic, shuffled his books and muddled his papers, opened his letters and pried at his diaries. When I gave him the newspapers – carefully hoarded those past few days for the sake of the arts pages – he took it as an insult and had a tantrum. I watched him rip the papers apart, throw them to the floor and trample on them, weeping with frustration, ridiculous with rage. He was in a dark and dangerous mood but we had to wait until supper was served before he revealed the cause of his anger.

It was early when we gathered in the dining room – there was a TV wrestling spectacular later in the evening and mother was determined to have a ringside seat. The Wandsworth dining room had lost most of its ornamental plasterwork and the brilliant, illustrated window had sagged and fractured and been repaired with ugly panels of grey, knobbled glass, creating the effect of an unfinished jigsaw puzzle. But the room was large and warm and contained the original dining table served by a group of press-ganged chairs. Franklin came down and took the most comfortable chair for himself, sitting opposite Janet who kept watch over him with love in her eyes. It was a good supper. A big beef stew spiked with Guinness, served with carrots and baby dumplings.

Franklin looked around and waved his fork at an empty chair. He was wearing a velvet jacket with a large but flaccid bow tie, giving him the air of a rampaging game-show host. 'Do we find ourselves deprived of Mr Marvellous tonight?' he growled at the assembly. 'How shall we entertain ourselves without the light of his wit and wisdom?' He never forgave an insult, real or imagined, and had written Marvel's name large in his book of enemies.

'He doesn't take supper,' mother said gently. Marvel had returned to the house, damp but undamaged, and promptly retired to his room. He'd asked for nothing throughout the day but coffee and sultana biscuits.

'No doubt he dines on his own bile,' Franklin muttered, filling his mouth with buttered carrots.

Janet blinked and looked startled. 'That's not a very kind remark,' she said, blushing at the sound of her own voice and hoping to hide her embarrassment by hooking her hair behind one ear. She was wearing tiny crystal earrings that sparkled and flashed as they caught the light.

Franklin was in no mood to be criticised by an uppity shopgirl, no matter how much she might adore him. 'I strongly advise you to concentrate!' he barked. 'If you eat and think at the same time you'll do yourself damage.'

'Are you upset about something?' Janet asked him nervously. She was sitting beside me. Whenever she squirmed in her chair she brushed my sleeve and set fire to my arm from wrist to elbow.

'*Poke*!' Franklin shouted, making me drop my dumpling. He was in a most peculiar temper.

'What?'

'*Poke*!'

'Poke what?' I said.

'Language!' father said sharply. He rapped his fork against the rim of his plate in a bid to restore law and order.

'*Poke*!' Franklin repeated, his face seemed bruised by the fury that the word provoked in him.

'What are you talking about?'

'It's the Dwarf!' he shouted. '*Poke*! It's the Dwarf! He's written another damned novel!'

There was a long silence. The Dwarf, aka Maxwell Bizarre, was a rather clever young man fresh from Oxford who had written a string of bestselling novels. His first book, *Muck*, had featured a rather clever young man fresh from Oxford and set adrift in a crude and stupid world. The rather clever young man is cast into a twilight zone where people are beastly to him. I don't know what happens because I couldn't find the energy to read beyond the third chapter. It was one of those books that has the power to make everything else in the world seem suddenly more interesting. You pick it up and read a page and find yourself thinking about the length of your fingernails, or the temperature in the room or the odd little burbling noise in your stomach. So you slip an envelope or an old bus ticket between the pages and close the book for a moment to stretch your legs and make a sandwich and you walk away and never return. Bookshelves are filled with these unwanted guests, waiting years to be boxed and discarded. But Senior Franklin despised the book as much as he despised the author. He declared that (1) the Dwarf was a plagiarist; (2) that the Dwarf knew next to nothing about the horrors of life at street level since his own short span had been one of comfort and privilege; (3) that the Dwarf had such a loose grasp on the language his publishers had been forced to employ a team of editors to shape and polish his prose; (4) that the Dwarf had carnal knowledge of children and domestic animals; (5) that the Dwarf had contrived to include amusing portraits of all his Oxford chums in the story, which had the desired effect of making said chums fight each other, tooth and claw, for the privilege of praising the book in every available literary organ. These were serious allegations. But nothing could stop the Dwarf's progress. His other books, *Spit, Jerk* and *Vomit* had been hailed as penetrating satires on the moral decay in urban culture. *Vomit* had been awarded the Stanley Butler Prize for its perky, pornographic prose.

'*Poke*!' I said, breaking the silence. 'That's a good title. What's it like? Do you recommend it?' I knew he was jealous of the Dwarf's success, it cut very deep and I wanted to twist the knife. Everyone seemed impressed by the Dwarf, including Franklin's most loyal friend, Polenta Hartebeest.

'It's dog dirt!' he shouted indignantly. 'It's a pompous prick-song from a dangerous, Priapic pygmy!'

'Language!' father warned again.

'It's dung! It's offal! It plumbs new depths of banality! It's a battological dirge of filth and fornication!'

'So you don't think much of it,' I ventured.

'I haven't read it!' Franklin shouted.

'That's very queer,' I said. 'I thought you read everything...'

'They dared not take the risk of sending a copy for review. The book was strictly reserved for his sycophantic Shirlies!'

'It's a lot of nonsense,' mother said, stirring her stew with a spoon. 'Books! A lot of nonsense.' She didn't trust the written word. Her only weakness was *Chinwag*, a weekly magazine devoted to Hollywood gossip, horoscopes and picture puzzles.

'Why don't you just ignore it?' father suggested. 'You should write a good adventure yarn. That's more like it. Everyone loves a good yarn. Think of Godfrey Bowman. I used to read a lot of Godfrey Bowman before I was married. You should write a good, old-fashioned yarn with speedboats and sports cars and poisoned fountain-pen ink and special exploding Havana cigars. Something with lots of action. A proper beginning, middle and end. Nobody wants it artsy farsty.'

Franklin looked infuriated and tried to cut his plate in half with the frantic work of his knife.

'You mustn't upset yourself...' Janet said kindly.

'What?' He cocked his head and glared across the table.

'Well, I was thinking...' she began nervously and felt herself frightened into silence.

'Come, what fragrant thought hangs suspended?' He leaned forward by digging an elbow into the table. He could sense her discomfort. It pleased him. I wanted to puncture his lungs with my fork.

'Nothing.'

But Franklin would not be discouraged. 'Speld yourself, my toothsome toady, and grant me a glimpse of your moist cogitation!' he coaxed softly and then sneered, revealing his long upper teeth.

'Language!'

Janet braced herself to try again. 'You really shouldn't upset yourself because one day you're going to finish your own book and it's sure to be a tremendous success and then you'll be so famous they'll want you on talk shows and everything to meet film stars and all sorts and you won't even want to know people like me...' she said quickly. This pathetic confession made me prickle with jealousy. It was utterly wasted on Senior Franklin.

'Is that it?' he gasped, clutching at his drooping bow tie in a pantomime of astonishment.

'Yes,' Janet whispered. She set down her knife and fork and stared forlornly into her gravy. Her eyes were too bright. She puckered her mouth as if she were sucking on gristle.

'I'm astounded by its simplicity!' Franklin shouted gleefully. He began honking with laughter, leaning back in his chair and staring around at his audience as if he wanted to share the joke. 'I hadn't understood that life was so little complicated. I shall press your advice into service at the earliest opportunity...'

Janet withered in the blast of laughter. She bent towards her plate and pressed her knuckles against her throat. I turned to give her a word of comfort but the crystal earring disappeared as her hair swung down to hide her face.

For a moment she seemed to hesitate, slumped forward in silence, and then she uncoiled, pushing at the table, kicking loose from her chair, catching me deliciously in the warm and perfumed draught of her skirt.

'Janet!' mother called anxiously.

We turned but it was too late. Janet had already rushed from the room and was running towards the stairs.

'Now look what you've done!' mother scolded. 'I hope you're satisfied with yourself.'

Franklin flared his nostrils and reached for the mustard pot. 'I did nothing!' he protested. 'The cut and thrust of common chitchat. The ebb and flow of fireside banter. No harm intended. None. Am I to take the blame if the girl is a hopeless neurotic?'

'You ought to apologise,' said father, wiping his mouth with a paper napkin. 'She was looking very upset.'

Franklin grew sullen and smeared the remains of his dumplings with mustard. 'I shall not stand accused of forcing an entry into her bedroom.'

'Someone should go after her,' I said, resisting the desire to volunteer myself without pause for a little encouragement. I didn't want to raise suspicion.

'Someone should do *something*,' father said impatiently. He didn't have time to become involved in another domestic quarrel. He wanted to eat and escape to the cellar.

'She's hardly touched her supper,' mother grumbled, frowning at Janet's abandoned plate. 'Do you think we should save it?'

'How should I know?' father snapped, screwing his napkin into a ball and making it bounce across the table.

Franklin looked uncomfortable and began to fidget in his chair. He was still angry but there was just a chance he'd soon feel guilty enough to submit an apology. I had to seize the advantage.

'It's a shame to waste it.' mother continued stubbornly. 'She didn't eat enough to fill a sparrow.'

'She obviously doesn't want it,' father said.

'Do you think she'd like me to make her a tray?' I said.

'Mr Romance accepts the challenge!' Franklin shouted sarcastically and forced a dumpling into his mouth. 'Scuttle forth, my curious capon, whilst Love still beckons thee. There are worse occupations in this world than feeling a woman's pulse.'

'Perhaps she'll want a sandwich,' mother suggested.

'I'll go and find out,' I said with a weary reluctance and shot from the room before Franklin changed his mind and stole my opportunity to have Janet weep on my shoulder.

7

'WHO IS IT?'

'Skipper!' I called softly, as I stood at her door, trying to comb my hair with my hands. My heart was thumping so hard and fast I could feel the rushing of blood in my ears.

'It's not locked.'

I hesitated, turned the handle and peeked into her room. It always seemed larger at night, perhaps because the curtains were closed and the lamps with their pleated paper shades, splashed light at the walls, dappled the rugs and pulled strange shadows from furniture, lending the room an unfamiliar geometry. I took a single step forward and glanced towards the dressing table where the mirror shone like a sunlit window into another, parallel world. Through this window I could see Janet, pale and slightly luminous, turning away from her wardrobe and walking towards the bed. She was barefoot. Her blouse was unbuttoned. She was tinkering with the clasp on her skirt.

'What is it?' she asked. She seemed bewildered. Her eyes were pink, their lashes glued with melted mascara.

'Do you need anything?' I asked, closing the door and stepping deeper into the room.

'No,' she whispered. 'There's nothing. I'm fine.'

'I could bring you a tray,' I said hopefully. 'If you're hungry. It's no trouble to fix you a tray.'

She shook her head and made some attempt to repair her blouse. Her hands were shaking. She fumbled blindly in search of the buttons. She was crying. Her mouth sagged open as if she were drowning.

'I'm sorry!' she snuffled. 'I'm sorry!' She sat down hard on the edge of the bed and covered her face in her hands, sucking and blowing between her fingers.

'What for?'

'For making such a fool of myself!' She yanked a Kleenex from the box on the bedside table and used it to wipe her eyes, pausing to gasp for breath before teasing the tissue into a spike and neatly drilling her nose.

'I must have missed it,' I said. 'What happened?'

'You're sweet!' she sobbed, raising her head and forcing a smile. Her mouth looked swollen and petulant. She dragged her tumbled hair from her face, making her blouse pull away at her throat in a heart-stopping moment of carelessness that gave me a view of her collar-bone.

'And Franklin's a bully,' I said, trying to steady myself by taking charge of the Kleenex box and sitting beside her on the bed.

'No, he's not really a bully,' she gasped, plucking at tissues. 'He just gets impatient because he's so clever. Don't you think he's clever?'

'A brain the size of Belgium,' I said.

'And elegant,' she said, remembering her buttons. 'You can tell that he's special just by looking at him. Distinguished.' Her flicking fingers worked to secure the front of her blouse, making me shrink with disappointment as if an unspoken trust had been broken.

'I can't say that I've noticed.'

She didn't care to be contradicted. 'He's distinguished. And he must think that I'm so stupid,' she continued miserably. 'Honestly! The things I say! I can't help it. He must think I'm hopelessly ignorant.'

'It's not true,' I protested. How I hated him! I wanted to snip off his thumbs with scissors. I wanted to tear out his tongue.

'He makes me feel stupid!' she snorted. 'I hate myself. I'm so stupid and plain and ordinary.'

'You're not ordinary!' I said fiercely.

'I'm stupid!' she insisted, beating her knees with her fists.

'He tries to make everyone feel stupid,' I said. 'You should be flattered. It probably means that he likes you.'

'Do you really think he likes me?' She stared at me with brilliant eyes, squinting with concentration, as if I could soothe her misery, brew love potions, cast spells, heal the sick and raise the dead from their graves.

'Yes,' I said. 'I don't know.' I shrugged and felt hopeless. 'He doesn't seem to like anyone very much.'

'Whenever I try to talk to him I get tongue-tied,' she explained. 'It's horrible. I always make such a mess of it. I can feel him looking and laughing at me.' She had stopped sobbing and seemed now to be quite exhausted, like a small child after a tantrum. She yawned. She swung her legs from the floor and made herself comfortable on the bed, leaning into a pile of pillows. 'I was thinking of taking extra night classes. Do you think it might help?'

'It depends,' I said doubtfully. She already took Yoga and Needlecraft, Basketwork and Pottery.

'I might try Conversation. I could learn to become more interesting by improving my conversation.'

'They have night classes for that?'

'Oh, yes. They teach you to express yourself in a variety of popular situations. It lends you greater confidence.'

'Perhaps you should try a different approach,' I suggested.

'How do you mean?'

I didn't have the faintest idea but I wanted to keep her attention. 'Well, the next time he starts to make fun of you, try breaking his jaw,' I suggested. 'That should wipe the grin from his face. Spit in his food. Throw something at him. A little violence works wonders.'

'I couldn't do that!'

'It's worth a try,' I said, reaching across the bed to return the Kleenex box to the table and endeavouring to work a little closer to the object of my desire without giving her cause for alarm. But I was clumsy and brushed her naked foot with my hand. She fanned her toes in surprise.

'You're so funny,' she murmured, sinking deeper into the pillows.

'Why?'

'When you're serious.'

'I don't like to see you hurt. It upsets me.'

'He doesn't mean any harm.'

'How is your mother?' I said, hoping to steer the conversation away from the merits of Senior Franklin. Janet's mother enjoyed robust bad health and wrote regular letters describing the progress of her many and complex ailments, the opinions of various doctors and the names of the drugs and therapies prescribed.

'Liver and lumbago. Panic attacks. Dizzy spells. Tired scalp. Bad feet. Legs like balloons,' she said, reciting from memory.

'Is that serious?'

'The doctor said if they get any worse, he's going to have to drain them.'

'I hope you'll send her my regards.'

'You're sweet!' she said again and smiled, lifting and smoothing her skirt to give me a brief but spectacular view along the wonderful length of her legs, as if she wanted to demonstrate that her own fair limbs were in the very pink of condition.

'Would you like me to bring you some ice cream?' I managed to croak as I blinked my stolen glimpse of her thighs deeper into my eyes. I couldn't breathe! I was paralysed with danger. 'Chocolate and Vanilla Fudge. Strawberry Blonde. Mango and Coconut Surprise.'

'Lovely,' she said. 'But it makes me fat.'

'You could risk it,' I said, in a feeble attempt at flattery. You could risk a little ice cream. Surrender yourself and close your eyes as I feed you sips of scented snow. Abandon yourself and give me the night to stuff your mouth with flakes of ice and melt your frosted lips with kisses.

She shook her head. 'I'm tired.'

'It's early.'

'I think I'll get into bed with my book.'

'I can't tempt you?'

'No.' She picked Ronald the Rabbit from her harem of stuffed toy animals and smothered him between her breasts. Oh, lucky rabbit! His ears stood up on his head like exclamation marks.

'Anything,' I insisted. 'I'll get you anything.' A loaded revolver. Baskets of kittens. Diamonds as big as potatoes.

'No.'

'Well, goodnight,' I said reluctantly, as I threatened to remove myself from the scant rewards of her bed. I sighed and slapped my knees and stared at the floor.

'Goodnight, Skipper.'

'Shoes!' It was an inspiration. Rise and shine! I might still indulge my fantasies by stealing a souvenir. 'Do you want me to take your shoes?' I pleaded. 'Those ankle boots need some attention.'

'Tomorrow.'

'Well, goodnight.'

'Goodnight, Skipper.'

I stood up and sighed and dragged myself slowly across the room. I wanted her to block my retreat, cling to my neck and pelt me with kisses. I wanted something to melt her heart. I wanted some help from Katie Pphart. I wanted it to be different. But I gained the door without a fight and gently closed it behind me.

8

WHEN SUPPER HAD been cleared away I spent the rest of the evening in the back parlour, watching the wrestling with mother. We settled down with a box of cheese crackers and shouted at Keiji Muto, aka the Great Muta, as he battered the daylights from Thunder Lyger for the Junior Heavyweight Championship before a crowd of 60,000 screaming spectators in the Tokyo Dome. Mother barked and tossed crackers at the referee. She loved Japanese wrestling and Thunder Lyger, with his fountain of hair, spectacular horns and strange gauze goggles, was a particular favourite. She didn't mention Franklin's bad behaviour. The incident at supper had already been forgotten. It wasn't unusual. We had learned to accept Franklin's influence over the house in the manner we accepted the weather – there were squalls followed by calms, storms followed by frosts, and nothing could change it.

It was a good match. The Great Muta nearly took the belt in the first few minutes with a snap suplex converted into a scorpion death lock but Thunder Lyger turned the match by throwing his opponent clean through the ropes in a punishing counter-attack. Muta struck the steel barrier, scattering photographers, and Lyger chased him down to shovel him back into the ring.

'That nailed him!' mother shouted with satisfaction as the Great Muta was abruptly cartwheeled and his head driven into the canvas.

Muta looked bad. He must have been injured. His mouth foamed, his mad eyes were fixed and staring, one leg seemed broken and twisted beneath him. The referee hurried forward and gave him a kick with the tip of a patent leather shoe. Muta didn't move. The referee trod on his fingers. Nothing happened. The referee shook his head. It was finished.

Thunder Lyger turned in triumph and threw up his arms to salute the crowd. But in the blink of an eye, in the push of a heartbeat, the Great Muta sprang back to life, restored by some miracle into a demon and seized Thunder Lyger by the throat, spun on his heel and gave him a mule kick that sent him sprawling.

'Hit him with your handbag!' mother spluttered, firing cracker crumbs down the front of her cardigan.

Lyger went down but came up again. Muta hacked and chopped and battered him into the ropes. And then, when all seemed hopeless, when it was certain that the belt had been lost, Lyger lashed out like a cobra, pinned his opponent and snatched victory from the jaws of defeat. One. Two. Three.

We went to bed some time after midnight. We called father from the cellar and mother took him upstairs.

'What's the time?' he demanded, wrenching away his spectacles and peering blindly at his wrists.

'It's time you spent an evening with your family,' she said.

I checked the locks, switched out the lights and went to my room. The smallest and ugliest room in the house. The furniture I'd been given might have been chosen especially to trigger depression or violent despair. A second-hand wardrobe made from some kind of particle-board, painted brown to imitate wood and fitted with broken red plastic handles. A blue vinyl chair with tubular legs in a clumsy, old-fashioned space-age design. A cracked wall mirror in pokerwork frame, a grey metal bedside cabinet and a murky lamp in a pink paisley shade with badly scorched nylon tassels. If mother had bothered to name this room she might have called it the Orphanage.

I quickly undressed and climbed into bed. But I couldn't sleep. I lay awake and stared at the dark. I remembered my conversation with Janet, sitting beside her on the bed as she showed me her legs and fondled her rabbit. The thought excited and troubled me.

She threw back her lovely head and tossed her abundance of flaming gold hair in a gesture of angry defiance as she turned once more with glittering eyes to confront the tall, big-fisted young man who was standing silently over the bed.

'You should leave this instant!' she commanded but Mr Romance shook his head with a devilish chuckle. How handsome he looked in the candlelight! He was lean yet perfectly muscular with a dark and fascinating smile. Until that moment she had thought him to be a child but now she felt herself blush like a peach as she watched him unbutton his uniform.

'*Can't you see that I'm bulging for you!*' he murmured hoarsely. '*I'm straining like a gallant stallion!*'

Finally I switched on the bedside lamp, leaned overboard, poked my fingers under an edge of frayed carpet between the wall and the bed and recovered my copy of *Frolicking Fatties*. But nothing could bring me comfort and even the sight of pot-bellied Lottie Pout, with her slap-happy smile and elastic nipples, failed to work its nocturnal magic. *Frolicking Fatties* had provided me with many faithful companions during the long, cold nights of winter. Whenever I couldn't sleep I would hook out the magazine and let myself loose in its gallery of readers' wives.

I loved this exotic bestiary of fat housewives on parade in corners of suburban living rooms. The pictures were dark and badly composed and always included the furniture – a bag of knitting in a small armchair, a lava lamp on a chest of drawers, a paper lampshade in the ceiling, shoes and underwear spilled on the floor. The dimpled divas strutted on shag pile, hoicked up their skirts and pushed out their buttocks like cheerful African gods. They had snagged stockings and crooked smiles and bellies the size of prize-winning pumpkins. Yet they were nothing compared to the gatefold where Lottie Pout waited to pounce in her creaking, pink satin waspie. Lottie Pout was a porker! The sight of her always worked on me like a rush of opium. The symptoms were agitation and fever, followed by blissful narcolepsy. But tonight she failed to take effect as I fingered my bone of contention. Janet had immunised me against lewd Lottie's charm and although I tried to picture Janet – greatly engorged and thoroughly brazen – turning her into a frolicking fatty proved beyond my imagination.

I was struggling to return the magazine to its hiding place when I heard the floorboards creaking near the bedroom door. I froze in alarm, hanging upside down with my arm trapped beneath the bed. There was someone prowling on the landing. There was someone skulking outside my door. I let myself slide from the mattress, plunged across the room in search of my dressing gown and squandered precious moments cramming my feet into shoes.

When I pulled open the bedroom door I found Mr Marvel, shivering in his pyjamas, with a blue plastic flashlight in his hand. He seemed as shocked to meet me on the stairs as I had been to find him there. He fell against the wall and clutched his chest in distress.

'What's happening?' I whispered, raising a hand to protect my face from the flashlight.

'Intruders!' he gasped, rolling from the wall and trying to catch his breath. His face was mottled and bleary with sleep.

'Where?'

'Downstairs!' he whispered. 'They're downstairs. I do believe they've found their way into the kitchen.'

'But I've locked the house.'

'No matter! Bolts and chains mean nothing to these devils!' he said, wagging his head.

'Who?' I demanded. The house was large and draughty but the doors had been carved from seasoned oak and most of the windows were sealed by an elephant skin of enamel paint. We were so secure we would die in our beds if the house caught fire. There was no escape. It was guaranteed. And no one could force a lock or smash a window without making such a noise it would wake the neighbourhood. But Marvel could not be mollified.

'Listen!' he shuddered, waving his flashlight at the ceiling. The pale light fluttered, caught by a cobweb.

I cocked my head and listened. There was silence. Even on quiet nights in this house you could hear the sound of the sea in the traffic, aircraft rising and sinking above you, distant voices, the mumbling of pipes and ticking of timbers. Silence, when it falls in the city, is so rare and unfamiliar that it seems to have a sound of its own.

'Did you hear it?'

'No.'

'Do you have something to call a weapon?' he asked suddenly, glancing over my dressing gown in the hope that I might be concealing a bayonet or ammunition belt.

I shook my head and tightened the knot on the dressing-gown cord. Nothing came to mind short of rolling a truncheon from *Frolicking Fatties*. The knives and scissors were in the kitchen.

'Sticks! We'll find sticks in the umbrella stand!' he said. He scampered away, hunchbacked and dangerous, ran downstairs and tiptoed across the hall where he pulled a metal-tipped walking cane from the armoury.

'Wait!' I whispered as I hobbled behind him.

'What is it?'

'My shoes are on the wrong feet!' I complained, sitting down on the stairs.

He waited for me impatiently, flexing the cane in his hands, while I fumbled with my shoes. His fear was infectious. As soon as I could walk again, I took a weapon for myself, choosing a clumsy walking stick with a rubber stopper on the end but a handle as thick as a cudgel.

We rushed down the corridor, burst into the kitchen and snapped on the lights, hoping to frighten intruders into an easy flight. But nothing happened. We stood blinking at an empty room. The freezer trembled. A leaking tap spilled pearls. We searched the cupboards. We glared into corners. We moved to the kitchen window and shone the flashlight into the yard. It was empty. I checked the lock on the kitchen door. It held fast.

Marvel paused and looked puzzled, scratching his bristling chin. 'The parlour!' he whispered. 'They must have sneaked into the parlour.'

'There's no one here,' I protested, plodding after him.

We searched the front parlour and the back parlour, the cloakroom and the dining room, checked the locks on the windows and doors, and poked our sticks beneath chairs and tables, until Marvel had to agree with me that the house had been secured.

'It's very queer,' he said, switching off his plastic flashlight and sinking into a sofa. 'I could have sworn…' He looked old and confused, like an unhappy sleepwalker shaken awake in unfamiliar surroundings.

'Perhaps you were dreaming.'

'I don't know.' He frowned and stared at the cane in his

hand, running it through one fist and tapping it against the floor.

'It might help to talk to someone…' I suggested.

'Talk?'

'If someone was chasing you,' I said. 'If you're in danger. Who did you think was in the house?'

He shrugged and sighed and balanced the cane between his slippers. 'It could have been almost anyone. There seems to be so many of them.'

'Who?'

'No one to worry you, Skipper' he said gently. 'They've no grudge against you. It's me they want. It's me they're trying to find.'

'Do you want a hot drink?' The house had grown cold and Marvel shivered in his pyjamas. I thought I could coax him with strong, sweet tea into making a full and detailed confession. It seemed the perfect opportunity. I was wrong.

'How old are you, Skipper?' he asked for no reason, tilting his head and fixing me with a yellow eye.

'Eighteen.'

'I'm fifty,' he sighed. 'Do you know the difference between us?'

Well, I knew the answer wasn't thirty-two, so I shrugged.

'Sometimes I think that I'm eighteen,' he said sadly, 'but you've never felt you were fifty.'

'I might find some brandy…' I suggested.

'What are you going to do with your life?'

'I don't exactly know,' I said.

'But it's going to be something special, isn't it?'

'Yes!' I said. It was obvious. It was something I had never doubted. I might become anything in the world. I could be anyone. When the time arrived I might discover myself to be a famous TV talk-show host. A senior news-room anchorman. Or the cowboy in the Cadillac in the Mexican coffee commercials. In this age of loneliness, tele-vision celebrities are what we accept in place of heroes. In truth I lacked ambition. I had nothing to recommend me but optimism and innocence. I was confident that when the time came I could do anything in the world but I hadn't yet found my purpose. I was waiting to be summoned by trumpets.

He nodded and considered. 'Because there's a voice inside you that says you're different.'

'Yes!'

'A small voice whispering in your ear. And it seems to be telling you that you've been marked out by fate in some mysterious manner that you don't quite understand. Isn't that right?'

'That's right!' I said, astonished by his insight into my soul. How did he do it? This man was a genius!

'And one day you'll be famous for something,' he said with a distant smile. 'You'll make your impression on the world. You don't know how. But you'll do it. You'll change it. You'll get there.'

'How did you know?' I whispered.

'That's the difference!' he said with a smile. He spiked the carpet with his cane and used it to haul himself from the sofa.

'Let me find the brandy,' I said.

But I couldn't make him stay and confide in me. He shook his head. 'I'm much obliged,' he yawned. 'But I think that it's time I went to bed.' And he shuffled for the safety of the stairs.

9

'IT'S HORRIBLE!' MOTHER sobbed, pulling away and wiping her eyes in her apron. 'You wake up in the middle of the night and there's a strange man standing at the foot of the bed wearing nothing but his balaclava. It happens all the time...'

'It's never happened to me,' I said.

'You're not a woman!' mother said, snuffling and stroking her burning face.

'How do they get through the bedroom windows?'

'They carry ladders,' she said ominously.

We were in the kitchen, chopping onions for supper. I had been describing the previous night's events and Mr Marvel's fear of intruders. It wasn't much of a story but the thought of strangers in balaclavas had caught my mother's imagination.

'We're not safe in our beds anymore,' she said, returning to her chopping board and promptly blinding herself again.

'They're looking for drugs,' father said. They had always shared the opinion that the world was dangerous after dark. Beyond the safety of the privet hedge, in the great black yonder, terrible phantoms prowled the streets, corpses climbed over cemetery gates and lunatics barked at the moon. He was sitting at the kitchen table trying to make sense of his new security system, teasing wires into bundles and wrapping them with bandages of sticky, black insulating tape.

'They're not after drugs in the altogether,' mother argued, wanting to emphasise her special vulnerability as a frail and frightened woman.

'Well, that's what the drugs do to them,' father explained. 'It gives them enormous appetites.'

We'd spent most of the afternoon discussing our fortifications. The roof was so warped and dangerous that anyone scaling its peaks in the hope of gaining entry would certainly die in the attempt. The old stained-glass windows were formidable obstacles and needed no attention. We knew that most intruders would force an entry through the back of the house but since we also knew that most intruders knew that we knew, we reasoned they already supposed the back of the house to be secure and would make their assault from the front.

'You have to understand how they work,' father said. 'You have to enter the criminal mind. And then you can make their lives difficult.'

He rigged the battleship klaxon high up on the wall where even the most determined intruder would have trouble reaching it, and spent several dangerous minutes balanced on a ladder, arms stretched to the ceiling, while a power drill growled and jumped in his fist.

Mr Marvel came downstairs, attracted by the noise, and was soon involved in the work. 'You built this from your own design?' he asked father, weighing the box of tricks in his hands. He seemed fascinated by the contraption.

'It looks primitive,' father said proudly, 'but this is only a prototype. When we go into proper production it should be a little more compact.' He could already see it in every detail. The Wandsworth Security Watchdog. It stays awake while you're asleep. All rights reserved. More than a million sold worldwide.

'Remarkable!' Marvel muttered. 'It's most remarkable!'

'We thought it would help you feel more secure,' mother told him, snuffling and wiping the tears from her eyes.

'I'm much obliged,' Marvel said and looked overwhelmed by so much attention. He helped me run the cables from the klaxon as far as the front door and watched father connect the whamdoodles to the great oak frame.

When it was finished we gathered round and waited as father hurried back into the kitchen to switch on the power. I thought he looked flushed and rather anxious. He didn't like an audience when he was testing a new invention.

'Has anything happened?' he shouted.

There was a dull thump as the electricity kicked into the system and a beam of acid-green light crackled between the two plastic boxes, forming a shimmering curtain against the door. We couldn't speak. We stood astounded.

'It works!' he gasped, upon his return. 'It works!' He sounded surprised. 'Who wants to try it?'

No one answered. We frowned at the light and shrank

from its glare, shielding our eyes with our hands. There was something in its brilliance that suggested it could eat flesh and drill through bone.

'I think Skipper should test it,' father said at last, when it was plain that nobody wanted to volunteer. 'He's the youngest.'

'What's that got to do with anything?' mother demanded suspiciously, peeking at him though spread fingers. The light flashed on her wedding ring and glittered on her cardigan buttons.

'Well, if anything goes wrong, he's more likely to survive the shock,' father explained.

'I think we should ask Franklin!' I said.

'Why?'

'Because if anyone must die for science,' I said simply, 'he has the best education for it.'

'Good idea!' father said.

'We mustn't *kill* him!' mother said, as if she might accept a measure of mutilation.

'He won't come to any harm,' father promised. 'But, if something goes tragically wrong at least we'll have an opportunity to clean out his attic and give it a fresh lick of paint.'

So Franklin was summoned from the front parlour where he'd spent most of the day dreaming of ways to destroy the Dwarf's reputation, and stood scowling at the fiery cobweb while father explained the situation to him.

'We just want you to step through the front door,' father said. 'It shouldn't take you a moment.'

Franklin sensed there was something wrong. He

wanted to be the star attraction but he wasn't prepared to
risk losing his head to gain our undivided attention. 'I'm
flattered, nay, honoured in every extremity, for this generous invitation to be the first to demonstrate your
spinthariscopic bibelot,' he babbled. 'And yet, alas, upon
reflection, I feel the pleasure, nay, glory of the moment
should be strictly reserved for the eldritch Mr Marvellous!'
He made this little speech without once turning to look at
Marvel or showing any sign that he knew the man was
standing beside him.

Marvel looked doubtful but felt required to take the
risk since these extra security measures had been arranged
for his benefit. 'Does it hurt?' he inquired.

'You won't feel a thing!' father said confidently.

Marvel nodded and pulled a large white handkerchief
from his pocket to wipe the sweat from his palms. He
cleared his throat, adjusted his collar, puffed himself out
and boldly stepped forward. But before he could walk
through death's door it creaked open and Janet appeared
on the threshold.

'For God's sake, get back!' father shouted. The prevail-
ing atmosphere of doubt must have affected him for his
courage suddenly failed and he seemed to lose faith in the
enterprise.

'Don't move!' I shouted. 'Don't move and you won't get
hurt!'

Janet shrieked and floundered. 'I'm electric!' she
screamed. 'I'm electric!'

The light wobbled and shrank to nothing. But Janet
became phosphorescent. The light clung to her arms and

legs. It danced in her hair like St Elmo's fire. She opened her mouth to scream. Her teeth were green. Her tongue was a forked and flickering flame.

I was paralysed with fright. I should have done something. I should have scooped her from the fire's embrace. I should have borne her away in my arms. I should have carried her up to her room. I should have unbuttoned her shirt, slipped off her shoes, sipped at her tears, soothed her with kisses.

Oh, Skipper, she whispers, Skipper you saved me! I give you my heart. I grant you three wishes.

But it was Mr Marvel who found the courage to pluck at her sleeve and drag her to safety. She went tumbling into his arms and the light was abruptly extinguished. Far away in the kitchen, the klaxon sprang from its moorings and crashed through a cupboard onto the floor. Janet was still screaming but she wasn't hurt. Marvel helped guide her into the back parlour where mother gave her sweet tea for shock. Franklin smirked and drifted away towards Lilliput.

Father stared at the melting whamdoodles dripping plastic onto the carpet. His face looked grey. He clasped the back of his neck in his hands.

'It almost worked,' I said, standing beside him. 'It certainly scared the hell out of me.'

He shook his head. 'It must have been a loose connection,' he said quietly. He was very subdued. The disappointments of a lifetime seemed to crowd down upon him. This public demonstration of his own failure was almost more than he could endure. I helped him dismantle

the equipment and we threw the wreckage into the yard.
He never mentioned it again.

10

I WAS A disappointment to my father. He was a man ruled by principles and formulations, charts, tabulations, weights and measures. He could chant the laws of thermodynamics like pages from the Book of Common Prayer. He would recite, chapter and verse, the architecture of chemicals. He could measure the wind and forecast the weather, classify insects, label rocks and even perform minor surgery on a range of domestic animals. He was never called upon to exercise his skills as a surgeon but he had the manuals. He took an interest in everything. He was acquainted with engineering, electronics, plumbing and photography. He was familiar with geology, botany, astronomy and microscopy. Nothing escaped his attention. He might, upon request, name all the bones in a skeleton or guess the atomic weights of iridium and uranium. This thirst for knowledge made him pragmatic. He wasted no time in gazing at stars or trying to fathom the universe. He would rather build a radio or an automatic cat-food dispenser. He wanted me to share his interest but I couldn't tell a sprocket from a number three grommet. It was hopeless. His head was filled with the certainty of meticulous diagrams. My head was filled with the smoke of dreams.

Once upon a time he'd kept me enchanted with toys and gadgets made in his workshop. I remember rubber spiders, cotton-reel snakes and troupes of mechanical penguins that clattered their wings and staggered like sailors. I remember the robot that lost its head and the submarine that went missing in action. I remember, when I was seven, a steam-powered rocking horse, a horse from hell for a birthday boy, that flared its nostrils and rolled its eyes and could not be tamed but kicked and bucked and threw itself from a bedroom window.

In the damp, draughty days of autumn he would turn to the manufacture of fireworks, mixing sulphurs, salts and household bleach to his own particular recipe and producing volatile crystals that he packed into blue paper cartridges to fire from heavy, metal tubes. At the dead of night we would creep from the house and stand shivering in the back yard, wrapped in overcoats and mufflers, to watch my father bombard the city with Bengal lights and Chinese mortars. He tossed rainbows into the sky and showered the rooftops with sparkling cinders.

He had the violence of a magician and the patience of a craftsman. His fireworks exploded like thunderstorms. His toys were intricate creatures that came to life at the flick of a switch and tumbled and danced on tabletops. Yet he always dismissed these achievements as trifles. He wanted to create objects for a future world, miraculous household objects for the metropolis of tomorrow. He wanted to live in a labour-saving utopia of indestructible plastic shoes and personal jet-powered aerocycles. This plain, old-fashioned view of the future was something he must have carried with him from his own childhood and he would not rest until he had climbed its glittering towers and strolled through its shimmering thoroughfares. Yet no matter how he laboured to create the elements of this perfect world, his efforts seemed doomed to failure.

His most ambitious invention was the Life Expectancy Wristwatch. I was fifteen years old when he took me down to the cellar and introduced me to its sinister calculations. It was the size of a regular wristwatch, but rather heavy and square in the beam and secured with a thick leather band. The face of the instrument contained a cluster of white enamel dials designed to measure the minutes and hours, the days and weeks, the months and years.

'It's beautiful,' I said, holding the watch in the palm of my hand. The case was polished and finely engraved with acorns and clusters of oak leaves.

'Silver,' he said proudly.

'How does it work?' I asked him.

'It's simple,' he said, gazing down at his work with a soft and tender expression on his face. 'Regular wrist-watches give you the time of day. But this watch gives you the time of your life. The owner adjusts the calibrations according to his age, health, education and background. It will come with a full instruction book. When the instrument is properly set it provides an estimate of your life expectancy and starts to work backwards to zero. Do you follow me?'

'No.'

'Well, let's say, for example, that you can expect to live

for another sixty years. You're fit and healthy. You still have your teeth. Sixty years. What do you think?'

'Fine!' I said. Sixty years seemed like a good long time. It sounded like an eternity.

'If you wear this wristwatch it will help you keep track of the time. It's a friend for life. When you reach your fortieth birthday you'll look at your watch and know that you have another thirty-five years. When you reach sixty you'll check your wrist and know that you still have another fifteen years ahead of you.'

'Isn't it rather complicated?' I asked him.

'No!' he said, beaming. 'Anyone with a screwdriver, a complete medical history, a grasp of mathematics, a smattering of genetics, a family tree and just a little technical how's-your-father could get it going in a couple of hours. That's the beauty of it. You just set it and forget it.'

I thought it must be difficult to forget a biological time bomb ticking your life away, especially when it was strapped to your wrist. But it was a clever idea. You couldn't fault him. If you wanted to know the hour of your death, this was the wristwatch for you.

'What happens if there's an accident?' I ventured.

'It's shockproof and waterproof to fifty metres,' he said proudly.

'No, I mean, what happens if I get knocked down by a truck? What happens if I die in a plane crash or an earthquake or something? What happens if I catch some unknown disease?'

'It can't read your fortune,' he admitted. He took the timepiece from my hand as if it were some rare and valuable egg, placed it gently on the workbench in a little nest of rags, and wiped my thumbprints away with a cloth. 'You can't account for acts of God.'

'And what happens if it goes wrong?' I demanded. 'What happens if it runs slow, or fast, or suddenly stops?'

'You get it fixed,' he said, perplexed by my attitude. He wanted smiles and admiring glances, congratulations and coloured bunting. He hadn't expected to pick at the bones of an argument.

'But it's running backwards,' I protested. 'How do you know if it's running on time? You wouldn't know the difference. I mean, if it starts gaining or losing thirty seconds every twenty-four hours, that would turn into days over thirty years. You wouldn't know if you were supposed to be alive or dead!'

He blinked and frowned and clacked his nails against the silver case. He was beginning to have his doubts.

'And what about flat batteries?' I said. 'What happens when the batteries go flat because you forgot to change them?'

'It's a solar battery,' he argued. 'It's powered by sunlight. Solar battery. Quartz crystal. It will last forever.'

'But suppose,' I insisted. 'What would happen if you woke up in the middle of the night and fumbled for your watch and you *thought* it had stopped. You pressed it to your ear and you couldn't hear it. You would feel like you'd died in your sleep. Your life cut short unexpectedly. It would be like mechanical heart failure. I mean, the shock could kill you!' I knew I must be hurting him but I didn't know how to stop myself. I was out of control. I wanted him to throttle me. I wanted to bite out my own tongue. I couldn't stop talking.

'And if nothing goes wrong, if it just keeps running, that would be worse because you'd eventually reach the last few weeks of your life and you'd start counting the days and hours and final minutes,' I continued. 'It would drive you crazy. Watching your life slip away. I mean, you'd feel like a condemned man waiting for the moment of execution!'

He looked sick. His fingers trembled as they stroked the watch. His face had turned grey and the skin seemed to sag on his bones. He was growing old before my eyes. But I couldn't stop talking.

'If we all wore this kind of wristwatch there'd be panic in the streets!' I jabbered. 'We'd all be running and screaming, trying to keep ahead of ourselves. It would be terrible. Terrible. Nothing would get done because we wouldn't have the time to spare.'

He looked exhausted. He shivered and shrank away from me. He didn't want me there in the cellar. He didn't want me to be his son.

'It would drive you mad!' I shouted in horror. Here was a monstrous device, a diabolical manacle of slow but perpetual torture. 'Something like that. It would drive you mad. Watching it get a little closer every day. Hour by hour. Minute by minute. Terrible. You'd always be thinking about it.'

'No!' he said, shaking his head. 'No!'

'Yes!' I shouted. 'You'd go insane or get so depressed that you'd want to take an overdose just to forget about it.

And if you killed yourself before your time, if you committed suicide, it would make life worthless. All that hard work for nothing. It would be a waste of time.'

He didn't say a word. He looked down at his doomed invention for a long time. He could see now that the concept was fatally flawed. It was damned. It couldn't be rescued. And then he reached out, took a hammer from his toolbox and with a swift, deliberate blow, smashed the watch into fragments. He didn't speak to me again for two-and-a-half weeks. I know it was two-and-a-half weeks. I marked off the days on my Wrestlemania calendar.

11

DESPITE THE FAILURE of the Wandsworth home-security system, Mr Marvel never again prowled the stairs at midnight in search of phantom intruders. Perhaps he slept secure in his bed because he felt that we cared for his safety. Or perhaps the demons that taunted him fell silent during the hours of darkness. Whatever the reasons, he seemed to grow more confident. He would sleep late, take a pot of tea and a plate of biscuits at ten o'clock sharp, and spend the rest of the day in the parlour, reading any paper or journal that hadn't fallen victim to Franklin's scissors. Janet granted him the freedom of her Katie Pphart library and, in return, he taught her to play a nimble game of dominoes. He even began to join us for supper, pecking timidly at his food and chuckling at my mother as she tried to tempt him with tasty morsels of steamed beef pudding or cherry pie. He led a quiet and simple life.

But once a week he would undertake the same mysterious errand, leaving the house in the morning and returning in the late afternoon, bloated and raving, transformed from a timid, mild-mannered man into a flatulent, pot-bellied boggart. These wild excursions would be followed, late at night, by rapid bursts of activity on his ancient typewriter. It happened with such regularity and seemed to fill him with such a great violence of emotion that even my mother had to admit something was wrong.

'Drunk!' father declared, after one particular episode. 'Drunk as a toad in a brandy barrel!' He didn't sound in the least concerned that Marvel should want to drink himself blind. He supposed that crapulence was a mark of universal brotherhood and thoroughly approved of it, although he himself seldom took more than a glass of beer and never touched wine or spirits.

'Nonsense!' mother said. 'The drink has got nothing to do with it.' We had found Mr Marvel slumped against the front door with his head wrapped up in his overcoat and carried him upstairs like a piano.

'He still thinks there are people chasing him,' I said.

'So why doesn't he stay in the house?' father asked.

'He needs the fresh air,' mother told him. She rarely ventured from the fog of her own kitchen and thought the smoke of the city streets was a first-rate tonic, a natural restorative.

'He's convinced that someone out there wants to kill him,' I said. I knew it sounded ridiculous but that was the truth of it.

'Who?' father demanded. 'Who? Tell me. Who wants to kill him?'

'I don't know,' I grumbled, sucking air through my teeth. We were hiding in the back parlour, feasting on slabs of sultana cake with glasses of chocolate milk. The cake was still hot from the oven, the sultanas sizzled and popped in my mouth, making me gasp as they burned my tongue.

'I think he's lonely,' father said to himself. 'The poor old bugger. I think his mind is wandering.'

'He should be married. A man his age. It isn't normal,' mother agreed. She hated to see a man without a wife. She regarded such men as pariahs, free to prey on the innocent, cunning, hungry and dangerous.

For a few moments we were silent, our mouths glued with cake.

'He seems to have grown rather fond of Janet,' I said, with a pang of jealousy. Everyone fell in love with Janet. I imagined her beauty counter besieged by crowds of her smiling admirers. Dangerous men in dark suits stirred into heat as she bent to anoint their wrists with perfume.

'Janet couldn't look after him!' mother said, as she sucked her fingers.

'It's a shame that we don't have Dorothy here,' father said brightly. 'She'd soon have him as right as ninepence!' And to my surprise he blushed with pleasure and laughed at the mere idea of it.

'Who?'

'Dorothy. You must remember Dorothy. Dorothy Clark. Big, bright girl with a sense of fun. She used to have Janet's room when you were small.'

'He's forgotten,' mother said. 'He doesn't know what you're talking about. It must be more than ten years ago.'

It was true. So many people had passed through the house it was hard to remember their names and faces. A few had made an impression. I could still recall Trenchard Cox, the stuttering lepidopterist, who had filled his room with ten thousand tiny velvet corpses. I dimly remembered

Boswell Shanks, a man who had shocked me as a child by extricating his upper teeth and placing them in his jacket pocket. And I hadn't forgotten Jessica Proud, the bull-necked physiotherapist. The memory came rushing back to scorch my face with embarrassment. She had come to the house one dismal winter's afternoon and stayed until the following summer. I had been twelve years old and interested in growing biceps. Jessica Proud was three times my age and three times my size and possessed not an ounce of modesty. She had marched around the house in vest and underpants with a towel at her neck and a stopwatch in hand; and for a few brief but alarming months, she had turned our little backyard into a makeshift gymnasium.

For a week or more I had watched her pumping and grinding from the safety of my bedroom window, my nose squashed against the glass and a poltergeist in my pyjamas until, one morning, she had seen me there and coaxed me down for a programme of vigorous exercise. I'd stood in the frosty yard, trembling in my Jockey shorts, but the sight of her bending and touching her toes had filled my sprouting twelve-year-old limbs with such a confusing rush of excitement that I was required to throw myself into the exercise just to cover my embarrassment. By the time she left I was feeling as fit as a butcher's dog.

Oh, I remember Jessica Proud, with her close-cropped hair and her perky pecs and astonishing abdominals! I still remember her glucose tablets and pain sprays and vitamin drinks and the pleasure I felt in mixing those Hi-jump milk shakes for breakfast, and my first sight of her white sports bras and her health education magazines and the smell in the towels of her medicated lubricants. And after Jessica Proud came Percy Smart the ventriloquist with his constant companion Cheerful Cyril; and Violet Bush the telephonist and whispering Shirley Fudger the hospital radiographer. I could recapture a dozen or more of the faces that had passed me on the stairs. But Dorothy Clark was not among them. Dorothy Clark was missing.

'She went to live on the coast,' father said. 'I think I might still have the address somewhere...' He took a swig of chocolate milk, which gave him a foaming sugar moustache to be wiped away with his thumb.

'No!' mother snapped.

'What?' father said, looking startled.

'Whatever you're thinking, the answer is No!'

'There's no harm in thinking.'

'One thing leads to another.'

'You'll like Dorothy,' father whispered, turning to me for support. 'She was a dancer!'

'She *said* she was a dancer,' mother said darkly, licking the tip of one finger to dab at the crumbs on her plate.

'She was a dancer,' father insisted. He sounded very confident. 'She came here to rest. She was resting.'

'Well, let her rest in peace,' mother told him, sternly. 'And we'll have no more nonsense.'

Father didn't care to argue. He wanted more sultana cake. But the next day, when I followed him down to North Street Market, he felt free enough to mention Dorothy Clark again.

12

We had no business in North Street Market – we'd been sent out for soap and potatoes and there were plenty of shops within a short walk of the house. But we knew from bitter experience that the local shops could not be trusted. An Asian grocery might open for business and the second time you went there for cabbage or lavatory paper, it would have turned into Strictly Donuts or the Porno Mag Mart, and a month later would sink into a deep depression only to rise again as Paradise Pancake or an Irish pork butcher or a charity shop selling plaster-of-Paris novelties. In our local neighbourhood only fried chicken counters seemed able to flourish and three of them survived within spitting distance of one another, haunted by unhappy drunks, picking scraps from waxed paper boxes.

The market, by contrast, was constant. A sprawling maze of lanes and alleys carved from the oldest part of the city. You'd find everything in that shanty town. Beneath the faded canvas awnings there were Turkish florists, Indian doctors, Chinese grocers, Nigerian barbers and strange, brooding Babylonians who seemed to sell nothing but needles and buttons. If you picked a path through the brooms and buckets, bales of silk and brightly coloured plastic sandals, you'd find millet cakes from Togo, biltong from Zimbabwe, freshwater fish from Bengal and bottles of almond oil from Kashmir. There were baskets of cardamoms, red and green chillies, cloves, peppers and nutmegs. The air was charged with the smells of incense, fried apple fritters, cheap cigars, roasting peanuts, ripe fruit and the sour, smoky smell of tamarind paste.

'Guess what I've found!' father demanded, as he paused beneath a tarpaulin tent to poke through a pile of bananas guarded by a silent, staring Arab in a pair of winkle-picker shoes.

'What?' I said, half-expecting him to pull out a spider or scorpion. The Arab scowled and looked nervous, trying to brush father away with his sleeve.

'Dorothy's address. I knew that I hadn't thrown it away. It came to light in a box of spanners.'

'And you're going to write?' I asked, as I led him away.

He turned and winked at me. 'You wait, Skipper! You'll love it. When Dorothy was in the house we never stopped laughing. That girl was a panic. She'll soon have old Marvel sitting up and balancing biscuits on his nose.'

We pushed forward into the crowded lanes of the market, past the ancient Rangoon doctor with his remedies for the married man, and the sad Greek herbalist with the curious skin disease, and the fat man in the black cotton gloves who sold cracked plates and bundles of unwanted knives and forks.

'What are you going to say in the letter?' I asked, as he paused to pick through a box of tarnished silver spoons.

'I don't know. I'll think of something.'

'Are you sure it's a good idea?' I said. It was obvious that he'd given his scheme a lot of thought but sometimes the obvious seemed to escape him.

'Don't worry about your mother,' he grinned. 'That's no problem. I know how to handle women.'

'But if they don't like each other…'

'Everyone likes Dorothy!'

'You want them spoons?' the fat man asked impatiently, watching father with a small and deeply suspicious eye.

'They're filthy!' said father, dropping them in disgust and sniffing his tainted fingers.

'They're old,' the fat man replied. 'That's why they're smelly. Genuine antiques. You'll be smelly when you reach their age.'

Father wasn't impressed. He took me by the elbow and led me deeper into the market, past the Russians selling bottled mushrooms and the Cubans hawking combs, until we had reached the darkest corner where an old man in a knitted hat was selling small birds and animals. There were parrots, huddled like priests, on his shoulders and kittens that squirmed in his overcoat pockets. He was leaning on a long metal pole, tied with plastic bags of water. The bags were draped like dozens of teardrops and each teardrop contained a fish. They hung suspended like living baubles of red and black sequins. Their eyes were gold and their tails were trailing paper fans.

'You have to give them little surprises,' father explained, buying one of the prisoners and weighing the wobbling sphere in his hands. 'A woman needs to be coaxed and flattered. It's something you'll learn as you get older.'

He never managed to sound convincing, teaching his son these masculine secrets. Despite his bravado, it was obvious that he didn't believe the myths and fancies that men invent to explain the world. He lived entirely at a woman's mercy and he knew that he could no more influence her mood with a magic fish than control the planets with tossed chicken bones.

'It sounds like bribery and corruption,' I said, to encourage our sense of happy conspiracy.

'That's about the size of it,' he grinned.

'Do you think a goldfish will do the trick?' I said, gazing at our glittering captive.

'Your mother *loves* goldfish!' he said.

'And why doesn't she want Dorothy back in the house?'

He shrugged and said nothing. I couldn't guess what had happened but it must have left him in deep disgrace. I sensed scandal. I began to imagine Dorothy as a wild and dangerous woman. He wasn't an affectionate man. I never saw him flirting or making a fool of himself. But that merely added to his new role as man of mystery.

It was late when we arrived home and, despite father's predictions, mother wasn't impressed by the gift.

'What do you want me to do with this?' she grumbled, as if she thought we expected her to be ready and waiting to bone and fry it.

'Nothing,' father said, rather too loudly. He was rattled by such a poor reception. He'd been hoping for instant success. 'I bought it for you as a gift. It's purely for decoration.'

'That's something you have in common,' she said.

She poured the novelty into an earthenware mixing

bowl, scolded father and sent me out to buy soap and potatoes. The suffocated goldfish swam in circles and died the following morning.

Father was discouraged but he tried again. 'Women need time to get the idea,' he told me. Another of his lessons for life.

He offered sun-faded boxes of chocolates and jars of ginger steeped in syrup. He bought bunches of flowers and glass-bead bangles and miniature bottles of real French perfume. It took him another week of wheedling before mother gave him permission to write a letter to Dorothy Clark. And by that time she was proudly squelching around the house in a new pair of fancy Reeboks with air-cushioned soles and racing stripes.

13

DOROTHY CLARK ACCEPTED my father's invitation. She wrote to him on a single sheet of pale green paper, thanking him for his generous offer, inquiring after my mother's health and expressing her firm intentions to stay for at least a month.

'What did you say in your letter?' mother demanded at breakfast.

'I forget!' father said quickly, sorting through the rest of the morning's post and pretending to take an interest in a *Readers Digest* competition. Win a fortune. Trial subscription. Your name selected. No stamp required.

'A few days!' mother said, scowling at Dorothy's peculiar, cramped handwriting. She sniffed the page and held it against the light. 'You asked her to stay for a few days!' She snatched up the envelope, prised it open and gave it a shake, searching for an explanation.

'A few days. A few weeks. What's the difference?'

'The difference is perfectly obvious. We can't afford it! We're supposed to be renting the rooms, not giving them away.'

'She never had much of an appetite,' father argued. 'She's like Janet in that respect. And it's a damned big house. We'll still have plenty of rooms.'

'Not to mention the extra expense of heat, hot water and laundry.'

'We'll manage.'

'And how are we going to keep her amused?' she said, returning the letter to its envelope and slapping it down on the table.

'She can keep herself amused,' father said mildly.

'I don't want any monkey business,' mother warned him.

Father didn't flinch. He certainly didn't look like a man who had once been led astray by a lean and lewd-limbed dancer. But appearances can be treacherous. I began to imagine Dorothy as a glittering chorus girl in spiky, high-heeled shoes and a sweeping head-dress of ostrich feathers.

'She'll be company for Marvel,' he said simply, thumbing an opportunity to purchase a set of porcelain thimbles decorated with flags of all nations.

'And what happens if they don't take to each other?' mother asked him. She had a knack of finding problems. 'What happens if Mr Marvel doesn't want to be bothered? You can't force him to take an interest.'

'Everyone loves Dorothy,' father said absently, as he shuffled coupons for cut-price pizza, dog food, shampoo and life insurance.

'Suppose,' mother insisted.

'Well, if she gets bored, Skipper can show her the sights,' father said impatiently and shot me a glance that told me he'd take no arguments.

Mother complained but she wasted no time in preparing the house for our visitor. We washed windows, scrubbed floors, waxed tables and beat the living daylights from curtains while father found excuses to keep himself locked in the cellar.

'What's happening?' Mr Marvel demanded, finding himself trapped in a dust storm as we pummelled the front parlour cushions.

'A family friend,' mother warned him. 'She might be staying for a few days. Do you like dancing?'

'Is it required?'

She stared at him for a moment and frowned. 'No,' she said, with a baffling innocence.

We opened the big front bedroom called Belgium. I don't remember why mother called it Belgium but I think it had something to do with the carpet. It was a large room with a fine carved mahogany bed, two old armchairs stuffed with horsehair and a massive wardrobe with fogged mirrors. There was a dressing table, a chest of drawers and a decorated folding screen. The wardrobe was filled with cobwebs and the dust had settled beneath the bed like a perfect patch of snow. We swept the room from floor to ceiling, bullied the mattress, flogged the chairs and squirted Springtime into the curtains. We fetched glass knick-knacks for the dressing table and a blue china vase for the chest of drawers.

'It still smells strange in here,' mother complained, wrinkling her nose. She stood in the centre of the room, clutching her Springtime like a can of Mace.

'It's the house,' I said, wiping my face in my apron. 'The whole house smells strange.' A hundred years of soot and sorrow, wet foundations, blistered plaster, boiled bedding and kitchen smoke.

'We need an onion,' she concluded. 'Go and fetch half an onion.' She believed that onions had magic powers to soak up smells and disinfect the atmosphere.

'What are you going to do with it?' I was hot and tired and filthy. There were cobwebs under my collar and feathers sticking like darts in my hair.

'We'll hide it behind the wardrobe,' she said, as if we were setting a garlic trap for an unsuspecting vampire.

So I ran downstairs to fetch a peeled onion, which we wedged between the wall and the wardrobe. We found a bunch of faded crepe-paper flowers for the vase and filled the chairs with patchwork cushions.

'What do you think?' mother asked, when we had finished.

'It's good,' I said. 'It looks comfortable.' I tried to picture the room at night; candles flicker, music murmurs, wardrobe spills her spangled costumes. Dorothy struts the carpet laughing, satin slippers, bracelets glitter, long hair tied with living rosebuds. Tap-tap. Room service. Silver tray. Champagne. Lobster. Compliments of the management.

Mother shook her head and shivered. 'There's a nasty draught through that window frame,' she said with satisfaction.

14

SHE ARRIVED ON the Saturday afternoon with a suitcase the size of a cabin trunk. She was taller than I'd expected and heavier and wore spectacles and a raincoat and sensible shoes and pink lipstick and her hair was dark and tied in a knot and she wasn't the woman I'd seen in my dreams.

She kissed father and squeezed mother but seemed confused when I was presented and did nothing more than shake my hand.

'Skipper?' she asked, suspiciously. 'Is it really Skipper? I can't believe it! My scallywag! Is it really you?' Her fingers were cold and fleeting.

'Skipper,' I said, feeling foolish. We were standing in the hall, forming a circle around the suitcase, as if it were an object of worship.

'You've grown,' she said and blinked several times and looked disappointed, as if I'd failed her in some odd fashion.

I couldn't think of a sensible answer so I said nothing but shuffled my feet and grinned like a good-natured idiot. I was wearing a new haircut and my best shirt and the collar was squeezing my throat like a rope.

'It must be ten years!' father said after a while, and I fancied that he looked as disappointed as Dorothy, although he did his best to conceal it.

'A long time,' mother declared.

'Ten years,' Dorothy agreed.

'And that's a long time!' father said.

'Is it really ten years?' I said, hoping to encourage them. They seemed to be short of conversation.

Mother shrugged. Dorothy smiled. Father sighed and stared at the floor.

A saucepan bubbled in the kitchen. Far away in the parlour we could hear the sounds of Senior Franklin rustling newspaper like a rodent building itself a nest. Somewhere a clock chimed the hour.

Mother smiled. Dorothy sighed. Father shrugged and looked at the wall.

'Well, you must be tired!' mother said finally, breaking the silence. 'Skipper will show you the room. There'll be plenty of time to talk when you've rested.'

'That's the spirit!' father said, clapping his hands. He bustled back to life and helped me to drag the suitcase as far as the staircase.

'Follow me!' I said.

'Can you manage the weight of it?' Dorothy asked doubtfully.

'It's nothing!' I grunted. The suitcase was made from a dark blue leather secured with straps and bright metal buckles. It pulled my shoulders, wrenched my spine and twisted my stomach muscles.

'The trick is to find the right balance…' father shouted from the safety of the hall as he watched me haul the brute upstairs.

I took Dorothy as far as Belgium, unlocked the door

and dragged the suitcase into the room. 'I hope you'll be comfortable,' I wheezed as I staggered free from my burden and fell thankfully into a chair.

'It's perfect!' she said. She walked to the window and peeked through the curtains. She walked back across the room and peeped behind the folding screen. 'It's a lovely room.' She took off her raincoat and placed it carefully on the bed. There were no spangles, no ostrich feathers. She was wearing wool from throat to ankle.

'Tell me if there's something you need,' I said, standing up to make my escape. I felt nervous. I was anxious to be gone.

'I can't think of anything.'

'I'd better get back to work,' I said, bobbing like a bell-boy.

'Wait a moment!' she said and knelt down to unlock the suitcase. 'You've grown so tall, Skip! You're quite the young man.'

'I'm eighteen.'

'I'd forgotten. How the time hurries past. And I used to play with you in the bath.' She unbuckled the straps, snapped open the locks and retrieved a brown paper packet from the neatly folded jackets and skirts. 'I've brought you something,' she said, looking up at me with one of her bright, pink smiles.

'Thank you,' I said, taking the gift in both hands. It was limp and flat and smelt a little of lavender.

'Comic books,' she declared, removing the element of surprise. 'You always seemed to like them.'

'I used to have quite a collection,' I said. *Superman.*

Batman. Green Lantern. Cat Woman. A complete set of *Valiant Vigour.* A first edition *Captain Thunder.* It was true. Hundreds of precious, dog-eared comics stored in a box beneath my bed. I'd thrown them away, along with my cardboard X-ray specs and my membership to the Junior Space Commando Club, when a friend at school had changed my life by lending me his *Skirt Lifter* annual.

'I remembered,' she said.

'Thank you.'

'I think you'll be pleased,' she said confidently. 'They feature the world's favourite superhero.'

I didn't ask questions. I hurried away to my room, sprawled on the bed and tried to make sense of this strange encounter. Where was the laughing, lewd-limbed dancer? Where was the woman who loved to make mischief? Ten years was a long time but I didn't believe it could do so much damage. It wasn't until I'd taken the trouble to unwrap my gift that the terrible truth was exposed.

They were large-format comic books, harshly coloured and printed on cheap, hairy paper. They had titles like *Jesus & the Titan of Doom* and *Jesus Conquers the Universe.* A banner on each cover promised that every page was packed with thrills and adventures. Jesus looked a lot like Cary Grant, with broad shoulders and quizzical eyebrows. He marched from one adventure to another wearing smart red orthopaedic sandals and seemed to employ his own beam of sunlight to pick him out in the crowd. But it wasn't hard to pick him from the multitude – he was the one with the piercing blue eyes who spoke entirely in proverbs. He was quite a character! He was always healing the sick or raising the dead and he'd walk a mile to stroke a leper. He didn't cruise through the stratosphere, bite through iron bars with his teeth or cripple rampaging robot armies. But you can't have everything and Dorothy seemed to worship him.

So here was the answer to the riddle! Dorothy was transformed. She had found faith. She was a new woman. She had burned her dancing shoes and joined the new crusade for Jesus. I flicked the pages and made an effort to read the captions – in case she was tempted to ask me questions – and then ran downstairs to help in the kitchen.

'Is she happy with the room?' father asked when he saw me again. He was standing at the kitchen table with his hand up an oven-ready turkey. The bird was the size of a small child. He was cramming it with chestnut stuffing, scooping the sludge from a glass dish and forcing it home with his fist.

'Fine,' I said.

'Is she coming down?'

'She'll want to rest and unpack,' mother reminded him.

'She must be tired,' father agreed. 'But you wait until this evening. You wait. You're going to love it. She's a scream.'

'She seemed surprised by the way you've sprouted,' mother said as I washed my hands at the sink.

'She thought I was eight years old.'

'It's that stupid haircut,' she said. She was sitting at the table, scrubbing vegetables in a bowl. She grinned as she shaved a whiskery carrot.

'You *were* eight years old,' father said, rushing to Dorothy's defence. 'The last time she saw you. Eight years old with a passion for collecting button badges and fivepenny conjuring tricks.'

'She gave me some comic books,' I said.

'What sort of comic books?' father asked. He pulled his fist from the bird and smacked a gobbet of unwanted stuffing against the side of the dish.

'The life and times of Jesus in colour,' I said, fetching a saucepan for the carrots. 'Pages packed with thrills and adventures.'

'What's he talking about?' father demanded, wiping his hands in his apron. He picked up the corpse and cradled it in his arms, testing its weight and surreptitiously squeezing its thighs before placing it to rest in a buckled roasting tray.

'Don't ask me!' mother said cheerfully, chopping carrots into my saucepan. 'And stop fiddling with that turkey.'

'Jesus & the Titans of Darkness!' I shouted. 'Jesus Conquers the Universe! Heed your heart and follow the Shepherd. Give your money away to strangers.'

'He's as daft as a brush!' father snorted. 'I think I preferred him when he was eight years old. At least we had sensible conversations.'

'Ignore him,' mother said. 'And use the oven gloves.'

They were proving deaf to my warnings. I was casting my seed upon stony ground. I stayed in the kitchen for the rest of the afternoon, washing pans and boiling down giblets for gravy. It was going to be a difficult evening.

15

WHEN SUPPER WAS served, Dorothy made her entrance wearing a white cotton dress printed with bluebells. It was high at the neck, pinched at the waist and the skirt was packed with petticoats. She had been transformed. She was Debbie Reynolds! She was Doris Day! She looked so robust and healthy you really thought she might kick off her shoes and start to dance on the carpet. Father took her arm, led her into the dining room and presented her to the company. Franklin whinnied and flared his nostrils, Janet blushed and Mr Marvel, with his fear of strangers, looked so alarmed that we feared he might panic, leap from his chair and damage himself as he tried to escape. But she smiled a pink smile as she sat down beside him and patted his hand and stared serenely into his eyes until he grew calm, his jaw fell slack and he seemed quite mesmerised.

Mother kept a watch on them as she scampered up and down with mustard pots and jugs of gravy. Father, at the top of the table, stood behind the turkey with a carving knife in his hand. He was already grinning, anticipating the moment when Dorothy would pull some prank to send us spinning in fits of laughter. Always when you least expected. What a performer! She was a scream.

It was a good supper. The plates were loaded with turkey and stuffing. There were roast potatoes with wedges of parsnip, sugar-glazed carrots and baby sprouts. There was gravy the colour of creosote and wrinkled rashers of salty bacon. There was ginger pudding to follow with four different kinds of ice cream. There was fruit and a very doubtful cheese.

'For what we are about to receive may the Lord make us truly thankful. Amen!' Dorothy said loudly, beaming at the assembly.

Father gave a great bark of laughter but choked it down when he sensed that nobody shared the joke and pretended to have a coughing attack.

'Where's your napkin?' mother said sharply.

Father slapped open his napkin and used it to cover his confusion.

'And what do you do for a living, Mr Marvel?' Dorothy inquired. She didn't seem in the least concerned by father's unfortunate outburst.

'Oh, this and that,' Marvel mumbled. 'This and that.' He was bent over his plate, nibbling at crumbs of potato. He paused and raised his head, as if he were going to speak again, and then decided against it.

'How fascinating!' Dorothy crooned.

'And may we beg leave to inquire how you spend your time, madam?' Franklin demanded, taking command of the conversation.

'I live in the Lord,' Dorothy said with a bright pink smile.

'Where's that?' Janet whispered, leaning hard against me. It was a rare and precious moment. I should have buried my face in her hair and babbled sweet nothings into her ear. It was a gilt-edged invitation. The perfect opportunity. But I couldn't answer. I was busy staring at Franklin who had dropped his knife and fork and was clutching his throat in a gesture of horror.

'No! Say 'tis not true! A student of cant and comstockery? And yet so fresh and comely! A dabbler in bibliomancy? An unreconstructed triskaidekaphobe?' He shook his head and shuddered. 'I would I had not asked the question. I would it were bedtime, Hal, and all well. Curiosis fabricavit inferos!' he added mournfully.

'What's wrong with him?' father demanded. He didn't have the faintest idea what Franklin was talking about, but bitter experience had taught him that these sudden outbursts meant trouble.

Marvel growled and glared across the table. He gestured at Franklin with his knife but he couldn't find the words he wanted.

'Do I take it, Mr Franklin, that you don't yet share the good faith?' Dorothy inquired.

'I don't bother God, madam, and I find that He seldom bothers me!' he shouted, dramatically. He seemed so pleased with this remark that he grinned and filled his mouth with turkey.

'Ah, but that's where you're wrong,' Dorothy insisted. 'You may not believe in the Lord but, rest assured, He believes in you!'

This news seemed to bring no immediate comfort to Franklin. 'If He cared at all for my welfare, madam, I would not be afflicted with scrivener's palsy! A condition

I've suffered with some forbearance since my earliest days at Oxford. English. Honours. First class.'

'We are all miracles of the Creator,' Dorothy reminded him gently. 'And to keep ourselves in good repair we should never fail to read the manufacturer's handbook.'

'How's that?' father asked, as he battled to follow the conversation. I think he was still hoping for fun and games but his voice had an edge of desperation.

'The bible,' Dorothy explained.

Father missed his mouth with his fork and stabbed his chin with a parsnip.

'Napkin!' mother sang happily.

As we struggled through the meal, mother's good humour increased in direct proportion to father's tragic decline. While I watched him wither away in the glare of Dorothy's shining light, so mother brightened and blossomed.

'Now tell me,' Franklin continued, 'for here's something that often troubles me: if Adam and Eve dwelt in innocence, without the knowledge of Right and Wrong, how might they be blamed for eating fruit from the Tree of Knowledge?'

'It was forbidden.'

'Indeed! And yet, I trust you'll agree, that to understand the concept of obedience demands a fundamental, nay, comprehensive grasp of the differences 'twixt right and wrong and Adam and Eve were both idiots. Whimsical puppets in the good Lord's garden. Witless stooges in the paradise pantomime. Amiable automata in the cosmic theme park.'

'The serpent tempted them.'

'And thus they were betrayed by the burden of innocence that God had bestowed on them.'

But Dorothy merely smiled at his mischief. 'I think you're playing a little game with me,' she twinkled.

And there the argument rested while the plates were cleared away and the ginger pudding brought from the kitchen.

'And what do you do for a living?' Dorothy asked Janet.

'I'm a beauty consultant for a well-known department store,' Janet whispered, licking ice cream from the back of her spoon.

'How fascinating!' Dorothy gasped.

Janet looked up in surprise and seemed so startled by Dorothy's bright pink mouth that she blushed and grew confused and found nothing more to say on the subject.

We took coffee in the front parlour. Janet retreated to the safety of the table beneath the window where she soon settled down with Mr Marvel for her evening game of dominoes. Franklin spread himself across the sofa and Dorothy was left alone to choose herself an armchair. She circled the room several times before she made a decision, prodded the cushions and dusted the little lace antimacassar before she gave herself to its embrace.

'Do you play dominoes?' mother asked hopefully as she squelched up and down with the coffee tray.

Dorothy smiled but shook her head and spent a little time fiddling with the pleats of her skirt as she tried to hide her petticoats. She crossed her ankles and stared at her shoes.

'Mr Marvel's a wonderful teacher,' Janet said.

Dorothy looked interested and glanced towards the table but there was no time to introduce her to the pleasures and perils of the game before Franklin stirred from his torpitude and demanded more attention.

'So tell me,' he said, fixing her with a jaundiced eye, 'for here's something else that troubles me: does your church yet find itself open to the wind-jammer's powdered embrace?'

'I beg your pardon?'

Franklin propped his elbow on the arm of the sofa and moved his hand like a metronome. 'Wind-jammer. Shirt-lifter. Dung-puncher. Dirt-tamper. Pillow-biter. Chutney ferret.'

'Language!' father growled, as he passed through the room with the sugar bowl. He glanced apologetically towards Janet but she didn't seem disturbed. It must have been another topic missing from a Katie Pphart education.

'We are clearly told to forgive,' Dorothy said patiently. 'We are urged to practise tolerance and understanding. We must not condemn those souls who are made of a different persuasion.'

'Sugar?' father said, pausing beside her chair.

'No, thank you.'

Franklin stared at the ceiling and sucked his teeth as if he wanted time to consider the wisdom of her verdict. 'And the Lord spake unto Moses!' he thundered, lurching suddenly forward and slopping coffee into his saucer. 'Thou shalt not lie with mankind, as with womankind: it is abomination!'

Dorothy didn't flinch. She merely tipped her head and looked at him over the rim of her spectacles. Her dark eyes shone with sincerity. 'The Lord loves all His children,' she said firmly.

'And he brake the houses of sodomites, that were by the house of the Lord!' Franklin bellowed. 'The Book of Kings.'

'To them that love God, all things work together for good.'

'The saint and the sinner together?'

'He gave His only begotten Son that we might be forgiven our sins.'

'And so we continue to carry the guilt for God's little robots, Adam and Eve, but no longer need to feel any shame for buggering boys in lavatories! Is that how the winds of change bloweth?'

Dorothy blushed and hesitated for a moment. 'Knowledge puffeth up, but charity edifieth!' she said, at last.

'You're an oaf!' Marvel shouted from the table. He turned and glared at Franklin. 'An oaf and a scoundrel! And if I were twenty years younger I'd give you a damned good thrashing!'

Janet yelped and jumped back in her chair.

'Ah, Mr Marvellous speaketh!' Franklin roared, clearly delighted by so much attention. 'The Kraken wakes! Do we suppose he's found courage enough to enter an educated debate?'

'Your education, sir, for all its pomp and circumstance, seems to have failed in providing you with any common decency!' Mr Marvel punched the table, making his dominoes clatter, and turned around to confront his tormentor. His face was dark with rage and his eyes strained in their sockets. For a moment I thought he might spring forward, make a lunge for the sofa and seize Franklin by the throat. But Dorothy was there to calm and comfort him.

'Answer not a fool according to his folly, lest thou also be like unto him,' she said gently, turning her radiant smile upon him.

'What?'

'Proverbs.'

Marvel hesitated. He blinked at Dorothy. He scowled at Franklin. He turned once more to his game.

'I'm much obliged,' he muttered.

At midnight, mother was still in buoyant mood as we cleared the wreckage in the kitchen. Despite father's great disappointment, Marvel's gloomy silences and Franklin's bad behaviour, she declared the evening a great success.

'I think Dorothy took a shine to him,' she said cheerfully, plunging plates into water so hot it threatened to melt her rubber gloves.

'She's already found a friend in Jesus,' father said, wagging his head. He just couldn't believe it.

'It makes no difference,' mother insisted. 'She likes him.'

'I didn't notice anything,' I said.

'You're a man!' she said scornfully.

'Marvel's a man, in a manner of speaking,' father said wearily, picking at the skeleton of the turkey. He was searching for scraps to turn into rissoles.

'And he sprang to her defence,' mother said. 'When Franklin was making a fool of himself. He sprang to her defence like a proper, old-fashioned gentleman.'

'I thought he would explode!' I said, sorting through the mess of cutlery. 'I've never seen him look so angry.'

'That tells you something!' mother said with satisfaction.

'What?'

'You wait,' she said, smiling, wiping her rubber hands in her apron.

16

WE WAITED BUT nothing happened. Despite mother's best attempts, Marvel was not to be seduced by a woman with a bible in her handbag and for the next few days he contrived to remain in isolation. He continued to join us for supper but ate little and spoke seldom. Dorothy spent most of her time in the kitchen chattering with mother and devoted her evenings to reading the scriptures. Mother was stubborn and stayed optimistic but I lost interest in her plans for kindling romance because something sinister caught my attention.

Someone was mutilating my collection of *Grappler* magazines. It began with the issue featuring Junkyard Dog, the big New Jersey brawler who had recently been elected in a readers' poll as the Crazy Man of the Year. Someone had been cutting holes in him. The Junkyard Dog had lost one eye and part of a wrestling boot. It continued with the tag-team special. The battling Buffalo Brothers had been cut in half by a lunatic with a pair of scissors. Rampaging Randy Buffalo had been chopped away at the knees. His brother had completely lost his head.

There was no doubt that the culprit was Senior Franklin. But why would he bother with *Grappler*? He pillaged the daily newspapers for essays and reviews, poetry and political comment. He plundered the weeklies for Dwarf droppings, snippets of tittle-tattle and literary gossip. He couldn't be interested in the politics of the squared circle. It was a puzzle. And anyway, he hadn't removed complete pages or even paragraphs from the magazines but contented himself with random headlines, phrases and isolated words. He wasn't concerned with the photographs, of course, but the editorial on the back of them. He was making alphabet confetti.

When I confronted him with the crime he looked surprised.

'Were they of any particular interest?' he asked. He was sitting in the sofa, happily slashing the arts section of the giant *Sunday Superior*. The scissors flashed in his bony hand.

'I save them,' I said. 'I'm collecting them.'

'Wrestling magazines?' He looked astonished, as if the idea that I took such an interest had never before occurred to him; as if the magazines somehow came and went like mushroom rings. 'You're collecting them?'

'That's right,' I said. 'They're mine.'

'Did you never suppose that the agony of your adolescence might best be served by the random application of drugs, self-abuse and rock and roll?' he said impatiently. 'Why can't you be a crackhead like any respectable child of your age?'

'I study wrestling to provide myself with a totally unrealistic view of violence and its consequences,' I said, in my own defence. 'At the earliest opportunity, I plan to go out and hurt old ladies.'

He frowned and then honked with laughter. 'Ah, my squidgy bumblestrop, but the game is rigged, the lottery itself is lost! These warriors of your circus world are nought but acrobats, tuppenny tumblers, valgus vagabonds!' He chuckled to himself as he went back to work with the scissors.

'It doesn't make any difference,' I said defiantly. It just wasn't good enough. I wasn't going to be bullied into submission by a man who didn't know a camel choke from a chin lock.

'But these battles are nothing but comic routines, theatrical performances, carefully scripted, doubtless rehearsed and designed for no greater purpose than to pick the pockets of noodles, numskulls, nincompoops and simpletons,' he continued, still hoping to shame me. 'Shatterpates, jobernowls, loony-heads and dizzards. Drivellers, babblers, sappy-straws and halfwits.'

'I know that.'

He paused and stared at me. The scissors dangled on a crooked finger. He was waiting for his venom to take effect. 'I do declare I can't fathom you!' he said, at last, and wagged his head as if he were disappointed.

'I don't care!' I said fiercely. Damn his eyes! 'I don't care for your opinion. And I'll thank you for keeping away from my property.'

'Why don't you follow a real sport?' he demanded, with a fair degree of prickliness.

'Because it's not the same,' I said. 'I mean, when you watch a tennis match you know that the champ is going to win because he's a better tennis player than his opponent.

And because he's the champ he's probably a millionaire with his own sportswear company and an aftershave named after him and everything. And if he doesn't win, well, it makes no difference because the new champ will get his own brand of sportswear and his own range of personal hygiene products to peddle. So nothing really happens. It's a fake. It's just millionaires playing bat and ball. But if there was an element of danger, if you knew there was the possibility of a 300-pound, pot-bellied monster in wrestling boots with his name tattooed on his forehead crashing onto the court, shredding the net, eating the ball and then beating out the champ's brains, well, you'd have something to catch your imagination. There'd be risk. And romance. And a real sporting chance that the golden boy would get his Rolex rammed up his arse.'

'And that's wrestling?'

'Yes,' I said. 'And zombies and werewolves and giants and dwarves and fire-eaters and missing links and mad monks and Pacific island cannibals and Caribbean witch doctors and tattooed ninjas and rampaging Russians and moustachioed Mongols and tumbling Turks and fighting Fijians and cartwheeling cowboys and Syrian stranglers and masked men of mystery and caped crusaders and gladiators from the grave.'

He opened his mouth but said nothing. He sat transfixed, his skin was wax and his eyes were glass. It was a curious sensation to watch him endure his own silence.

'So why are you cutting up *Grappler*?' I demanded.

His eyes flickered as he came back to life. 'Alas, my frumious bandersnatch!' he barked. 'I'm flummoxed. I'm confused. I'm shocked to the core. I'm all thrown down in a heap! I wasn't aware that I'd trespassed so far from the pastures grown for my grazing.' He gathered together his torn newspaper and tried to stuff it under a cushion. 'The scissors, I confess, must have gathered a life of their own. I'm hardly aware that I'm doing it.' He snapped the scissors together and dropped them into a jacket pocket. 'I trust you'll accept my apology.'

'Have you finished with that newspaper?' I asked.

He lifted the cushion and watched me remove the rubbish.

'Thank you,' he said meekly.

And that was that. He continued to shred the newspapers every day, although he never again touched the *Grappler*. But the mystery remained.

17

DOROTHY RESTED FOR three days before she sought to ask questions about the Jesus comic books. I'd almost forgotten them. They'd been hidden away in my room as if they were copies of *Frolicking Fatties*. But Dorothy must have been waiting for me to study and absorb their lesson.

She found me down on my hands and knees, picking old Burger King boxes from the roots of the privet hedge. It was a brilliant morning, the air was warm and high clouds streamed from the west with an early promise of summer. The privet was packed with empty beer cans, broken polystyrene cups, cigarette cartons, burger boxes, chicken bones, desiccated dog turds and scraps of discarded underwear. I'd once found an empty leather wallet, a bunch of keys and a cucumber wrapped in polythene. We lived in an interesting neighbourhood.

'Did you look at those comic books?' she inquired carelessly, strolling from the house and standing to watch me work. She was wearing another Doris Day dress, banana yellow with lots of buttons, a scoop neck and pretty soft brown shoes. Her dark hair was loose and whisked her shoulders. She was dangling a satchel on her arm.

'Yes,' I said, turning my head to find myself brushing against her skirt. 'Thank you.' I stopped rummaging in the hedge, stood up and wiped my hands on my apron.

'And did you take the time to read them?'

'Yes,' I said.

'Did you like them?' she asked anxiously. 'I'm afraid they're rather too young for you.'

'No!' I said. 'I found them very interesting.'

She smiled her big, pink, open smile that stretched her mouth against her teeth, squeezed her eyes and tugged at her nostrils. She gave herself to these beautiful smiles with the shamelessness of a yawning cat. They were smiles that suggested such rapture, such abandoned pleasure, that you wanted to perform handstands in an effort to make her smile again. 'Did you learn anything?'

'Give your money away to strangers?' I suggested.

'Not exactly,' she said.

'I'll read them again,' I promised.

'Are you doing anything?'

'No,' I said innocently, rattling my sack of flotsam and jetsam. 'I was trying to clean out the privet.'

She walked to the corner of the hedge and glanced up and down the street. 'I was going out for some fresh air,' she said, wrapping the strap of the satchel around her wrist. 'It's such a lovely morning.' She paused and watched me pack down the sack with my foot. 'Why don't you come with me?'

'I should be working…' I said doubtfully.

'I'm sure you can spare a couple of hours,' she coaxed. 'I'd appreciate the company. You can tell me all about yourself.'

'I don't know,' I said, dumping my booty beside the porch. There were windows to wash and laundry to fetch and the best of Janet's shoes were begging for a whipping with duster and polish. 'Perhaps Mr Marvel would like to go with you,' I said, rather reluctantly.

'That's strange. That's just what your mother suggested. But I haven't seen him this morning.'

'Well, I'd have to go and get changed,' I said, plucking apologetically at the front of my filthy apron. I was easily persuaded. 'I'd have to find a clean shirt and get washed.'

'I'll wait,' she said and smiled again and looked so pleased to have me as her escort that I would have followed her anywhere.

As it turned out I followed her on a guided tour of the city's churches. Armed with nothing more than a tourists' map to places of worship, we took the bus to Pickle Street, crossed the open cobbled square where people had stopped in the sunlight to gossip, and plunged without pause into the gloom of St Febronia the Martyr. It was cold and very dark and filled with the smells of incense and polish with a faint yet disturbing rumour of drains.

'Perpendicular with Classical and Gothic additions,' she whispered, gazing up at the massive ceiling. She shivered and sighed with pleasure at the sheer weight of masonry.

At first I thought the church to be empty, but as my eyes grew accustomed to the shadows I found figures looming everywhere. Apostles stood sentry high in the walls and angels watched from their perches in pillars. They gazed down upon our intrusion with dark expressions made from granite. The long windows were filled with the heavenly host, a thousand of them blowing trumpets and banging the daylights from tambourines. We brushed against the tombs of priests and trod on the graves of squires and crusaders. We were crowded by the good and the dead, their statues and monuments.

'Beautiful!' Dorothy whispered.

She walked me down the nave and into the south transept where she paused at the gates to a small chapel and introduced me to a marble woman. The woman was chained by the wrists to a rock. She was languid and lovely. Her opalescent hair tumbled as far as her waist and her robes were so finely polished and draped they might have been moulded from ice. Her trusting eyes were turned to Heaven. The shaft of a great sword had been planted in the pale divide of her pudding-basin breasts. A dove sat and preened itself on her shoulder.

'Saint Febronia,' Dorothy smiled.

'Is she buried here?'

'No. This is merely her monument.'

'Was she famous?'

'She was a young and beautiful maiden who lived in Mesopotamia during the time of the persecutions. And she was a Christian. But, although she was a Christian and should have been martyred, the prefect Selenus offered to grant her freedom if she renounced her faith and married his nephew.'

'And what happened?' I whispered. It sounded like a fair bargain, depending on the nephew having rugged good looks and a decent villa in the country.

'Febronia refused,' Dorothy said proudly. 'So Selenus ordered her to be seized and taken away to be mocked and humiliated and tortured and horribly mutilated and finally battered to death.'

'Terrible.'

'Yes,' said Dorothy breathlessly. 'And shortly afterwards, Selenus went mad with remorse and killed himself.'

'Dreadful.'

'But there's a happy ending,' she said, summoning the ghost of a smile, and as she spoke she reached out to stroke Febronia's stricken face with fluttering fingertips. The nose of the saint, her toes and her nipples had been burnished black by the fingers of pilgrims.

'How's that?'

'The nephew became a Christian!' Dorothy said happily.

'God works in mysterious ways,' I said.

We went from the Church of St Febronia the Martyr to the Church of St Rock the Healer and hence to the Church of St Gregory the Wonderworker. I was worried at first that we might have to pray and I should be seen to disgrace myself by demonstrating an ignorance of verse and chapter, sudden curtsies and genuflections. But nothing was expected of me. I fancy now that Dorothy had gone that day to worship the buildings themselves, the majesty of their buttressed walls and their sombre interiors. We gawped at the stone memorials, peered into pulpits, choir stalls and vaults. We lit candles wherever we happened to find them for sale and Dorothy wrote her name in St Gregory's visitors' book. *We were privileged to ponder your rood screen*, she scrawled in her spidery hand. *May the Lord keep you and bring you his blessings. Very best wishes. Dorothy Clark.*

I discovered later that she took instruction from no church in particular but sought inspiration from the Glad Tidings Bible Tract Company of New York, an organisation with liberal views and a full colour mail-order catalogue.

We had lunch in the little church of St Godfrey the Convert, between a cinema and an office block. Dorothy had packed a modest picnic of fruit and biscuits in her satchel. We strolled through the empty church and sat down to eat before Godfrey's Finger. The relic sat on a blue, braided, velvet cushion in a glass box with a gold frame on an ivory stool in an iron cage on a stone shelf in the wall. It was small and shrivelled and a rather peculiar shade of brown. It looked for all the world like something I might have found beneath the privet hedge.

Dorothy fed me chocolate biscuits and recalled how I had once shown a great fondness for chocolate eggs. I must have been five or six years old and had often glued myself to my chair, which reminded her again of the time when she'd played with me in the bath, making me squirm with embarrassment to know that the woman who sat beside me had once been given the freedom to strip me down and bully my buttocks in her soapy hands.

'You were such a little scallywag!' she said, plucking an apple from her satchel. 'You wanted to be a Robot Commando.'

'I don't remember that.'

'Robot Commando. I think that's what they were called. It was quite the rage at the time. They were little plastic dolls in all sorts of different colours. You must have had the whole collection.'

'I've forgotten.'

'You've grown,' she said, as if that would account for my memory loss. 'You must have found other interests.'

'Housework,' I said. 'I like housework.'

She turned the apple from hand to hand and gave me a look that suggested she didn't believe me. 'There must be something else,' she said. No one could believe that I found satisfaction in household chores.

'There's no time,' I said. Housework is a task without purpose, a labour without reward. Dust settles as soon as you've whacked it. But chasing the dust brings a chance to dream.

'You'll have a sport!' she said confidently. 'A healthy young man will always play sport.'

'Well, yes, I like professional wrestling,' I said helpfully. 'I like watching the TV tournaments.' I might have mentioned that I also enjoyed the spangled world of synchronised swimming, but I didn't want to cause any trouble.

'And Jacob was left alone; and there wrestled a man with him until the breaking of the day. Genesis 32. Verse 24,' she said peacefully, rolling the fruit against her thigh with the palm of one hand.

'Is it true that you were a dancer?' I ventured, watching the apple begin to blush as it nuzzled into her leg.

'Yes,' she said. 'A long time ago. I belonged to the Big Boy Bad Boy Company. It was an experimental dance and music workshop. It had quite a reputation. Did you ever happen to hear of it?'

I shook my head.

'Well, it wasn't the Kirov. We once did a modern interpretation of Swan Lake dressed as a striptease tap-dance troupe with a cappella singers.'

'I suppose it was symbolic,' I said.

'I don't know. The choreographer was a Swede.'

'Why did you stop?' I inquired, half-expecting to be told that the Lord had appeared in the orchestra pit and told her to cover herself with a towel.

'I fell off the stage dancing Cinderella on stilts,' she said.

And so we talked.

I asked her questions about her dancing years and she did her best to describe them to me. She asked questions about Franklin and Janet and Mr Marvel and I told her what I knew of them. It was good to be sitting with Dorothy in the twilight of that empty place, sharing her picnic in full view of Godfrey's holy digit. She had a simple view of the world that made her shine with confidence. Nothing could tarnish her optimism. She was strong. She felt invincible. She had faith that passeth all understanding. And as I sat beside her I began to feel a strange attraction. I was fascinated by the lazy movements of her slender hands, and the tidy way that she crossed her ankles, and the way that her long, heavy hair looked so polished, and the way that the cords stood out on her neck when she sank her teeth in the flesh of the apple. And her eyes, behind the black wire spectacles, were so bright and friendly and her eyebrows so dark and luxuriant. And she had a good, sweet smell of sandalwood soap and orange-blossom shampoo and a perfume called Pandemonium with which she liked to anoint her wrists. And she was elegant, yes, and well-made and retained the grace of her dancer's limbs that the drab, yellow dress couldn't quite disguise.

'It's time to go home,' she said at last, wrapping her apple core in a Kleenex and dropping it into the satchel. 'I've kept you far too long. Your mother will think that I've kidnapped you.'

I was disappointed. 'We can do it again,' I said, brushing biscuit crumbs from my sleeve. 'I mean, if you'd like the company. I can always find the time and there must be a lot of churches to visit.'

It hadn't been too bad. Considering. It was cold and dark and the pews were hard but Dorothy's obvious enthusiasm for these sacred piles was reward enough for such small discomforts. And I fancied a sort of conspiracy, a pleasant intimacy, in our whispered conversations as we'd tiptoed around the marble tombs.

Dorothy buckled the satchel and raised the strap to her shoulder. 'I'd like that,' she said with a smile and took my hand as we walked back towards the sunlight.

18

I WAS FIRST introduced to God at around the time I was told about Death. The two spectres arrived holding hands. Until that moment I had crawled and dribbled a path through the world believing myself to be immortal. My universe was a small bed in a wooden cage, a blue plastic chair and the carpet. I was new and resilient. I would eat anything that reached my mouth. I could fall asleep hanging upside down. I laughed when you squeezed me, bounced if you dropped me. My eyes were blue and my bones were made from rubber. The news that Death brought an end to life was impossible to imagine. I couldn't remember a time when I hadn't existed. How could I confront such a time in the future? And this moment after life, this darkness called Death, intrigued and frightened me. It made a nonsense of being born. It made a mockery of life.

God followed hard on the heels of Death, introduced, I suspect, in a bid to soothe and diminish my fears. It didn't work. It was hard enough to live with Death without living in the knowledge that after Death you might have to make your way to Heaven. And Heaven remained a doubtful prospect. Invisible and unexplored. A lost continent in the clouds. The end of the rainbow. The silent land of no return. There were so many practical questions with no satisfactory answers.

'Does anything happen in Heaven?' I would ask of my mother, still strong in my simple belief that this woman must know everything.

'Nothing,' she would say, wearily. 'People go there to rest.' It was usually at breakfast when these questions came into my head and they never seemed to find her in the mood for spiritual inquiry.

'How old are we in Heaven?'

'It depends on your age when you get there.'

'How?'

'It depends.'

'But if a baby dies on earth will it remain a baby in Heaven?'

'I don't know.'

'And if you die when you're very old, will Heaven help to make you grow younger? I mean, if you've lost all your teeth, will they grow back again?'

'I don't know.'

'How do they measure the time? Are there any clocks in Heaven?'

'I don't know!' she would shout at me, suddenly losing her patience. 'Shut up and eat your breakfast!'

Father couldn't answer my questions, although he often made half-hearted efforts. His own view of the afterlife was even more obscure than my own. He saw it as some sort of beautiful white stage-set filled with actors like Roger Livesey and David Niven, drifting around in period costume. He added a lot to the general confusion. But as soon as I began to read, God in His Heaven was promptly retired and in His place came the books about Jesus.

They were large, improving storybooks, written in a gushing prose and filled with sentimental pictures. I remember very little about these books but for some black-and-white illustrations by a woman called Emily Bagley, in which all the characters seemed to be wearing striped towels and fake beards.

And it came to pass that in those days Jesus came in several disguises.

There was Jesus the Pied Piper, stealing children from their mothers and leading them away to the Father. I didn't want to go with Him. I didn't want to follow.

There was Jesus the Watcher, the bogeyman, the magic eye at the keyhole that never stopped staring and staring at you, even when you needed to be alone to pick your nose or sit at peace on the lavatory.

There was Jesus the Tyrannical Uncle, who was always right, who was never wrong, who argued with everybody and had an answer for everything.

There was Jesus the Ghost, appearing and disappearing, with a polished gold plate behind His head and His arms outstretched and holes in His hands and His sad eyes rolled towards Heaven.

The crucifixion troubled me – God who sacrificed Himself in the flesh. And some little time later, although we weren't Catholics, the news that Mary, mother of Jesus, was also the mother of God created another confounding puzzle for a boy intent on bringing some organisation into a disordered world. If Mary was the mother of God then it followed that Mary's mother was the mother of the mother of God and this thread, by a child's logic, would lead directly back to Eve who would, by the same logic, be the mother of all the mothers of God; and God, who had created Eve, would also be Eve's creation. It was very hard to imagine.

Despite such serious doubts, I tried to reach God in my prayers. I prayed, of course, to be spared from Death and be granted certain advantages, such as X-ray vision, the power of flight and the cloak of invisibility. These small gifts – the fantastic dreams of boys – would be nothing for the Almighty. He never replied to my pleading and even when I became less ambitious and begged for more humble favours – a proper penknife, a gas-propelled rocket – he didn't appear to show any interest. I tried to strike bargains. A lifetime's obedience in return for saving me from the dentist. A promise to become a monk in return for a bicycle. He didn't listen. The last time I'd turned to the power of prayer I was trying to manipulate Jessica Proud into acts of gross indecency, but they were such disgraceful requests I didn't deserve an answer.

19

'SO YOU'VE FOUND a friend in Jesus,' Mr Marvel said that evening, when I smuggled supper to his room. I think he knew that Dorothy had been introduced to the house for some particular purpose and now he supposed that I was the target. He grinned as he took the tray and found a place for it on the table. It must have been his first meal of the day.

'We went to look at the sights,' I said. 'It's a long time since she saw the city. She wanted someone to show her around.'

He peered at the fat slice of pie on his plate and knotted a napkin under his chin. 'Pork pie!' he declared, as he broke through the pastry crust with his spoon.

'Home-made,' I said. Hacked from the freezer the previous night by a mad woman with a hunting knife.

'Apples!' he said, trawling his nose through the steam. 'I smell a rumour of apple and onion.'

'For the sake of the pork,' I explained.

'Allspice?'

'And nutmeg.'

'Cider!' he announced.

'Cider!' I agreed.

He smiled and, having identified the principal ingredients to his own satisfaction, set to work with confidence.

'Oh, my, but it's good!' he said, blowing steam through his teeth.

He was wearing his pyjamas beneath a faded, blue dressing gown. Despite the fair weather he'd not found a reason to leave his room. Yet how did he keep himself amused? As he tackled the pie I took time to survey the surroundings. It was a bleak prospect. The room itself was comfortable after the Wandsworth fashion, but there was nothing to occupy his time beyond the radio. He must have spent hours surveying the walls like some forgotten prisoner. It was remarkable. How did he manage to keep from screaming? He must have the patience of a stone.

'Where did she take you?' he asked, having taken care to demolish the greater part of the pie.

'We went to visit some old churches,' I said. 'It wasn't so bad. Considering. She has a real interest in architecture.'

'Architecture is it?'

'What's wrong with that?' I demanded.

'Nothing!' he said. 'Entirely innocent.'

'But you have your doubts.'

'It's a doubtful world, Skipper,' he said, tilting his plate to scoop up the last of the gravy. 'Beware of having the world explained before you've fashioned a view of it. It's important to know your own mind. And Christians are such a happy breed they can never resist interfering and making your life a misery. Naturally, I don't expect you to heed this advice and, by the same token, I trust you'll ignore any other advice that people may try to thrust upon you. Know your own mind and follow your bliss. Believe in your secret destiny.' He smiled and belched and wiped his mouth in the napkin.

Despite her cheerful disposition, it seemed Dorothy threatened everyone. We were all afraid of a bible-bashing. We dreaded the prospect of finding ourselves trapped in a scripture class.

Mother attempted to keep her amused by letting her work in the kitchen. She wasn't a bad cook if you didn't mind eating party food. She had a secret for guacamole and a dozen ways to stuff a pepper. We ate whatever she cared to prepare and there were evenings when mother's hot beef stews were served with cheese and pineapple cubes on plastic cocktail sticks.

Janet tried to pacify her with small gifts of eau de cologne and several expensive red lipsticks. But this encouraged Dorothy to return the kindness in comic books and Janet quickly learned her lesson.

Marvel stayed in his room and even father kept his distance, as if it had now been agreed that keeping his guest entertained was work for a much younger man. He gave his blessing by offering to pay my expenses.

Franklin alone tested her patience with his relentless sarcasm and quoted as freely from the bible as he might from Goethe or the Marquis de Sade, supporting his claim that he could absorb any book by sleeping with it beneath his pillow.

'What do you make of our guest?' he demanded of me, during one of his friendlier moments.

'Dorothy?'

'The same.'

'She seems very pleasant.'

'Pleasant!' he echoed. 'The woman seemed excessively pleasant! She died from a surfeit of pleasantness!' He bared his teeth and poked a finger into my chest. 'Are you acquainted with the works of William Wilkie Collins?' he inquired.

'No.'

'Novelist, companion to Dickens and slave to the mistress Laudanum,' he continued, as if these clues might help me place him.

I shook my head.

Franklin snorted at my ignorance. 'Well, be warned, my tremendous testicle, that your pleasant Dorothy Clark seems most suspiciously similar to a character in *The Moonstone*,' he said darkly. 'I don't like it. There's something very queer abroad! I would urgently recommend, should you care for some educated advice, that you don't get involved with the woman.'

'There's no harm in it!' I protested.

'No harm in it?' Franklin thundered, very much enraged. 'You tell me there's no harm in it? The church is the simpleton's soporific, Mrs Grundy's breeding box, divider of nations, palace of prejudice, tomb of tolerance, death of reason, poverty's favoured promise!'

But Dorothy never once tried to make me embrace the faith as I followed her tour of the city's churches. She neither preached nor prayed. She seemed happy enough to have a companion. We paid our respects to the lofty Church of St Barbara with its fine Victorian brass and echoing blue brick pillars. We walked the arcades of St

Theodore with their grieving pink alabaster angels. We saluted Boris the sufferer and the hermit Hilarion.

We paid particular attention to the saints of sorrow and tragedy. Scholars and kings held scant attraction. Popes and bishops meant nothing. Dorothy had a passion for martyrs. She lit candles for the blessings of Blandina who was tossed by bulls and St Agatha who had her breasts removed and was seen to carry them in a dish, high in a stained-glass window. Pantaleon was decapitated. Chrysanthus was buried in sand. Lawrence was roasted. Jonah was crushed. Julian of Antioch was sewn in a sack and drowned.

While she counted the roads to martyrdom I found myself developing a fondness for relics and, as we wandered from church to church, I searched eagerly for the phials of black blood, the varnished bones and miraculous fingernails that were part of the holy mystery. This sacred memorabilia could usually be found in shrines of splendid design but occasionally we were forced to squint through the keyhole of an iron casket for a view of a yellow tooth or holy cobweb of human hair, and this measure of voyeurism would add melancholy to my fascination. These morbid fetish objects, these tiny scraps of charred skin and bone, seemed as remote as dragons' teeth, as ancient as fossilised shell.

Sometimes, grown chilled in the gloom of nave and transept, we took our picnic to the cemetery of St Gilbert at the Gate and stretched ourselves on the clipped lawn beneath the cypress trees. Here we would unpack the satchel and nibble on fruit, wedges of cheese and slices of pressed sultana cake. And when she had eaten and finished a little flask of coffee, Dorothy would yawn and bask in the sun, flat on her back like a stone knight, eyes closed, arms crossed and her long legs locked at the ankles, while I sat contentedly at her feet and followed the breeze as it rummaged beneath her petticoats.

Marvel's poor opinion of my friendship with Dorothy seemed unusually pessimistic. But after several days in her company I began to notice symptoms of a strange malaise. There were moments when, having pressed myself against her in some confined chamber as we searched the walls for faded inscriptions, I would find myself stammering uncontrollably, as if a demon had seized my voice and were shaking it like a rattle. My face would begin to burn, my mouth turn dry and my heart push painfully into my throat.

And there were other, more alarming signs. Whenever she joined us for supper my appetite would shrivel to nothing and no tempting titbit or fancy morsel had the power to revive my flagging interest. I sat and stared at my plate in confusion. I dipped my fork but I could not eat. My stomach might have been filled with pebbles. At the same time I felt exhausted yet found it difficult to sleep. I roamed the house like a shadow. The dust settled. Janet's shoes lost their shine.

Mother, suspecting malingery, gave no sympathy to my condition.

'You don't get enough exercise,' she complained, when I'd unexpectedly fallen asleep during one of our wrestling evenings. No matter how hard I worked in the house, her remedy for any complaint was always more vigorous exercise. She was half-submerged in a pile of old cushions, eating leftover coconut cakes from yellow Tupperware.

'I feel so tired,' I mumbled, yawning and rubbing my face in my hands.

'Fresh air and plenty of it.'

'What happened in the clash of the titans, Nasty Harris and Scrubber Norton?' I said, peering at the TV screen. A woman was smiling back at me, wearing a swimsuit, selling toothpaste with spearmint stripes.

'You were here,' she said.

'I missed it,' I said. 'I must have shut my eyes for a moment...'

'It was a cracker!' she grinned. 'I've never seen anything like it!'

'What happened?'

'You wouldn't believe it!'

'What happened?

'I don't remember.'

'I couldn't help falling asleep!' I protested.

She sighed, set down her Tupperware and made several sharp little tutting sounds as she tried to suck coconut strands from her teeth. 'Head butt. Head butt. Slap. Gouge. Rake to the eyes. Head lock. Back-breaker. Body slam. Atomic drop. Chin lock. Roll over take-down. Body scissors. Figure four. Elbow. Elbow. Flying head butt. Chair. Belt. Bucket. Chair. Mid-air collision...'

I nodded and tried to stay awake, but even the wrestling, for the moment, had lost its power of enchantment. Hulk Hogan's farewell performance did nothing to

stir my imagination. Gilda Galore, the thunder-thighed
female champion, failed to revive my flagging interest.

I did my best to resist, yet the fever continued to rage
and the more time I spent with Dorothy, the brighter the
flames that consumed me. The torment became relentless.
She could set me ablaze with a smile or dampen me down
with a frown. When she granted small favours or blessings
I flared like a human torch. I made feeble attempts at a cure
but gained no relief from my sickness. Did I claim as much
for Janet? Did I tell you that Janet distracted me? Well, I
must have exaggerated. There was no comparison. And
the truth, when it dawned, was terrible.

I'd been seized again by Mr Romance!

20

DOROTHY BRUSHED BACK *her glossy dark hair and lay daydreaming in the daisied grass, drinking in the abundant scent of sun-warmed flowers where bees were dipping their furriness, and thought again of the young Mr Romance and the mysterious darkness that brimmed his beautiful eyes whenever he watched her enter the chapel for daily devotions. What was the terrible secret locked in the living depths of his soul that took him to the far shore of the ornamental lake on moonlit nights and why had she overheard Janet, the simple yet deceptively pretty chambermaid, describe her master to the cook as His Satanic Majesty? Dorothy sighed and opened the strings of her bodice to let the sunlight caress her bosom. Since her arrival at the old house the brooding young nobleman had treated her every whim with grace and gaiety, and yet there was something distracted about him, a haunted look to his countenance that suggested he wrestled with demons in pursuit of his strange, nocturnal desires.*

21

I DON'T THINK Dorothy was to blame for my ultimate disgrace. She did nothing to encourage me. And in the beginning I struggled as best I could to shrug off my infatuation. I felt obliged to offer myself as an escort but, after ten days of viewing churches and monuments, I returned to my household duties. She didn't protest and I was happy enough to retire to a routine of cooking and cleaning. There were new and more exotic pleasures to be explored. I knew that when I reported for work I'd be sent up to Dorothy's room with my duster. And there, alas, despite my very best intentions, deaf to reason and blind to danger, I would step inside her wardrobe and, hidden away in that perfumed chamber with my heart pounding against my ribs, I would grant myself the freedom to push my head up her Doris Day skirts or practise the delicate art of unpicking buttons and sliding my fingers into her shirts.

How can I explain the misery and excitement of my fascination? I was doomed to love shadows and phantoms. But stealing into her room, disguised as an imbecilic cleaner, I would quickly become the invisible man. No one would challenge or question me. I could strike up a love affair with her shoes, her brushes and combs and necklaces. I might trace with infinite tenderness the hollows she made in the armchair cushions or draw to my sensitive nostrils the intimate scents of her skin from the discarded sheets and pillows. Dorothy everywhere! Seek and ye shall find. An impression of her mouth pressed in lipstick and softly printed onto the edge of a water glass. Teeth marks in the stub of a pencil. The smudge of a thumb on a make-up mirror. A single glittering strand of hair. Ah, sweet pain of that shadow world! The stealth employed by the secret admirer! Where God hath a temple, so the devil will hath a chapel.

But on my first morning, as soon as I'd tied my apron strings, mother came running into the kitchen with news that Franklin had gone to spend the day with Julian Fancy, the poet and social historian. Julian Fancy was husband to Clara Fidget, the influential editor, and we knew that Franklin would cling to her skirts and remain attached until he was dragged away screaming. It was a rare opportunity. So we dashed upstairs to raid the attic with brushes and buckets of hot soapy water. I was forced to postpone my invasion of Belgium. China and Mexico lay forgotten. We couldn't waste this chance to cast some light into Lilliput.

The attic rooms smelt stale. There were dozens of newspapers strewn on the floor. The chairs were gritty with biscuit crumbs. We had stripped the bed and cleaned the carpets before I inspected the great oak writing desk. And there, spread before me like a treasure map, was the answer to the mystery of the mutilated magazines. A pair of scissors. A large pot of pungent paper glue. A box of alphabet confetti. Franklin had been mounting a poisonous attack on the Dwarf's reputation! He was sending anonymous letters to every literary editor and critic in the country. And every word of these scandalous diatribes had been cut and assembled from newsprint and glued to sheets of coarse blue paper. The enterprise must have taken him days of painstaking labour.

He maintained that the Dwarf **HATed woMEN, huRT DOgs** and had recently grown addicted to **Xtreme FORMs of cHiLD PornoGraphY**. He claimed that the Dwarf was a **PlagiarIST** and had s**Tolen IDEAs & eNtirE PASSages of pROSE** from **OtheR distinguiSHED WriTErs**. He described the Dwarf as a **turD a THief** and a **tosSPOT**.

'He's barking mad!' I complained.

'What is it?' mother muttered, without much interest, squelching to the desk and shuffling through the evidence.

'Poison-pen letters!' I said, stabbing at **turD a THief and a tosSPOT**. The **tos** came away on my fingertip and I had some trouble restoring it.

'He's always writing something,' mother said, shaking her head. She screwed up her eyes as she tried to read one of the blue paper sheets but, to my relief, she didn't have enough patience for it.

'We've got to stop him!' I said. 'It's criminal. He'll probably get himself arrested.' Police swoop at dawn. Break down door. Scramble upstairs. This is a raid. Men barking. Women screaming. Franklin bending the bars at the window. Accused of libel on divers occasions. Threatening behaviour. Defamation. Malicious wounding of English language.

'Arrested?' mother said, bewildered by the excitement. 'But they're nothing but a lot of nonsense!' She surveyed the letters with a new interest. 'Let's throw 'em away!' she said finally. 'I don't suppose they're important.' She began searching her apron pockets for a roll of plastic rubbish sacks.

'No!' I said, trying to shield the desk with my arm. 'This is serious. If we interfere he'll know that he's been discovered.'

'So what?'

'Well, anything could happen,' I warned. 'We'd be involved. And if he's caught we might be held responsible for him. And we don't know how many of these things he's already sent. He could have been doing it for weeks!'

'So what's your advice?' she demanded.

'I don't know,' I said feebly. 'I suppose, under the circumstances, we could always pretend that it isn't happening.'

'Good idea!'

'We'll forget that we've seen them,' I said, pulling away from the writing desk. 'Did you move anything?'

'I don't remember.'

'He probably won't know the difference.'

'Scribblers!' mother said in disgust.

We finished cleaning the rooms but were careful to leave the desk undisturbed. There was nothing we could do to save him. The letters were anonymous. And the Dwarf, unknown to Franklin, was beyond the range of his rage, on a triumphant book-promotion tour of America to trumpet the merits of *Poke* – an episode he would turn into his next sensational novel in which a rather clever young man embarks on a triumphant book-promotion tour of

America. That book would, in its turn, provide the material for another novel in which a rather clever young man sets himself the challenge of writing a novel about a man writing a novel about a man selling a novel on a triumphant book-promotion tour of America. You couldn't stop him. The critics and camp followers clung to him like flypapers. 'Seek only to write from your own experience,' was Katie Pphart's advice to rookie writers with no elastic sewn into their imaginations and, by God, the Dwarf had taken the maxim and made it his life's work. No hagiographer could have larded his name with more glory than the praise he heaped upon his own head.

Franklin might have chosen from half a dozen fashionable writers as the target for his abuse. The arts pages were stuffed with swaggering braggarts and hobbledehoys shouting and spitting and posing for pictures.

There was Mad Max Mullah, resident fellow of Oxford, son of a French industrialist and Moroccan socialite, who used his writing to insult people on two continents and in three different languages; and whenever challenged by his enemies to stand and fight, would claim diplomatic immunity by switching his country of origin. 'A professional darkie,' is how Franklin had once described him, 'wrapped in a flag of convenience.'

There was Big Bertha Mappelthorpe, aka E B Morris, the drama critic, art collector, traveller, translator, gardener, wine expert, classical scholar and TV personality. A woman with a brain almost the size of Franklin's huge pudding and who used her monstrous organ to write nothing but detective novels (or 'puzzle books' as Franklin called them) set in a world of classical scholars. She regularly infuriated Franklin by announcing from her rambling country estate that, although a literary genius, she was really just like any other plain and ordinary housewife in a string of pearls and an outsized, floral-print kaftan.

Franklin despised Mullah and Mappelthorpe but concentrated his hate on the Dwarf. I think he loathed him with such a passion because he saw in his rival some dim reflection of himself and his own vain aspirations. Whatever the reasons, Franklin was mad and dangerous.

I watched him closely over the next few days and although he remained bombastic, beneath his brittle carapace he seemed unusually nervous. The telephone startled him. A ring at the door would make him flinch and look around anxiously until the visitor had been safely identified as harmless. Even Marvel grew sorry for him, but this amounted to nothing more than a sullen silence between them. I don't know what he'd hoped to achieve from his campaign of mischief. If the charges against the Dwarf were hollow insults then the author of the letters would be dismissed as a heckler, an idiot, another lunatic in the crowd. If the charges were published and proved to be true then the Dwarf would almost certainly enjoy a massive surge in his sales and be sent forth on a fresh publicity campaign. He wouldn't for a moment feel ashamed. He would probably write another book. His reputation as a wildly dangerous and rather clever young man would be complete. And that reputation would be his shield. He couldn't be slain by his enemies. But in trying to damage him it was clear that Franklin had injured himself. He grew queasy with guilt. Paralysed by his own poison. It was terrible to watch him suffer.

22

THE NEXT MORNING I tried to raid Belgium again. The house was quiet. Marvel was still asleep in China. He was trying to summon the strength to pursue his mysterious weekly errand and was not to be disturbed. Franklin was in the attic putting the **B** into **BasTArd**. Janet had gone to work at the usual time. Dorothy, with a little coaxing, had returned to St Boris the Sufferer to purchase a full set of colour postcards. Father had taken himself to market. And mother, tired of waiting for me to finish clearing breakfast away, had already gone into Mexico. It was perfect. Mr Romance loitered in the kitchen for a few minutes, trying to gather his courage and at nine-fifteen precisely, armed with a bucket of dusters and polish, he finally tiptoed up the stairs and slipped across the Belgian border.

The room was still charged with her perfume. A shot of Pandemonium that drifted on the air like mist. The heavy doors of the wardrobe had been closed but left unsecured. Her make-up stood crowded among the many glass knick-knacks scattered about the dressing table. There were books arranged on top of the polished chest of drawers. A travel alarm on the bedside table. A Glad Tidings Bible Tract paperback bible. A water glass. Spare spectacles. A half-eaten bar of hazelnut chocolate. It was everything I'd imagined. Dorothy was everywhere.

There were one or two disappointments. She had made her own bed, depriving me of the heart-stopping pleasure I had anticipated in driving my arms, with shirt-sleeves rolled, between the fading warmth of her sheets to smooth out the night tide of folds and wrinkles. She did not abandon her clothes on the floor, which might have allowed me some insight, with no more work than to walk the carpet, into her taste in underwear. These items were of more than passing interest since I fancied she must gird her loins with garments made from nothing but cotton, pure and simple, uncompromising and durable, with sensible, warm designs built on secure, unyielding foundations. The buckle-down Invincible. The Dreadnought draughtproof superior. Thou shalt not wear a garment of divers sorts, as of woollen and linen together, as you'll know from Deuteronomy. No pagan panties for Dorothy, with their soft silk ribbons and beards of lace. But I saw not a shred of evidence. The carpet was bare. The chairs were empty. Perhaps it was enough, for the moment, to be in her room and to sense her presence surrounding me.

I set down my bucket beside the chest of drawers, plucked out a duster and flicked at my face in the wardrobe mirrors. I folded the duster into a pad and bullied the mottled glass to a shine. It was hard work. I pummelled until the wardrobe creaked and all the catches sprang open. There! I took a step back to allow the doors to swing on their hinges and stared towards forbidden country. A faint trace of sandalwood leaked from the darkness. The little colony of frocks and jackets swayed in surprise at my rough intrusion. In the far corner of the wardrobe a few empty coat hangers jangled together. Here before me dwelt Dorothy's shadows, the soft, empty shells of my heart's enchantment. How vulnerable they appeared, hanging there, secured by their shoulders! How delicate their pleats and buttons! My mouth was dry. I felt my legs tremble with my desire to fall to my knees, lift up her skirts and bury my face in her petticoats.

'Take us,' they whispered. 'Take us, shake us and heal yourself in our soft embrace'.

For several moments I was conscious of nothing but the despicable urge I felt to clamber into the wardrobe and ravish its hapless inhabitants.

Ah, but doctor, I was too strong to be led astray by these wanton strumpets! I closed the doors and turned my face away from temptation. I slapped the duster against my knuckles and settled down to concentrate again on my work.

But very soon the chest of drawers began to beg for my attention. It sighed and whispered and flexed its joints. I tried to resist but I couldn't ignore it. So I went across and fondled its heavy, polished carcass.

It groaned and spoke in a husky tone. 'Pull open my drawer,' it murmured. 'I'm suffocated. I feel so tight I can barely breathe.'

No. I shook my head. No.

I tried to harden my heart as I lingered to wipe the blue china vase and dust the little stack of books; but the chest of drawers continued to moan and I felt obliged to obey its instructions. I hooked my fingers into its handles and gradually guided the top drawer towards me. It opened with a reluctant shudder and there, neatly folded and interleaved with sheets of tissue paper, I found myself confronting Dorothy's most intimate companions!

And now, having ventured so far on my voyage of discovery, tell me what should I have done? Doctor, don't spare your advice. Was I to remain unmoved by the sight of this forbidden orchard? Was I to retreat from that place, if not in fear of my mortal soul then for risk of discovery? Believe me, I ignored the dangers and feasted my eyes on those fragile morsels!

There was white cotton, yes, and shades of white in ivory and pearl. But there was saffron, lavender, peppermint and cinnamon. And beyond the Christian comforts of cotton there was wickedness in slithers of silk and titters of lace and satin that shone like a silver frost. Here were the panties, scanties, slips and stockings that had played such a long game of hide-and-seek with my imagination. And who would have guessed at this hoard, with its wealth of colour and sweet variety! Never once, when anchored to Dorothy, had they ever betrayed a hint of themselves. They were so very secretive and I was a stranger to them. Yet how eagerly they beckoned to be caressed, to be lifted up and nursed for a moment in my hands.

I waited until I could hear the sound of the vacuum cleaner sweeping a path across Mexico before I dared chance my arm. Then I closed my eyes, dipped between sheets of startled tissue paper and awoke to find myself, bleary as a drunkard, holding one of Dorothy's bras in my hands.

It was larger and more majestic than anything I'd encountered cast upon Janet's floor. It was made from some miraculous thread, smooth and translucent, embroidered with shimmering patterns of flowers. The straps were ruched and the cups, soft and seamless, trimmed with prickly toppings of lace, had been cunningly engineered with a pair of supporting, padded-wire crescents.

I fumbled to fit the hooks and eyes, one-two-three, and held it up by the shoulder straps. It dangled between my thumbs, empty yet fully-fashioned, a delicate, sculpted bust, strewn with flowers, inflated with sunlight: the living image of Dorothy. I staggered. I mewed. I was overwhelmed by the heat of my passions. Unable to restrain myself, I pressed myself to the chest of drawers, crushed her bosom pals to my mouth and collapsed the cups with kisses.

The first warning of my imminent arrest was the sound of footsteps on the stairs. It would have to be Dorothy! I was trapped. The stolen article promptly turned nasty, melted against my wrists, tangled itself in my fingers, quick as cobweb, stubborn as glue, refused to be shaken from my embrace. I struggled and sweated. I managed to fight myself free, stuff the wretched object into a nest of torn tissue paper, slam shut the drawer and turn myself on my heels at the same moment as the owner walked briskly through the door.

'Skipper!' She looked surprised. She hesitated. She stepped into the room and dropped her satchel onto the bed.

'I'm sorry!' I shouted, crazy with fright, catapulting around the walls. 'I was looking for something!'

'What?'

What? Love letters. A bottle of gin. What else could I hope to find hidden away in her underwear drawer?

'Why don't you sit down, Skipper?' she suggested gently. She had left the bedroom door open a fraction but now moved across the room to close it. Click. Caught. There was no escape.

I was still bandy with fright but I managed somehow to guide myself into a chair and fall among the cushions.

'I don't know what happened,' I stammered. 'I came up to tidy your room and then something seemed to come over me.' Guilty! Yes. Guilty. I plead insanity. I'm ready to confess my sins. It's the pillory for you, my lad. Take him away. Shave his head. Bind him with bodice and panty girdle. Drag the dirty dog in chains. Parade him for public ridicule.

'You mustn't feel ashamed,' she said, kneeling before me on the carpet. I was cornered. She had settled so close I could smell the peppermint on her breath. 'Why, look, you're trembling!'

'You startled me,' I said, grasping at my knees in a desperate bid to control the chorea. When my legs were quiet my teeth would chatter.

'Skipper, calm down,' she said urgently, taking my hot and heavy hand and pressing it between her palms. 'I think I understand what's been happening here.' Her touch was cool and deliberate.

'You do?' I whispered.

'Certainly,' she smiled.

'I couldn't help myself!' I bleated. Liar! The drawers protest. He was helping himself to your fancies.

'You must never forget that the Lord can look into our hearts and already knows our most intimate secrets. You've grown into quite a young man and you have a healthy young appetite. The Lord has been watching you, Skipper. You are never alone in the Lord. And He understands that you've reached an age when sometimes you're overwhelmed by certain strong feelings, powerful emotions, a driving force you don't understand. There's nothing wrong in that. It's perfectly natural.'

'It is?'

'Certainly,' she said again, giving my hand an encouraging squeeze. 'The world is beautiful. We are beautiful. We are the intricate works of creation. And now you're preparing yourself to explore that glorious mystery.'

'I am?'

She nodded and gave a little toss of her head to flick the hair away from her eyes.

Oh, but she looked handsome! Her face was flushed and her mouth, no longer painted pink, was a full-blown scarlet pout. If you hadn't known the circumstance, you'd have sworn she was trying to flirt with me.

'You're not angry?' I ventured. Good grief! This woman was a saint. An angel. She was so understanding it scared me.

'Angry? Skipper, I'm flattered!' she laughed.

'You are?'

'Yes! When you love someone, you want them to share all the joy that you feel in your heart. When they reach out their hand, you want to stretch forth and embrace them.'

'Thank you,' I said, entirely baffled. By this time I had

managed, more or less to recover my wits and was giving myself to the conversation. But it didn't help. I couldn't believe my ears.

'I think the Lord has thrown us together, Skipper,' she continued. 'Everything has a particular purpose. But you must give me time. There are many obstacles to be confronted. There may be ridicule and rejection. Have you thought about these things?'

I couldn't get my mouth working so I frowned and wobbled my head in a pantomime of indecision.

'Take your time. Listen to your heart. I'll wait for you,' she promised, releasing me at last by leaning away from the chair. 'You know that my door is never locked,' she added confidentially. She stayed on the floor with her legs folded neatly beneath her skirt and propped her hands on her hips. Elbows sharpened. Spine erect. She was looking very pleased with herself.

'I'd better be going,' I said. I glanced quickly at the bucket, half afraid that my dusters had been transformed by magic into a big bouquet of panties. Stop thief! They cry out in shame and humiliation. He's trying to steal us away for his dark and devilish purposes.

'We'll talk again.'

'Yes.'

'Don't be ashamed of your feelings.'

'No.'

'By the way, did you find them?' she asked. She seemed suddenly bashful, head cast down, combing the carpet with her fingers.

'What?'

'I think you know what I mean. Whatever you were searching for when I came into the room.'

The fear seized me again. I tried to rise but I couldn't move. I stared at my feet and shook my head until my brains rattled.

'Why don't you look in the bottom of the chest of drawers?'

'The chest of drawers?' I said, with innocent surprise, turning around to look at that broad-shouldered brute as if I'd never seen it before.

She nodded and waited. 'Aren't you going to fetch them?'

'Now?'

'Why not?'

I prised myself from the chair and shuffled miserably to the chest of drawers, source of all my humiliation. And there – you'll have guessed – I found her secret stash of Jesus comic books. There were dozens of them. *Jesus Abroad. Jesus Returns. Jesus Rebukes the Pharisees.*

'Take one,' she said. 'And God bless you.'

23

'WHAT HAVE YOU got there?' Marvel inquired as I passed him on the stairs. He was dressed for the street in his best suit and waistcoat. He nodded at the comic book, poking through the dusters in my cleaning bucket.

'*Jesus Returns*,' I said.

'I thought as much,' he said, pushing his hands in his trouser pockets. He nodded and sucked on his teeth.

'How did you know?'

'I've got *Jesus & the Scarlet Women*,' he said gloomily. 'That woman pushes them under my door.'

'I've read it,' I said. Despite its promising title, the comic was identical to all the others in the collection. Cary Grant in sandals. Blue eyes and proverbs.

'Is it good?' he inquired, rocking gently on his heels.

'Give your money away to strangers.'

'Fat chance.'

24

DOROTHY, SENSING AN opportunity to lead a sinner towards salvation, was soon in full pursuit. I managed to evade capture throughout the afternoon but after supper that evening she trapped me in the kitchen.

'Do you have a few minutes, Skipper?' she called through the smoke and the steam. She wore a pale, loose, cotton frock and stood timidly at the door like an angel peeking into the furnace.

'I'm working!' I shouted, banging a pair of saucepans together. I raised a fat rubber fist and waved my scouring brush like a hammer.

'I'll finish here,' mother said helpfully.

'But it's going to take you hours,' I protested.

'I'll fetch your father,' she said to me, beaming, pushing me away from the sink.

'He's working in the cellar,' I said stubbornly.

'I'll call him. You go and keep Dorothy amused.'

So I peeled the rubber gloves from my hands, surrendered my apron and let Dorothy take me from the kitchen.

'What is it?' I said, when we reached the hall.

'There's something I want to discuss with you,' she whispered, leaning so close that she accidentally kissed my ear. 'Can we go up to my room? It will only take a few minutes.'

I nodded. Yes. And meekly followed her up the stairs. Had she discovered the burglary? My thumbprints scorched on the wardrobe door! Guilty. A duster embroidered with my initials buried beneath her plundered panties! Guilty. I stumbled and slithered, clumsy with fright, as I clambered up in the draught of her skirt.

'Can you smell anything peculiar in here?' she asked, as soon as we'd reached the scene of the crime and she'd settled me down in a chair.

'No!' I squawked. 'What?'

'I don't know.' She seemed puzzled. She wrinkled her nose and glanced around the room. 'It's a strange smell. Almost like onions.' And she licked her mouth with the tip of her tongue as if she could taste it.

I shrugged. 'It must be coming up from the kitchen,' I said miserably. 'It's an old house. The smells travel.'

'Yes. I suppose so.' She smiled and seemed entirely satisfied with this explanation, strolled to the chest of drawers and began to finger her stack of books. She looked very calm and concentrated.

I sat and watched the back of her head, waiting for something to happen. Her long hair had been tied in a knot that exposed her ears and the nape of her neck. A gold necklace, thin as a thread, gleamed as it caught the light.

'Is that it?' I said, after a long time. This silence frightened me. There was something wrong. The guilt began to gnaw at my stomach.

'No. There's something I have to ask you...'

'Yes?'

'Where do you think we come from?'

I knew the answer to this conundrum. 'From the stars!' I said brightly. 'Stardust. We're made entirely from stardust.'

'And who made the stars?'

My heart sank. 'God made the stars,' I said obediently.

'God made the stars,' she repeated.

I was tempted to ask her who had made God but I didn't want to give her the pleasure of telling me that God had made God in that breathtaking leap of faith that only the innocent understand.

'Do you have a bible?'

'A bible?' My head was spinning. I had grown exhausted waiting for this interrogation. 'I had a bible. But I must have mislaid it.' A popular pocket edition with black, mock leather cover and pages as thin as butterfly wings. And Whodat begat Doodat and Doodat begat Whatdat. It was long lost and little lamented.

She turned towards me again and now she had a book in her hand.

'Here! I want you to take this,' she said, smiling the radiant smile that made her face seem to shine with pleasure.

'No!'

'Yes! I want it to be a friend to you. I want you to study it carefully. I want you to spend some time reflecting upon its meaning and purpose.'

'Thank you,' I said, receiving the unwanted gift with both hands. It was a modern, illustrated edition by the Glad Tidings Bible Tract Company of New York, featuring Cary Grant as Jesus and a Hollywood cast of thousands. It was large and heavy and wrapped in a bright, plastic jacket.

Dorothy moved to the opposite chair, sweeping her hands behind her legs to avoid crushing and spoiling her skirt. She sat down and promptly crossed her ankles. 'Did you ever feel that you were put on this earth for a purpose?' she said, confidentially, watching me flick through the illustrations. Garden. Flood. Sodom. Salt. Jacob. Joseph. Pharaoh. Moses.

'Housework!' I said breezily, glancing up and quickly looking away from the dark intensity in her eyes. That ancient battle. That noble pursuit. Man's eternal struggle to raise himself from the dust. I enjoyed the absurdity of the work. In our daily sweeping and polishing I could sense the perpetual fight against change, the doomed desire for the world to be constant, the struggle we make against death and decay. There is something powerful and primitive in this urge to establish order. We are always repairing our fragile world, sweeping the paths and restoring the fences, filling the cracks in the walls that we raise against the terror of life. When we stop chasing dust, when we stop washing windows, even for a moment, then the dust settles, the glass grows quickly dark again, and we are confronted with the folly of our endeavours. There is no reward in the labour of housework but for the certain knowledge that tomorrow the enemy will briefly take flight as we engage in vainglorious battle with broom-handle lances and dusters. And when we cast down our weapons and fall away exhausted, we sleep secure in the certainty that our familiar enemy creeps back under cover of darkness.

Dorothy wasn't impressed. 'But you have a much greater purpose in life, Skipper. Housework is fine, of course, but God also has work for you,' she said, tilting towards me. The gold thread dangled away from her throat.

'What is it?' I asked suspiciously.

'He wants you to praise Him and walk in His ways.'

'I'll do my best,' I promised. I smiled and closed the book and waited for permission to leave.

'That's not enough. You can't be expected to struggle alone. Jesus is waiting to save us from ourselves but to find Him we must open our hearts and become as small children. We're asked to confess our sins in order to wash away the past and gain the forgiveness we need to proceed towards the light of salvation...'

This declaration left her flushed and slightly breathless. She looked delicious. 'Do you understand what I'm saying?' she said, raising a finger to tap at the bridge of her spectacles.

'Yes,' I said solemnly. 'What sins?'

'We are all by nature born in sin.'

'How's that?'

'It's the nature of the world,' she said sadly. 'We are grown unlovely to the Lord.'

She shrugged and gently joggled her breasts.

'But why?' I said. What was wrong with me? I should have counted my blessings, stashed the bible under my shirt and been glad enough to escape. But the devil had stitched me into that chair and pricked my tongue into argument. 'Because we came from Adam and Eve?'

'Not exactly. We must think of our own disobedience.'

'Everybody? Does everybody sin?'

'Oh, yes!' she said, beginning to brighten. 'You're not alone. It's the human condition. I suppose you could say that life is like a wrestling match. Good always struggles with evil and God is the referee.'

I found no comfort in this idea. If God the Referee was anything like Rhino Black we all had something to worry about.

'Are you ready to confess your sins?'

'I can't think of anything,' I said nervously, glancing towards the chest of drawers in a rush of embarrassment. 'At the moment. Just like that. I'd need some time to think about it.'

'Well, let's start with the seven deadly sins,' she said helpfully. 'Greed, anger, sloth, lust. That sort of thing.' She reached out and took my hand. She seemed very fond of holding my hand.

'Yes,' I said quickly.

'Yes, what?'

'All of them.'

'Good!' she said, giving my fingers a friendly squeeze. 'That's good!' She began to look quite excited. 'Do you have the courage to tell me about them?'

'I don't know…'

'We need to confess our sins before we can be forgiven…'

But I was struck dumb. I wagged my poor head. Despite her tender encouragements, I found I had nothing to declare.

She sighed. 'Why don't we talk again tomorrow?' she said, at last, reluctantly returning my hand. 'Read the Good Book, think about the things we've discussed and come to see me tomorrow.'

25

LATE THAT NIGHT, as I sat in bed with Lottie Pout, I heard a scuffling at the bedroom door. I pulled myself reluctantly from hot Lottie's elastic nipple and went to investigate. The mysterious visitor had fled but left a large brown envelope on the floor. I took the envelope into my bed and found it contained, to my great disappointment, a dog-eared copy of the Glad Tidings Mail Order Catalogue. Dorothy must have felt that I needed some extra encouragement.

I settled back in my pillows and flicked with dismay through the glossy pages. The catalogue was the size and weight of a telephone directory and contained all the booklets and magazines, the tokens and charms, that helped the struggling missionary to travel safely among the heathens.

There were many bibles, as you might suppose, in different editions, and books of prayer and popular hymns and crucifixes and candles. But there were also comic books, posters, postcards, libraries of tapes and several pages of button badges. And there were T-shirts, sweaters and baseball caps embroidered with comical Christian slogans: *Christ I love Life!* and *God Knows Why I Picked This T-shirt!* And Jogging for Jesus tracksuits – pure cotton, one size fits all – and John the Baptist shower caps and Samson-strength luxury bath towels embroidered with your choice of proverb.

And there were novelty, cast-iron, Moses in the Basket doorstops and Christmas carol door-chimes and apostle key rings and Noah's Ark jigsaw puzzles and Nativity tapestry kits and giant inflatable rubber globes printed with maps of the bible lands. And there were crucifixion holograms, framed and ready to hang on the wall, with Charlton Heston as Christ in a crown of thorns and a twinkle of blood on his neatly trimmed beard. And there were reproduction brass rubbings and Ten Commandment coffee-mug sets and Three Kings in a snow-shaker and Queen of Sheba pot-pourri and Galilee bath salts and sinister glow-in-the-dark Baby Jesus in a Manger bedside ornaments and handy pocket Madonnas, with Ingrid Bergman cast as the Virgin, finished by hand in genuine hall-marked silver.

There was no end to this stuff! Pages and pages of mawkish knick-knacks, wall plaques and souvenirs. It was quite a revelation! And, as I had feared, Dorothy was working on some sort of bonus incentive scheme. She earned a small commission on every Jumping Jesus she sold, a good deal more on the leisure-wear and a tidy amount on the jewellery. If she procured ten new names for the catalogue's mailing list she received a free, nylon travel bag.

The catalogue itself was an article of worship and held the unspoken promise that Heaven would be a Disney World in which all your favourite characters – Abraham,

Judas, Jonah, Herod and the rest – would come out to greet you every night in a grand illuminated parade. You could shake hands with Mary and Jesus (don't forget your camera!) and try the latest white-knuckle rides. The Great Flood. The Flight from Egypt. Horsemen of the Apocalypse.

The Glad Tidings Bible Tract Company was a formidable industry. An influential financial power with considerable tax advantages. A major employer of clerks and accountants, an important consumer of wood pulp and paper. The New York headquarters, pushed like a stake through the heart of Manhattan, had been designed by a team of prize-winning architects. Marble and bronze. No expense spared. The Glad Tidings Bible Tract Company was a powerful organisation. And because it broadcast the word of God you couldn't fault its credentials.

26

I WAS A good student. I worked hard. I began with the first book of Moses and stubbornly worked my way forth towards the Revelation of St John the Divine. After supper each evening I'd slip away to Dorothy's room where she monitored my progress and tested my knowledge of saints and sinners. It was true, yes, that I'd trapped myself into taking this long and arduous path but I saw the advantages. I sat with Dorothy every night and claimed her undivided attention. We spent the time together, engrossed in intimate conversation, and no one complained or dared to come forward and challenge my purpose. As rumours of my conversion spread I was treated with caution as if, in my pixilated condition, I might infect others with divine contagion. And so I was granted the freedom to lay siege to the object of my desire without raising the least suspicion.

Dorothy trusted her faith without question, but when I grew in confidence I became more argumentative. As I struggled through the Old Testament I found God was bad-tempered and dangerous. He demanded living sacrifice. He devised countless traps for his followers and when His flock plunged into them, concocted terrible punishments. There were so many rules and regulations, so many curses and obligations. The fat years and the lean years.

The right path and the wrong path. The clean and the unclean. So many riddles to be explained.

'Why does God permit famine and earthquake and war and plague?' I demanded one evening.

Dorothy was ready for me. 'They're part of His terrible mystery,' she declared. 'If we understood, we should be like Him.'

'You mean angry?'

'No, Skipper!' She looked rather shocked. 'Praise ye the Lord, for He is good: for His mercy endureth forever.'

'But look what He did to the poor Egyptians,' I complained. 'He turned their rivers to blood, slaughtered their cattle, blighted their crops, killed their first born and sent down plagues of frogs and lice and flies and boils and hail and locusts.'

'Well, they were disobedient. They had hardened their hearts against His children.'

'I thought we were all God's children.'

'Except the Egyptians,' she said serenely.

'But He drove out the Canaanites, the Amorites and the Midianites,' I continued, blazing with indignation.

'For thou shalt worship no other god: for the Lord, whose name is Jealous, is a jealous God,' she said. 'Exodus 34, verse 14.'

'And He sent a flood to swallow the world!'

'But He sent His Son to save it.'

'I haven't found Jesus,' I admitted. I was still sloshing through the blood of kings with Joshua.

'That's obvious!' she said. 'But you'll find that life without Jesus is like a three-minute egg served without a spoon. If you try to crack it without His help you'll always make a mess of it. Why don't you try the New Testament?'

'I don't want to miss anything.'

It was far more complicated than I'd imagined. God sent Moses on the glory trail but still I grieved for obstinate Sihon, king of Heshbon, and Og, the giant king of Bashan, with his iron bedstead nine cubits long.

'If you die in an act of God, do you go to Heaven?' I said and I might have been four years old again, asking my mother the same question.

'Yes. Almost certainly.'

'But remember how Joshua waged war against Adonizedek, king of Jerusalem, and Hoham king of Hebron and Piram king of Jarmuth and Japhia king of Lachish and Debir king of Eglon and there was a great battle and God Himself came out though the clouds to throw stones at them?'

'Yes.'

'And Joshua utterly destroyed all that breathed, the armies were slain, the land was laid waste and the kings were hanged from trees?'

'Yes.'

'Were the slain taken up to Heaven? Were the unlucky kings to be forgiven once they'd been hanged and taken into God's kingdom?'

'I don't know.'

'I mean, if you saw Joshua coming at you shouting proverbs and swinging a sword, it would be an act of God wouldn't it? And you'd automatically qualify for a place in Heaven?'

'It would be an act of God,' she agreed.

'Well, that's what I mean!' I said.

'What?'

'Well, if God had sent someone to kill you and rape your women and make slaves of your children, and butcher your cattle and cripple your horses, you'd suspect that He wasn't pleased with you and this act of God was a sign that He didn't want you in Heaven.'

'In a manner of speaking,' she said, rather confused. 'But this all happened a long time ago in a faraway place called bible land. We have to understand its message for the modern world.'

'What is it?' I asked.

'We must love one another,' she said.

We had more success with my confessions. Encouraged to unburden myself without fear of restraint I now began to hint at the monstrous cravings that poisoned my blood and choked my heart with the agony of a violent and ballooning lust. Slowly. Slowly. I gave myself to her mercy.

She developed a little ritual for these delicate encounters. At the end of each bible lesson – conducted in the comfort of the two armchairs – we would sit side by side on the carpet, propping ourselves against the bed, and hold hands in silence, staring at nothing, waiting for me to open my mouth and incriminate myself. It might have worked, given time, but the weight of her hand, the warmth of her thigh and the lickerish nature of her perfume, left me tongue-tied and nervous.

Dorothy was not to be defeated and, in order to spare my blushes, had soon persuaded me to sit behind the folding screen to whisper my confessions through a crack in the canvas. It had the desired effect. Huddled in the twilight of that secluded corner, with my knees beneath my chin and broken cobwebs in my hair, I began to give voice to my strangled emotions.

'Do you have anything to tell me?' she prompted, kneeling on the floor with her face gently pressed to the screen.

'I've stolen food from the kitchen.'

'Forgiven.'

'I've made cruel remarks about Senior Franklin.'

'Forgiven.'

'I've failed to clean in this corner.'

'Forgiven.'

I fell silent.

'Is there nothing else?' She sounded disappointed at the banality of these crimes. They certainly didn't justify the hours she'd spent coaxing them out of me. But I wasn't finished.

'I have hot and fleshly thoughts,' I whispered.

'Forgiven.'

'But I have dreams!' I protested.

'What sort of dreams?'

'Voluptuous dreams.' I twisted and dipped my head to sneak a peek through the crack in the canvas. She had pulled herself away from the screen and was leaning against the back of a chair. She looked slightly flushed but remained self-composed. She sat in a pool of petticoats, picking at the pleats of her skirt.

'Tell me about them,' she said softly.

'I beheld a strange and wonderful woman!' I croaked, with my eye to the canvas keyhole.

'A young woman?'

'Yes.'

'Is she sent to lead you into temptation?'

'Yes,' I said. Yes! Tease me. Tempt me! Lead me astray. Deliver me into the arms of a cunning succuba in sensible shoes and wire-rimmed spectacles. For the lips of a strange woman drop as an honeycomb, and her mouth is smoother than oil.

'What happens?'

'Behold, she comes to me in my sleep and beckons me forth to render her garments asunder. And she prevails over me, yea, unto the trembling of my haunches and I cast open her raiment, even unto the last button thereof, and am bewitched and fondle her intimate portions...'

Dorothy brushed at her skirt with both hands, jerked up her head and frowned. 'Is this just a dream?' she asked, suspiciously.

'It's just a dream,' I said, sadly, from the gloom of my makeshift confessional.

'Forgiven.'

27

AND WHAT WAS happening while Mr Romance was locked away with his bible? Nothing happened. A sinister silence seemed to descend upon the house.

Father, absorbed in some new and fantastic invention, spent more and more time in the cellar. He became a shadow, a silent spectre that drifted from room to room and was gone again before we could challenge him. His eyes were clouded with dreams. His head was filled with immense calculations and fabulous conjectures.

Franklin, having completed his campaign of hate against the Dwarf, seemed to hesitate, listening, holding his breath, waiting for the screams of outrage, the battery of protest, the full fury of public indignation that he confidently expected to explode around his rival's head. He loitered in unexpected corners, barked when anyone rang the bell and cringed at the sound of the telephone.

Janet, despite my good advice, enrolled for Conversation at night class. She now took Yoga on Monday, retired from Wednesday's Basketwork, retained Pottery on Thursday and sacrificed her Needlecraft to practise chitchat on Friday. The precious few evenings she spent at home were usually reserved for Katie Pphart or games of dominoes with Marvel.

Mr Marvel, no longer so threatened by Dorothy, returned to his favourite roost in the front parlour, sleeping through the afternoons with his belly wrapped in *The Trumpet*.

He ventured abroad once or twice a week, returning battered and bilious, and continued to bang out messages on the old typewriter after each mysterious journey. I persevered in my attempts to trap him into surrendering these secret documents and he continued to outwit me.

The house seemed to grow unnaturally quiet, as if waiting for a storm to break. Nothing stirred. During the day the rooms slumbered beneath an oppressive weight of sunlight. At night they remained stubbornly indifferent to our circulation, muffled our voices and deadened our footsteps. But the storm gathered and finally broke as Janet's infatuation with the odious Franklin again made itself manifest in a new and most original fashion.

It was long and barrel-shaped. It was hollow. It was crooked. It was broad at the base and slightly twisted towards the mouth. It was moulded from clay and dribbled with a thick, white, blistered glaze. It might have been a stump of walrus tusk or a lump of eroded coral. It was beautifully wrapped in scented paper and tied with a glittering pink and white ribbon.

'What is it, my cringing concubine?' Franklin demanded suspiciously when Janet presented him with this gift. It was heavy! The weight startled him and he nearly let it slip through his fingers.

'Surprise,' she said quickly and blushed. She obviously hadn't made a lot of progress from her art of conversation class.

It was a Wednesday evening, supper was finished, and we were sitting in the front parlour recovering from an especially virulent spiced chicken pie. Dorothy was helping mother in the kitchen, where she made a nuisance of herself with cheese balls and cocktail onions. Father was locked in the cellar. Mr Marvel was at the table with his box of dominoes and I was in the armchair with *Jesus Rebukes the Pharisees*. Franklin cast away the ribbon and scratched at the wrapping paper until he'd uncovered the curious object. He frowned. He weighed the pot in his hand as if he were holding a human skull.

'It's for your pencils,' Janet said hopefully, smiling and knitting her fingers together.

'What's that, my pert pudendum?' he asked. He looked perplexed. He cocked his head and squinted along the length of his nose. He speared the pot with two fingers and sent it into a wobbling spin by striking it with the palm of one hand.

'I made it for you at night class,' she said, very flustered. 'It's supposed to be a pencil pot...' She hung her head to hide her blushes and stared stubbornly at her feet. It had taken all her courage to perform this little ceremony and now she was trapped, paralysed, waiting for his approval.

Franklin sniggered. It hissed from his stomach and squirted through those long and loathsome teeth. His eyebrows bristled. His mouth sprang open. His face trembled and he started to laugh. It was a hot, volcanic shout of laughter that whirled from his throat and would not stop. It gusted about the room, punching the curtains and lifting the lace on the antimacassars. It seized him by the arms and legs and made him thrash and kick in the sofa. He twisted. He bucked. He clutched his bursting head in his hands. His lungs, tortured by these convulsions, withered and collapsed, shrinking down to the size of walnuts. He began to suffocate. He gulped at the air like a fish, swallowing great greedy draughts as he tried to keep himself afloat. His face changed colour, grew dark and swollen with blood. His tongue was black. His eyes began to bulge in their sockets. And still the laughter came out of him.

'Quick!' Janet shouted in alarm. 'He's choking!' She stood, transfixed, and stuffed her knuckles into her mouth. She started sobbing. The tears filled her eyes and flooded her lashes.

'Let him choke,' Mr Marvel said with absolute indifference and emptied his box of dominoes on the table.

'Skipper!' Janet screamed, jumping from foot to foot in terror. 'Skipper! There's something wrong with him!'

She cried for help and I couldn't resist. The sound of her screaming pierced my heart. So I jumped from my chair and ran to the rescue. I'd read enough Katie Pphart to know that the cure for hysteria is a sharp smack in the face. The heroine has hysterics and the hero slaps her face. Scream. Slap. As simple as that. So I rushed to the sofa, pushed Janet aside and clubbed Franklin with *Jesus Rebukes the Pharisees*. He yelped, shook his head and continued to laugh. A terrible, mocking laughter that howled and moaned like a tempest inside him.

I clubbed him for a second time, a cruel smack across the mouth struck with such force that it buckled my weapon. He stopped shouting and gasped in surprise. He threw back his head, fixed me with an evil eye and grinned like a Halloween pumpkin. And then he trembled, his eyes fluttered, he spluttered, giggled and laughed again.

'It's no good!' I shouted at Marvel. 'I think he's having a fit!' It was horrible. He looked tormented. He flared his nostrils and clawed at his stomach. His laughter became a lamentation, a dreadful wailing that screeched and swooped around our heads and filled the room with its poisonous odour.

'He's a bugger!' Marvel grumbled. He clambered from his chair, stamped across the room, recovered the pencil pot from the carpet and brought it down sharply on Franklin's head. He didn't hesitate. He picked up the pot and smacked Franklin's head as if he were hitting a nail with a hammer.

Franklin grunted, his jaws clacked together, but still he couldn't stop laughing. He crawled into a corner of the sofa and tried to hide among the cushions, shielding his face with his arms. He looked like a giant insect, a brittle mantis with gangling, broken limbs. 'Hit him again,' I suggested.

Franklin honked and shrieked the louder, wheezing with panic and pain. He scrambled among the cushions in a feeble attempt to escape his tormentors.

Mr Marvel shook his head. 'We don't want to kill him.'

'Water!' Janet shouted from her hiding place behind the door. 'Throw a bucket of water on him...'

'That's for dogs!' Marvel grumbled.

'I'm going for help!' I shouted impatiently and started running towards the back parlour. We needed a blindfold and ropes to restrain him. We needed something to stupefy him. We needed someone to call a doctor.

'What's happening?' mother complained. 'It sounds like bedlam out there!' She was sitting with Dorothy watching TV as they plundered a packet of store-cupboard biscuits. I think they were watching *Random Harvest*, with Ronald Colman looking bewildered and walking into the furniture. They were both sobbing and squeezing pink paper handkerchiefs.

'Franklin's gone mad!' I panted, clutching the back of a chair for support. 'He's finally gone mad!'

Dorothy looked startled. 'Is he possessed?'

'I don't know.'

'Is he foaming at the mouth?'

I shook my head.

'Is he talking in tongues?' she demanded, brushing sugar grains from her fingers. 'Is he shouting obscenities?' She seemed frightened and rather excited, as if she fully expected an evening of amateur exorcism.

'He's laughing!'

'I don't believe it!' mother said, pushing away from the table and pulling her cardigan closed.

We rushed into the front parlour but we were too late. It was finished. There was silence. Marvel and Janet had vanished. The dominoes remained scattered across the table. Franklin was sitting in the sofa, pale, exhausted, drenched with sweat but no longer screaming or clutching his brain. He was calm. He was smiling. His eye were bloodshot and staring.

He nursed the pencil pot in his hands.

28

He was never seen again without that pencil pot. He carried it with him everywhere. It became his talisman, a charm against the Dwarf's revenge. I watched him waste hours each morning scouring the papers for rumour and scandal, some tangible sign of the Dwarf's disgrace. But as the days passed and he found nothing, he began to sense that something was wrong. Here was an unexpected twist to the plot! A conspiracy of silence! It never occurred to him that his poisonous letters might be dismissed as the work of a madman. He grew more hunted and unpredictable. His language became more convoluted, peppered with obscure words, snatches of French, clots of German, bizarre oaths and highly coloured phrases that flowered and withered and sprouted again until they entirely choked his conversation, permitting no daylight to penetrate, and he fell silent, lost, unhappy, watching us with bewildered eyes.

'Poor, tortured soul!' Dorothy said whenever we spoke of him. 'He needs to find comfort in the Lord.'

'He's past salvation,' I said.

'No one is lost forever,' Dorothy corrected and it worried me for a little while that she might find Franklin, in his present tortured condition, so challenging that she'd ask him to join our bible classes.

'Perhaps we should try the subtle approach,' I said. 'We don't want to frighten him. I could lend him my copy of *Jesus Conquers the Universe*.'

'Do you think it might help?'

'It worked for me,' I said.

I continued my studies. I struggled through Judges, Ruth and Samuel, battled through Kings and Chronicles. But I found the desert landscape increasingly depressing, with its long monotony of goats and thorn trees. A cruel and barren land filled with an ugly, quarrelsome people. Why had God chosen Palestine for the Holy Land when He had the freedom to pick and choose anywhere in Creation? What if Christ had been born in another part of the world? Entirely. Far away from the squalor of Roman occupation, dried figs and open-toe sandals.

He might have been born in the glittering snow fields of the north or the tropical islands of the blue Pacific. God could have snapped his fingers and everything would be different! No more squabbling Jews and Gentiles. We'd have inherited the parable of the doubting musk ox and the story of the prodigal polar bear. Jesus would have performed his miracles using the local ingredients: coconuts, yams and flying fishes. Consider the Nativity lit by the Northern lights, the wind whipping snow, the howl of hungry wolves on the ice and the clanking bells of the reindeer herds; or the wise men bearing gifts of turtle meat, orchids and cowrie shells, surfing a coral reef in a ceremonial canoe. A twist in geography could have made all the difference.

The landscape shapes a religion, drenches its stories and characters. Where there are mountains, the rocks and the rivers are touched by magic. Giants inhabit the caves and sprites command the water-courses. Where there are forests, the spirits and demons inhabit the trees, disguising themselves as birds and animals. And where there is nothing but heat and dust even the gods of that place retreat, allow themselves to become remote and watch from their palaces in the sky.

And what would have happened if another brand of faith, from a different tribe, had become the dominant force in the world? How did we find ourselves trapped in a church with a crucifixion for a trademark? Was it an accident of history that Christianity had spread into Europe and then to all nations, carried upon the colonial ambitions of powerful, military governments? Or was it one of God's jokes? Christ's message of tolerance delivered with sword and musket.

If the early maritime trade between India and the Persian Gulf had taken the gods of the Indus into Syria and Europe, we might now be celebrating 4,000 years of happy marriage with some powerful river god from the Ganges flood plains. Imagine the possibilities! If we hadn't adopted a desert blood cult we might have taken, instead, a jolly rain god. A god not of fire and brimstone but of fog and thunder.

And if the Hindus had been crusaders it might have been Nandi the divine bull or Ganesh the elephant-headed god sitting on the parlour table, wreathed in flowers and lit by candles. Ten thousand gods from a gaudy heaven of warrior-kings and beasts of burden. Enough gods to suit every taste. A different god for each day in the year. A god for every occasion.

And what if Africa had emerged triumphant and con-
quered the rampaging Arabs and Romans, chased them
north and subdued Europe with animistic cults and
ancestor worship? We'd be happy fondling stones,
sewing fetish bags and talking to spirits in trees. Trust
me. We'd continue to live in a perfectly well-ordered
world. Our lives would not feel impoverished for our
ignorance of the plagues brought down on the Philistines
or the battle honours of Judah. We could sleep without
knowing the sons of Levi, Issachar, Ephraim and
Benjamin.

And if there were no gods, if we were at last agreed that
we were created from stardust animated by the miracle of
molecular self-assembly, we would continue to ride
through the cosmos. The planets would still turn. Our lives
would still be terrible.

Dorothy wasn't interested in this kind of free-floating
speculation. She grew impatient with so many questions.
She wanted me to do nothing more than raise my bible and
praise the Lord.

'Living your life without Jesus is like finding yourself at
a Schoenberg concert,' she declared, with a fair degree of
passion. 'No matter how hard you strain your ears, none
of it makes any sense.' I didn't care to argue. Schoenberg, it
seemed, was in league with the Devil.

Actually, she had a huge fund of these Christmas-
cracker wisdoms, in a range from the painfully obvious to
the deeply obscure.

Life without Jesus is like a television without an aerial –
you must be content with only half the picture – was cer-

tainly one of her favourites, suggesting, as it did, that she alone in the house received perfect clarity of vision.

Jesus is like a big ball of wool – you can try to knit Him to your own design but you'll find that He's always too short in the sleeves – was one of her more baffling observations.

Franklin became rather good at this game and, when the mood took him, would construct maxims of such breathtaking complexity that their meanings could never be deciphered. His sarcasm was wasted on Dorothy, of course, who didn't waste time in listening to him but simply smiled as she waited for the opportunity to reply with a maxim from her own collection in the hope that it suited the circumstances.

I hadn't yet found my own comfort in Jesus but I began to look forward to evening confession. I depended upon her determination to wash out my sins and save my soul. It was crucial to my stumbling courtship: these blissful interludes in which she indulged my fantasies and encouraged me to describe my dreams.

'Do you have anything to confess?'

'Hot and fleshly thoughts,' I would whisper, hidden behind the shelter of the folding screen.

'Again?'

'It's my age.'

'It's not enough to confess these sins,' she warned me. 'God is always there to forgive, but He wants you to stay away from temptation.'

'I can't help it,' I complained. 'I'm seized by wicked and earthly notions.'

'Do you want to tell me about them?'

And so I would spin fantastic yarns of my struggle with the forces of darkness. I was obliged to tread a most delicate path between delight and debauchery and took great care to protect my tormentor's identity for fear of arousing suspicions.

'Do you know this woman?'

'She wears a mask.'

'A mask?'

'For she stealeth in secret through the night and maketh me to lie down with her strange persuasions.'

I was more candid when I spoke of my weakness in temptation, introducing scenes of cheerful violation, bondage, fetish objects, food abuse and elaborate moonlit rituals. I would watch Dorothy through the hole in the screen as she sat on the floor to hear my confession. She sat serene, hands clasped, head bowed, eyes half-closed and dreaming. Far from being scandalised by the chattering of my demons, she gave the impression of falling asleep.

I tried to keep her entertained. In an effort to sharpen her interest I would invent new and amusing locations for these erotic encounters. Carnival rides. Wax museums. Windmills. Aquariums. Aviaries. Theatre balconies. Department store windows.

The results were not encouraging.

'Have you finished?' she would ask eventually, when I'd fallen silent, having exhausted myself by committing every crime of passion available to my imagination.

'Yes,' I'd say bleakly.

'Forgiven.'

29

'BY THUNDER, BUT I must have you this night or let me perish in the attempt!' Mr Romance shouted as he whirled forward in a storm of passion, abruptly seizing her small, dainty waist and jerking her into his broad violent arms to confront the terrible madness that flashed in his dark and mysterious eyes.

'My heart has already been given to Jesus!' she gasped defiantly, touching her beautiful, naked throat in search of the missing gold crucifix, yet she knew she had betrayed herself and trembled beneath his hands as she felt the excitement of his brandied breath on the half-exposed globes of her polished white breasts.

'Be warned, madam, I have no patience with your reluctance!' he snarled as she felt his long, strong fingers invading the soft, silk embroidery of her delicate, hand-stitched underskirt. 'For I am a creature of the night and dawn is fast approaching...'

She cried out in great distress as she found herself pulled from her bed and dragged across the rough oak floor towards the looming shadows of the diabolical contraptions that had lately been constructed in the secrecy of his private chamber. 'Believe me, sir, I would rather suffer Hell's torment than give myself to your monstrous embrace!' she panted as she twisted and struggled against the restraint of the cruel leather harness.

But he merely threw back his head and laughed. 'Rest assured, my lady, for in this house they are but one and the same!'

30

It was time for my mother to grow suspicious about my friendship with Dorothy. Perhaps she felt in some measure responsible for the situation. It had been her idea – when Marvel had failed to show any interest – to make me Dorothy's companion. She had thrown us together. She had encouraged me to keep our guest amused with a pilgrimage through the city's churches. But as the courtship developed and I retired each evening to Dorothy's room with a large-print bible under my arm, mother began to show signs of alarm.

She waited until we had settled down together to watch the TV wrestling before she began her interrogation. I hadn't bothered with the wrestling for more than a week. But Dorothy wanted time to write postcards and mother insisted that I keep her company in the back parlour for the battle between Abdullah the Turk and the unpredictable Junkyard Dog.

'You should have been here last night!' mother said, as she savaged a cold bacon sandwich. The spectacle of half-naked men attempting to throttle each other always gave her an appetite.

'Why?'

'Grudge match. Rage in a cage. Submission or knock out. The Great Muta was fighting the Crippler.'

'I wish I'd seen that'

'It was a corker!' she chortled.

'What happened?'

'You should have been here.'

'I was looking after Dorothy.'

Abdullah the Turk took the Dog by surprise, grabbed him by the ears and hammered home a series of punishing head butts. The Dog shouted and sprayed blood. As he fell to his knees, Abdullah spilled forward and hit the deck. The Turk was big but he was clumsy. When he struggled back to his feet, the Dog catapulted from the ropes with a flying drop kick that sent the Turk sprawling. Abdullah roared and scrambled across the ring on his hands and knees. The Dog chased him into a corner and tried to wrench a leg from its socket.

'You seem to be spending a lot of your time looking after Dorothy,' mother said casually.

'She's going home at the end of the month,' I said.

'Is that what she told you?'

'Yes.'

In his excellent book *Complete Science of Wrestling*, published in 1909, the Russian champion George Hackenschmidt describes some fifty basic wrestling moves, from standing throws to ground combat. It was a rough sport – even in those early days. During a 1906 championship tournament in London, Hackenschmidt took the belt by breaking the arm of Monster Mandrali. Hackenschmidt was a tough guy. But even he could not have imagined the modern fighter performing backward somersaults from the top of the corner post, with his opponent's head locked between his knees and the ring ropes wrapped in barbed wire. These moves defy death. They challenge belief. They require a breed of ring warrior with steel nerves and liquid bones.

'Kick him where it hurts!' mother shouted, shaking her sandwich in fury. Abdullah had managed to insert his fist into the Dog's mouth and was trying to snap off teeth with his fingers. The Dog squirmed. He hacked and chopped at Abdullah's belly. It was like slapping tripe with a paddle. The crowd hissed and bellowed. The referee danced and waved his arms.

'She seems to be very fond of you,' mother continued.

'I'm a very likeable sort of person.'

She grunted and took a bite of her sandwich. 'What do you find to talk about locked away in her room every night?'

'We're not locked away!'

'Then why don't you talk downstairs in the parlour?

'Jesus. She wants me to find a friend in Jesus.'

Mother frowned and shook her head. 'I don't know where we went wrong with you. We've always tried to do our best. We've tried to make you clean-living. You don't smoke. You don't take drugs. And now this happens!'

'What?'

'Dorothy,' mother said. 'Dorothy and this other business.'

'There's no harm in it.'

'She's a lot older than you, Skipper.'

'She's not that old!' I protested. A few years. It was nothing. Why were people so concerned with age? What difference did it make?

'It's a question of experience. You've still got a lot to learn. I wouldn't want you to do something that you'll live to regret.'

'How do you mean?'

'Well, if she gave you certain ideas…' mother said carefully, peeling the crust from the sandwich. 'Peculiar ideas. If she tried to persuade you into doing something that, you know, that made you feel uncomfortable…'

'Uncomfortable?'

'You know that I'm talking about!'

I stared in panic at the TV screen. We're talking dirty! Is it possible? Mother and son. We're talking filthy. We're talking fantastic and dangerous. Forbidden acts. Peculiar practices. She was warning me of the perils that lurk in the locked room, the hall of mirrors, the little circus of horrors. What did she want to tell me? Quick! Tell me the truth. Don't spare my feelings. What did she know about Dorothy that made her fear so much for my safety?

The Turk had left the ring in search of an interesting weapon and returned with a fire extinguisher. He discharged a volley of freezing fog, knocking down the referee and blinding the Dog who howled and staggered, lost his sense of direction and blundered into the ropes. The Turk seized the advantage, dragged him down to the canvas and smothered his victim's face in his arms.

'It's easy to make mistakes,' mother said.

'Yes.'

'In the heat of the moment, when passions are high. Especially if you're young and innocent and trying to please a person. It's too easy.'

'I'll be careful,' I promised.

'They come at you with their silly smiles and their promises,' she continued bitterly. 'They string you along with their fancy talk. But one thing always leads to another. One thing leads to another.' Her face looked pinched by memories and for a moment I saw her as a skinny schoolgirl pursued by smirking romeos demanding the price of her favours.

The Dog had survived the choke hold and smother. He was handcuffed to a corner post and gasping for air while the Turk set to work, changing the shape of his head with a hammer.

'Go for his goolies, you big nancy!' mother shrieked in disgust.

The referee was shouting for help. The bell was ringing. Officials came running. The Turk was cornered and wrapped in a net by men with electric cattle prods. Paramedics were called to haul the Dog from the ring and carry him away as the audience hissed and pelted him with hotdogs and popcorn cartons.

'They know how to play on your emotions,' she grumbled, returning to the conversation. 'They get you excited and feeling confused. They try to work you into a frenzy. And then, before you know it...' She fell silent, lost for words, and waved the remains of her sandwich at me.

'What?'

'It's too late! You only make one little mistake and you have to live with the consequences...'

The consequences! I was too frightened to think about them. Interfere with Dorothy and taste the revenge of a

jealous God. Ten times more violent and terrible than anything yet devised by a vexed and jealous husband.

She turned and gave my hand a squeeze with fingers
glossy with bacon fat. 'I'm glad that we've had this little
talk, Skipper.'

'Yes,' I said.

'You must consider the future,' she added. 'I don't want
you to throw it away for the sake of a fleeting love affair. I've
met Dorothy's sort. They're sweetness and light. They're
sunshine from the back passage. But once they've got their
teeth into you, they never leave you alone. They'll always
follow and pester you. They'll make your life a misery.'

I nodded.

'You might think that you're ready to experiment but
don't rush into anything you might regret. You'll be surprised how quickly your feelings can change. Especially at
your age…'

'I'll give it some thought.'

'Your father was the same. Before we were married. His
friends had some very kinky ideas. He became quite
obsessed. You wouldn't have recognised him. He was
moody. He was secretive. It became a sort of sickness.'

I was shocked. I couldn't imagine my father with a
hoard of *Skirt Lifter* annuals. A secret subscriber to *Corset
Creakers*. A slathering slave to *Rascals in Rubber*. My
embarrassment turned to wonder. What secrets dwelt in
the heart of that man? The chemistry of love potions. One
drop secures her affections. The blueprint for a mechanical
woman. Life-sized and lovely. 'What happened?' I
demanded.

'I shouldn't tell you.'

'I won't breathe a word,' I said.

'Promise?' she demanded.

'Promise,' I said. 'I've already forgotten you've told me. What happened?'

She snorted and brushed down her cardigan. 'He met some girl who tried to turn him into a Moonie.'

31

I COUNTED THE days to the end of the month when Dorothy would slip from my grasp. I'd be lucky to reach Jeremiah. Time enough to qualify for a button badge, my mail-order salvation medal. But no time left for love's delights to fatten and sweeten on the bough. I needed Cupid's rapid shot. I needed a miracle.

In the chaos of my lovesick dreams I plotted Katie Pphart kidnaps, smuggling my true love away to far-flung islands, secret castles and isolated mountain cabins and she, in this wild and primitive state, surrendered herself to my dubious care. How simple these storybook seductions! The heroines become hedonists as soon as they're through the gate to the garden of innocence. Allow them a moment to stand in the sun and they throw away their modesty with their button boots and their crinolines. And so in my dreams we became naked children. We collected honey and fruits of the forest. We hunted crayfish and chased the wild rabbits.

These wholesome views of nature degenerated soon enough into scenes of robust copulation. I corrupted my trusting captive into a freckled concubine, my sun-kissed nympholept, my naked acrobat, a slave to her master's monstrous whims. When she failed to amuse I was lavish with her punishments, I gave her no mercy, I spared her no cruelty. She was spread. She was spanked. She was forced to endure unspeakable acts of debauchery.

1. *He commandeth her to be laced in a corset that be drawn so tight her buttocks do swell to prodigious proportions, whereupon he doth make his cruel designs with a goose feather dipped in ink.*

2. *He shaveth her whiskers most carefully and maketh her squat as to watch her piddle into a pot.*

3. *He bindeth her wrists and listens not to her pleading but causes great mischief within and without her chemise.*

4. *He doth blindfold her eyes and commandeth her enter on hands and knees to sippeth milk from a dish like a beast.*

5. *He spoileth her with wine and then stealeth upon her at night to feast on her fingers and toes.*

6. *He dresseth her for a nunnery and maketh her jump on a trampoline.*

7. *He catcheth her by the throat and though she do struggle and cry out he leaveth many tremendous hickeys.*

8. *He delivereth her to a Nubian who tickleth her extremities.*

9. *He bareth her tender hindquarters and spanketh them with a strap two cubits long, fashioned from leather and knotted silk.*

10. *He doth pluck and plunder her titties while she singeth Victorian battle hymns.*

11. *He filleth her palm with silver and stuffeth her ear with flattery until she kneeleth as a harlot to suckle his privy member and yet she careth not.*

12. *He doth fatten her with sweetmeats until she swelleth to a noble size and cannot rise from the bed but must tolerate his rummaging.*

Shake your head. Turn the page. But allow me the comforts of speculation! What else do we have but imagination to separate ourselves from the brutes? We are human because we have learned the skills to turn our desires into dream, fears into fantasy, curiosity into art. We are human because we alone have the gift to make love with our minds and our hearts. We are mad with love. We are sick with love. These erotic obsessions do not reduce us to the state of beasts but only serve to make us human. And because we are human we are quick with invention. We create the rituals, myths and magic. We fill our dreams with forbidden strangers, cruel caresses and strange encounters. We punish ourselves. We adore ourselves. We abuse ourselves. We confuse ourselves. We cry out to be teased and tantalised. Pornography is a figment of our own imaginations. We feed the fire with our fantasies and fears. How can it be smothered or stifled? We spread the flame as we trample it.

And besides, in this tug of war between the forces of good and evil, Dorothy had the advantage of angels pulling on her team.

32

IT MUST HAVE been the angels who eventually allowed Dorothy to fall so dramatically into my arms. It was certainly beyond her control and far beyond my influence. I was crouched inside the confessional, describing my hot and fleshly thoughts and watching Dorothy through my peephole as she sat listening in one of the old armchairs, head bowed, eyes closed, hands clasped between her breasts, when something most peculiar happened. At first it was no more than a slight shivering in the air, a trembling of wings on the window panes, a vague premonition of danger.

'She stealeth forth in the night,' I mumbled. 'And entereth my private chamber and withholdeth nothing from mine sight but delivereth mine unworthy hands even unto the glory of her hindmost quarters and the raiment thereof which is choice silk yet not withstanding cast asunder so that I tremble in myself and feel sore afraid...' I paused as I tried to gather my thoughts. It was hard work. I fancy my voice lacked conviction, but I stubbornly clung to my battle plan in the hope that these lewd incantations would finally melt my ice maiden's heart.

'She scorneth all manner of modesty to dwell in mischief and her bodice breaketh open and she confoundeth me with the whiteness of her bosom while she plucketh at mine terrible engine of war...'

When I squinted again through the torn screen to monitor my progress, I saw Dorothy had left the armchair. There was something wrong. She was still sitting with her eyes closed, in an attitude of prayer, but she seemed to be floating, held aloft on a slender cushion of air. Her feet drifted free from the carpet. Her shoes were loose. Her skirt ballooned with the force of inflating petticoats. I blinked and stared. She had started to levitate!

'And behold, she delivers me into temptation, yea, even unto...' I stopped and gawped in astonishment as Dorothy's shadow climbed the wall and filled the confessional with darkness.

'And, lo, my strength faileth me and my heart doth break for I am grown fermented in the sight of her...'

She floated silent and serene above the top of the folding screen. She didn't struggle. She seemed to be held in a trance. Her eyes were closed. Her hands were still clasped in prayer. She was wearing a ponytail that now stood rigid and erect as if she were being hauled to Heaven by the very roots of her hair. I reached out my hand to save her but she drifted slowly beyond my reach until she hung, helpless, beneath the ceiling.

I crept into the centre of the room and peered up into the open umbrella of her skirt. The novelty of viewing her from this angle occupied me for several minutes. She was a rare and lovely sight! Her arms and legs were bent in the attitude of a swimmer. She was moored beside the lamp-shade and swaying slightly from side to side against the influence of the tide.

As I watched, a shoe slipped from her foot and fell to earth, cartwheeling across the carpet. I reached up to clasp the remaining shoe and pulled it from the hook of her toes. It felt warm and soft in my hand. A dark-green leather moccasin. I wrapped one hand around her ankle and gently pulled her foot towards me. Her long leg straightened, the muscles stretched, but she continued to float against the ceiling.

'Dorothy!' I whispered. 'Dorothy!' I summoned my courage and pulled on her leg like a bell rope. But nothing happened. She sank and promptly rose again. Her lungs were filled with helium.

I managed to grasp her other foot and struggled to hold her fast, with my head beneath her skirt and my face between her knees. And still she floated above me. Gasping for breath and smothered in peppery petticoats, I groped for her waist and tried to make a snatch at her wrists, but the violence of my attack disturbed her buoyancy and she dipped and rolled away, caught on some invisible draught and sailed towards the top of the wardrobe.

I gave chase, secured her ankles and discovered, after a little experimenting, that pulling and pushing her feet like pistons could drive her forward, making her paddle across the room. In this manner I guided her across the ceiling, careful to avoid the lampshade, until she floated over the bed where I tried once more to find a method of bringing her down.

Despite my rough treatment she hadn't woken from her trance. She remained so calm and composed, she might have been hypnotised. I should have summoned help. I should have called for witnesses. But I hesitated. I didn't want to share the sight and I wasn't anxious to break the spell. It would be enough for the moment, I told myself, to find a way to moor her safely to the bed and wait for this enchantment to fade. A tether for her wrist. A shackle for her ankle. A simple anchor to keep her from danger.

She was wearing a narrow, black, leather belt. The perfect article! I clambered onto the bed, and standing on tiptoe, managed at last to unfasten the buckle. The belt slithered loose and her shirt came adrift from her skirt. A white silk shirt with six glass buttons. And here, I confess, I lost my reason. I grew confused. My thoughts were scrambled. To avoid the risk of suffocation it seemed important to loosen her collar. So I spread her arms and picked at the buttons. The shirt sagged apart and floated open. She was wearing a most impressive bra spun from some wonderful gossamer, embossed with delicate silver flowers that gathered against the shoulder straps and scattered across the creaking cups. Between the cups nestled three satin rosebuds, tied with a bow of sculpted ribbon. I gave them scarce a glance. There was no time to waste in admiration. Concerned with her general health and safety, I reached out and started to work my hands around her shoulder blades in search of the suffocating strap. There must be no restraint. Nothing must hinder her breathing.

It wasn't easy. The bed behaved like a trampoline, making me dance from foot to foot as I tried to keep my balance. I fell to my knees more than once as I struggled to set her free from bondage and grabbed at her arms and legs for support. She rocked and swayed against my weight, sweeping the ceiling, drifting in circles. But I was stubborn, I was cunning, my fumbling fingers found their mark and the burgled bra came apart in my hands.

And then, all at once, the laws of gravity had their revenge and snatched the prize from my grasp. The angels lost interest in their game. The strings snapped. Dorothy shrieked and crashed to earth. She came down with tremendous force, flinging herself against my chest and knocking me to the bed.

I was stunned. When I dared to open my eyes again I found myself pinioned against the mattress with Dorothy sitting astride me. I was blind. It was hot. I was buried alive.

'What happened?' she moaned above my confusion. 'Skipper, what happened? Where are you?' She was coughing and sobbing and rocking herself back and forth on her heels.

'Don't be alarmed! You've had a strange experience!' I managed to shout through her petticoats.

She yelped in fright, yanked open her knees and lifted the hem of her skirt. 'Oh, my poor child! Are you hurt?' she cried, as I struggled in vain to lift my head from that dark and delicious bed of pain.

'No!' I whispered, wincing. 'Nothing broken.' My ears were alight, my shoulder was torn and most of my ribs felt cracked.

Dorothy, splay-mouthed and shivering, quickly rolled from the saddle and crouched for comfort among the pillows. 'Whatever happened?' she asked again, feeling her face as she searched for her spectacles.

'I don't know. You were praying. And then you were floating,' I said, by way of explanation. Oh, yes, a likely story! I didn't think she'd believe me. It was simply too fantastic. I didn't believe it myself. I lay there exhausted and stared at the ceiling. 'You floated in circles around the room...'

'I don't remember...'

'You don't remember anything?' And now the glimmer of hope. The faint possibility of escape.

'Nothing.' She shook her head. 'I was taking your confession...' She was still very drowsy and confused. She stared at her naked feet and frowned, as if surprised by the sight of her toes.

'It was like a dream!' I said. 'You were floating around the room. And the room was filled with a wonderful light! It was a miracle! It must have been a miracle. But when I tried to reach out and touch you...' I swallowed the words and fell silent, turning my face away, encouraging her imagination.

'Yes?'

'I don't know how to explain...'

'Take your time,' she coaxed. 'Tell me what happened.'

'You grabbed me and threw me down,' I said, at last. And I am poured out like water, and all my bones are out of joint: my heart is like wax, it is melted in the midst of my bowels.

'I threw you down on the bed?'

I nodded.

'I can't believe it!' She looked worried. Perhaps she'd been fingered by the Devil. These things happened in

Dorothy's world. 'Did anything unfortunate take place while I was under the influence?'

I didn't answer. I pushed myself up on my elbows and took time to look around the room. Her black leather belt had landed some distance away, curled on the chest of drawers like a snake.

'Tell me, Skipper,' she said, very urgently. 'It's important. Whatever happened. No matter how terrible. I want you to tell me everything.' She was frightened. She had woken suddenly from her trance to find herself mounting me in a frenzy. It was natural under the circumstance that she'd come to the wrong conclusion. And I was ready and more than willing to help her along that yellow brick road. I make no excuses for the deceit. My life depended upon it.

'You're not to blame,' I said, neatly avoiding the question. It was true. I found her missing spectacles lodged in the folds of the blanket at the bottom of the bed. The wire frames were bent but they hadn't broken. 'I know that you weren't responsible,' I continued indulgently. 'I suppose you just couldn't help yourself...'

'Did you hear me talking in tongues?'

'You didn't say a word. Your eyes were closed. You moved in a trance.'

Dorothy stared at me thoughtfully. Her eyes flickered. She was just beginning to get the idea. 'You know, I think it's important, for the moment, that we keep these wonderful signs to ourselves,' she said.

'But it might have been a miracle!' I protested. 'It might have been an important message.'

'All the more reason to pause and consider.'

I nodded gravely.

'We should say nothing about these things until we've offered them up in our prayers. We need some time to meditate. You understand…'

'Yes,' I said. 'It's our secret.'

'Look at me!' she cried suddenly, directing her audience to gaze in wonder at the sight of her unbridled breasts. 'I'm indecent!' She laughed. She blushed. She cupped her proud, pink nipples and tried to push them into her shirt.

'You're nothing but lovely!' I managed to blurt out, feeling awkward. This last act of modesty snagged my heart.

'Thank you,' she said and, to my surprise, rewarded me with a smile. 'I don't know what came over me….'

'You were having a ghostly experience.'

She shook her head. 'I don't know. But I'm sure there's a purpose. It's a sign. Nothing happens by accident. We're part of a greater design.'

33

GOD WAS A personal friend to Dorothy. She told Him everything and took Him everywhere. When she introduced Him to the house He stared into our hearts and He pried into our dreams. We found that we couldn't hide from His suffocating presence. The Cosmic Voyeur peered into cupboards and drawers, peeked under beds, ran His finger along the tops of picture frames in search of cobwebs and dust. Nothing escaped His attention. He remembered each transgression. He knew every small, sad secret, from Janet's hopeless love of Franklin to my past idolatry of the mighty Lottie Pout. He weighed our strengths and weakness and always found us wanting. He scowled. He thundered. He never laughed. He couldn't see the joke.

Dorothy meditated upon the night's events. The knowledge that she had been thrown into the air by some divine or demonic hand and then been granted the strength, more or less, to hurl me down on the bed, must have appealed to her vanity. It was a sign that she had been chosen for some special purpose. No doubt about it. She had been brushed by the wings of angels. And for reasons that passeth all understanding I was to share this mystery. I'd been elected to witness her flight and play a part in her plunge from grace.

She turned to the Good Book and, seized by a fit of bibliomancy, sought the advice of Daniel aka Belteshazzar, favourite of Nebuchadnezzar, child of Judah, master magician, man of night visions, interpreter of dreams. And was it not Daniel who was tested and plucked alive from a den of hungry lions? Exactly. Dorothy saw the connection. She was eager now to sew me into a lion's skin. I had been sent to test her faith. I was the wild and raging beast from which she would shortly be delivered. I was to be the pit into which she tumbled and the ladder she would climb towards her redemption. I would become her ordeal and her ultimate salvation.

34

THE NEXT MORNING she seemed subdued. She came down to a late breakfast and spent the day in pious reflection. We didn't speak to each other. We barely exchanged a glance. Whenever we found ourselves together we quickly became uncomfortable, muttered excuses and fled to different parts of the house.

There was no bible class that night. Dorothy complained of a headache and went to bed soon after supper. She was not to be disturbed. Mother worked in the kitchen and father escaped to the cellar. Janet gossiped with Mr Marvel and Franklin went aloft to scribble mad secrets in Lilliput.

I loitered for a while in the front parlour, flicking through Jesus comic books while listening to Janet chatter to Marvel as they set out their box of dominoes.

'How is your mother,' Marvel inquired.

'It's been nothing but liver and lights for a month,' Janet reported. 'Frozen shoulder. Pain in the neck. Legs like balloons and panic attacks.'

Marvel made little clucking sounds. 'She seems to suffer with her legs,' he said. 'I thought the doctor was going to drain them.'

'Yes,' Janet said sadly. 'But every time he empties them,

they start filling up again. He said he's never seen anything like it.'

'Poor woman,' Marvel said, shaking his head and clucking like a demented chicken. 'It's a terrible thing to be old.'

I slipped Jesus under a cushion. The conversation depressed me so much that it drove me into the heat of the kitchen where mother was checking the horoscope page in her star-studded copy of *Chinwag*.

'Foreign travel is on the horizon. You'll find a new hairstyle working wonders,' she announced, as I sat down beside her at the table.

'Is that me?'

'No. It's your father.'

'Aquarius,' I said. 'Tell me about Aquarius.'

'A handsome new man will enter your life. He could be a construction worker.'

'It doesn't sound very likely.'

'What have you done to Dorothy?' she said, pausing to scratch in her cardigan pockets in search of stray peppermints.

'Nothing.'

Mother frowned and shook her head. She was clearly worried. 'She looked dreadful at supper. I hope she's not sick. We can't afford it.' She found a solitary peppermint ball and flicked it neatly into her mouth.

'It's nearly the end of the month,' I said.

'What's her star sign?' she demanded suddenly.

'I don't know.'

'I hope to God it's not Virgo!' she muttered darkly, scanning the stars in search of trouble.

It was late when I finally went to my room. I had finished my regular midnight patrol, testing the windows, locking doors and switching out lights. The world was silent and secure. But I found it difficult to sleep. I lay awake in the dark and thought of my tumble with Dorothy. It seemed impossible. An hallucination. A fever's dream. A cunning illusion brought to life by the heat of my own desire. I settled down to revisit the dream but failed; nothing substantial remained, and I very nearly persuaded myself that Dorothy's enchanted flight had been no more than a flight of imagination.

When I woke up it was still dark. My heart was racing. The sweat prickled against my scalp. Something had dragged me from uneasy slumber. There was some strange presence in the room. I lifted my head from the pillow and peered fearfully into the gloom. At first I could make nothing from the dancing shadows that swarmed in my eyes. But there was just enough moonlight through the half-drawn curtains to distinguish a figure standing at the foot of the bed. I sat up, startled, and stared. It might have been Marvel, come to bring news of phantom intruders tapping against his bedroom window; or the wretched Franklin, sucked from his lair in a whirlwind of anger to smash in my skull with his pencil pot.

It was Dorothy! She was naked. Her hair was loose, her hands were clasped and her eyes were turned to Heaven.

I wiped my face in my palms and stared. I was too astonished to speak. It was several moments before I tried to open my mouth. The sight of her standing there, stiff as a saint, was enough to shrivel the tongue in my head. 'Dorothy!' I hissed. 'What are you doing here?'

She stopped offering up her prayers and turned to squint at me through the darkness, leaning forward on tiptoe. She had come without her spectacles, as if to enhance her nakedness or perhaps to merely protect herself by sparing her eyes unwholesome sights. 'Why aren't you asleep?' she whispered at me. She sounded rather disappointed and crossed her arms against her chest, holding herself by her lovely shoulders.

'You woke me up,' I said, feasting my own dim eyes on her beauty. She seemed to be made entirely of shadows, arms folded, face obscured in a cowl of black hair. Between the blades of her hips and the swelling of her thighs I searched in vain for the prickly valentine heart of darkness. 'Is anything wrong?' I managed to mumble.

'Behold, I cried out for help in my prayers,' she whispered.

'Were they answered?'

'I turned to the Book and was given a sign.'

'What sort of sign?'

She tried to explain it to me. But I wasn't paying attention. It was difficult to concentrate on her theories of mortification while I watched her stepping towards me, her long legs plunging through murky moonlight and her big breasts clasped like gifts in her hands.

'Oh, Lord,' she whispered, as I felt her slip beneath the sheets to press herself, warm and naked, beside me. 'Oh, Lord, he deviseth mischief upon his bed; he setteth himself in a way that is not good; he abhorreth not evil!'

Yes, it was true! How was I to resist temptation? Can a
man take fire in his bosom and his clothes not be burned?
My bed was narrow and she was large and profoundly perfumed. Ah, sweet Pandemonium! I set about my task
willingly and with as much vigour as I could manage in
such confinement. The serpent slithered from its nest and
nuzzled its snout against her thigh.

Dorothy stiffened and growled. 'The Lord shall smite
thee with consumption!' she warned urgently. 'And with a
fever, and with an inflammation, and with an extreme
burning, and with the sword, and with blasting, and with
mildew; and they shall pursue thee until thou perish…'

I shrank. I considered. So that was the game! I was the
sword of iniquity, the mouth of the lion, the storm that
howled and broke itself upon the rock of her faith. I closed
my eyes and buried my face in her hair, discouraged. But I
wasn't yet discouraged enough to stop my hands from
wandering in the hope of leading her further astray. I murmured gently into her ear, apologetic and comforting, as
my fingers traced the curve of her thigh before scrambling
up the slope of her ribs, in the hope of seizing a breast by
stealth and sucking some titbit into my mouth.

But she was too quick for my crafty fingers. 'The Lord
will smite thee with the botch of Egypt, and with the
emerods, and with the scab, and with the itch, whereof
thou canst be healed…' she threatened, catching me by the
wrist as my fingertips fluttered against a nipple, and twisting my arm back into the mattress.

I might have risked the itch and the botch but I didn't
like the sound of unhealing emerods. I retreated, shifted

my weight uncomfortably, and pressed myself against the wall while she arranged to protect herself with elbows, knuckles and ankle bones. But how could I escape my fate? Oh, save me not from the sweet temptations of this world, rather let me rejoice in all the workings of creation; for we are but flesh, a wind that passeth away and cometh not again.

As soon as she had settled, my fingers sneaked forth in a different direction, hoping to take her by surprise. A nimble raiding party sent scampering invisible through the narrow, no-mans-land in the sheets. A bony spider set loose to pounce upon her proud and extravagant arse.

But Dorothy was waiting for me. 'The Lord will smite thee with madness, and with blindless...' she sang breathlessly, yet allowed me time enough to reach around and fondle the rise and fall of her buttocks before she checked my bungled advance by driving her elbow into my stomach.

'And upon the wicked He shall rain snares, fire and brimstone, and a horrible tempest!' she added.

I searched for some well-turned phrase to use in my own defence but the only words that came into my head were warnings against the unclean flesh. And these are they which thee shall have in abomination among the fowls; they shall not be eaten, they are an abomination: the eagle and ossifrage and the ospray, and the vulture and the kite after his kind. It didn't sound suitable.

We lay in a tangle of arms and legs, shipwrecked and drowning. I closed my eyes. I threw kisses at her throat, her neck and shoulders as if I were destined to peck her to death. The abomination of fowls. She softened and squirmed and seemed to sink beneath my caresses. I drew strength from these little sighs of surrender and searched for her mouth but she jerked her face away, indignant. I should have been content to lay there crushed, with her breasts pancaked against my chest and her breath in hot gusts against my neck.

But it wasn't enough. I was half-mad with excitement. I hadn't yet earned my full measure of fiery brimstone and after all, win or lose, I would probably still have the Devil to pay for this night of stolen pleasures. So I wriggled loose from her grasp again and made a final, clumsy assault by forcing my hand between her legs. She quivered and grunted in surprise. She was lost. For a brief moment she was sprung wide open and beneath her brush she was hot and swollen and slippery.

'Be warned!' she gasped, snapping her ankles together and trapping my fingers between her thighs. 'He that is wounded in the stones, or hath his privy member cut off, shall not enter into the congregation of the Lord!' And with these words she identified my stones by seizing the pair of them in her fist and giving them such a wrench, such a sudden and brutal squeeze, that it left me blinded and wheezing with pain.

The agony of that embrace! The memory of it brings tears to my eyes. I choked and wept like a miserable sinner and cradled my broken stones in my hands. Do you think that Daniel tormented the lions by cracking their nuts together? No! If that was the secret to his success he should have been disqualified.

And so we remained entwined while I gurgled and tried to stifle my sobs as Dorothy prayed and gave thanks to the Lord for having been spared from the worst of my pagan cruelties. She sounded so very pleased with herself! When she finally stopped chanting she yanked her face from the smother of sheets and stared peacefully at the moonlight drifting across the ceiling. She yawned. She stroked my face. She murmured little endearments to show that she'd now forgiven me. But I said nothing. Did she think me a fool? I wouldn't be tempted. I was feeling too bruised to risk another stolen embrace.

'Yet a little sleep,' she whispered, taking me into her arms, 'a little slumber, a little folding of the hands to sleep....'

35

'AH, TOO LOVELY! Too lovely! 'Tis but a dream!' she whispered sadly through trembling lips as she sank once more into the warmth of his sheltering arms and allowed her fingers to lightly trace the noble curve of his strong and finely fashioned thighs. ''Tis but a dream and waking shall find us parted.'

He said nothing but turned his beautiful face to gaze at the glittering ceiling of stars that swarmed in the velvet dark of the tropical night that surrounded them with its lush and sweet-perfumed embrace.

'Nay, 'tis but a dream come true and I pray we may never be woke from it,' he said with a smile that betrayed a measure of melancholy.

They were lost for a time, adrift in the marvellous majesty of that secret and steaming jungle arbour. Were they tribal drums she could hear in her head or the savage melody of her heart? How deep the night! How bright her fever! She felt she must quickly swoon with love. She feared she might die from its rapture. And then, without a word between them, he had gathered her up in his gallant embrace and pressed her surging loveliness against the smouldering heat of his loins, so that she gave a little gasp of surprise and melting into his flame of desire, cast all her *modesty aside to yield to the urgent appeals of his mouth and the vigorous work of his nimble hands as a panther barked in the moonlight.*

36

IT WAS ALMOST dawn when I woke again. The bed felt empty. When I looked around I was just in time to catch Dorothy as she stumbled towards the door. She was luminous. Her hair was so dark and her skin so pale that she seemed to shine in the gathering light.

'Where are you going?'

She stopped in confusion, staring at me over her shoulder. She looked bewildered to find me there. 'Thirsty!' she mumbled. 'Want something to drink…' She frowned and wriggled her toes against the chill of the old, grey carpet. Her hair was in her face. Her voice was still thick and blurred by sleep.

'Wait!' I said, scrambling from the ruins of the narrow bed. 'Stay here and I'll fetch it for you.'

But it was too late. She had already reached the landing and was staggering blindly downstairs.

The kitchen was filling with early sunlight. It covered the floor and lapped at the legs of the big, scrubbed table. It licked a stripe on the dismal walls and pressed along the doors of the cupboards. A smell of onions, soap flakes and tea leaves. An empty casserole pot on the stove. Aprons hanging on metal hooks like the washed-out skins of butchered skivvies. Two a penny. Boned and peeled for pies and gravy.

Dorothy moved towards the fridge, her bare feet making little sucking sounds on the sticky, checker-board tiles. She looked so tall and elegant, with her spine erect and her black hair loose and her long legs shining in the pale light; and those wide shoulders with her broad hips, lending her the wasp-waisted grace of some lost Edwardian beauty. She clipped the back of a kitchen chair, gave a yelp and clutched an elbow. I think she was missing her spectacles.

'Do you want some help?' I whispered.

She turned in my direction and scowled. 'Go away!' she insisted, brushing at the air with her hand.

'Shall I make coffee?'

'Cold. I want something cold. I'm looking for orange juice.'

'It's in the fridge.'

'I know that, stupid!' she growled. She reached the fridge and pulled violently on the door, releasing a blast of freezing fog.

'There!'

'Where?'

'There. Bottom shelf. Next to the grapefruit juice.'

'Thank you.' She held the door open and bent forward to peer down among the cartons and bottles, bending neatly from the waist, feet together, legs very straight, but carelessly leaving her backside exposed.

'Where?' she complained. She couldn't seem to find anything through the fog that billowed from the crowded shelves. She held one hand to her face and drew back a heavy silk curtain of hair. 'It's a mess!'

Oh, but the sight of her bending blindly there, with her buttocks raised to the sun and her breasts dangled in frost, was a provocation past human endurance and sensing my chance, with the privy member in good repair, I darted forward and slipped my arms around her waist, skirting her belly, plunging my fingers into the whiskers between her thighs. For a moment we were blissfully engaged and then I found myself clinging, amidships, as she snorted and staggered and tried to throw me to the floor.

'No!' she roared. 'No!'

I was torn from my feet, tossed against the side of the fridge, knocked to the ground and trampled.

'I can't help it!' I spluttered. 'I love you… I love you…!'

Dorothy toppled down on me and began to slap me about the face. 'All men are liars!' she shouted, grabbing my hair by the roots and trying to yank my head from my shoulders.

What a woman! She had a scripture for every occasion. And she looked so fierce! Her teeth were clenched and her ears flushed scarlet with anger. In a desperate attempt to protect myself I grabbed her wrists and fought to hold her arms apart, making her breasts swing and slap above me.

'It's true!' I protested, somehow scrambling to my knees. I was devoted. How could she doubt it? I was sick with love. I was crazy with passion and desire. Would I have taken such punishment if I'd been able to stop myself from falling victim to her charms?

'You're a child!' she said, sulkily, abandoning the struggle. She went limp and sagged forward, her face falling against my neck.

'I can't help my heart,' I said quietly. Slowly I loosened my grip on her wrists. She didn't lash out again. Her hands flopped to the floor and she listed sideways, leaning her shoulder into my chest.

'The heart is deceitful above all things, and desperately wicked!' she recited sadly. She raised one hand to the small of my back and sighed as she absently fingered my spine.

Encouraged, I tried to return the embrace, slipping my hands around her flanks and pressing her softly into my arms. But man is born unto trouble, as the sparks fly upward, and the moment she felt my furtive advance she prised herself free with a frantic kicking and slapping of feet that knocked her down and sent her sprawling into the open mouth of the fridge. She screeched against the shock of the ice and twisted about, frantically scratching among the shelves for some weapon to use against me.

She made a grab at a big glass bottle of mayonnaise but thankfully missed her mark and scooped by mistake at a slice of leftover chocolate cake, sweeping it from its plate and punching it into my face. It smacked coldly against my cheek and slithered down as far as my jaw before breaking up in a mess of sticky, black crumbs that scattered themselves on my stomach and legs.

Dorothy cursed and tried again. Now she pelted me with tomatoes and flogged me with wet sticks of celery.

'Calm down!' I gasped, raising my hands to protect my face. 'You'll do yourself a mischief!' But this pleading served to excite her violence.

'Committeth not thine iniquity lest calamity befall thee!' she thundered. A ham bone slapped the side of my head. She thrashed me with heads of lettuce and pelted me with pellets of cheese while I coughed and sneezed and slithered around on my hands and knees.

Exasperated, I threw myself upon her, hoping to engulf those flailing limbs, and managed to hook her by the armpits and pull her away from the fridge.

'Leave me alone, you monster!' She wriggled and kicked and threatened to scream but I dragged her over the treacherous floor and dumped her in the shadow of the kitchen table. She was furious. She jumped to her feet and glared down at me, bruised, bewildered, smeared with chocolate and gasping for breath.

'I hope you burn in Hell!' she hissed.

I stood up, groaning, and wiped my face. Enough torment! I turned to hobble away when suddenly she grabbed my ears, jerked me forward and filled my mouth with a heart-stopping kiss. I struggled. She tightened her grip, clutching the back of my head in her hands, driving her tongue between my teeth. I stumbled, the air was singing, the world was dark and surging around me. She turned me about, without leaving my mouth, and pressed me down on the tabletop.

Then she pulled away and stood staring at me, thoughtful and frowning. Her eyes glittered and filled with tears. She might have skewered me with a knife. She might have attacked me with bacon scissors. The kitchen contained a thousand weapons of torture and mutilation. Peelers and scrapers. Clippers and corkscrews. I was too tired to care what would happen. I gave myself to her mercy. I lay there helpless on the scrubbed table, naked, dazed and breathing hard, with my arms hanging over-board and my engine of war standing painfully to attention.

'Be not righteous over much…' she whispered hoarsely. She climbed onto the table, squatting beside me like a cat. 'And be not over much wicked,' she added, plucking my hand from her buttocks.

I reached up and kissed her eyelids, her melting mouth, followed her lean and outstretched neck until I could feast on the fat of her breasts. She complained, pushed me down and then straddled me, supporting herself on her knees and elbows, dragging her nipples against my face. She moved back and forth, slowly, tenderly, gradually working…

'Oh, my God!' father shouted.

Dorothy shrieked and sprang away, wrapping herself in her arms.

I twisted my head and there he stood at the kitchen door, gawping, astonished, with a big claw hammer in his hand. He was dressed in his working clothes, with a shawl to protect his shoulders and the top of his head rammed hard into a dirty, knitted hat. I'd forgotten about him! He'd been working late in the cellar and must have fallen asleep at his bench. I hadn't thought to check on him when I'd locked the house for the night. He'd been woken from an uncomfortable dream by the sound of intruders in the kitchen and scampered upstairs to investigate with a brain-smashing hammer in his fist.

'It's a mistake!' I blustered.

'What have you done?' he bellowed. 'What have you done?'

'Wait!' I shouted, leaping from the tabletop and allow-ing myself to fall unhindered to the floor. 'You're wrong! It's not what you're thinking!' I tried to crawl under the nearest chair.

'You dirty devil!' he thundered. His face was white. His jaw fell slack. He looked absolutely horrified, as if I'd been caught buggering a bevy of circus beasts.

'Do you want some breakfast?' I shouted.

But he wasn't listening. He was staring at Dorothy as she floated above me with her arms outstretched and her knees tucked beneath her chin. She was turning slowly head over heels as she drifted towards the smoke-stained ceiling. Her mouth sagged and her eyes were closed as if she were seized by a narcolepsy. Her hair unfurled and streamed like a flag.

The shock of being caught rude and romping on the kitchen table must have triggered her sudden flight. She struck the ceiling with a thump, kicked out her legs and started drifting towards a cupboard. The edge of the cup-board struck her heel, making her turn about and collide with a stack of wooden shelves, sweeping out jugs and bowls and plates. The china came down in a great storm of splinters, crashing about our startled feet. Plates bounced and rolled into corners. A jug hit the stove and exploded. Father yelped and shouted for help.

The noise woke up the house. Mother came running down with Janet and wrapped the wretched girl in her arms, covering her face with a towel to save her from lewd and disgusting sights. Mr Marvel appeared beside them, pale but defiant, armed with a brass-knobbed walking stick, to gaze in frank astonishment at the flight of this curious angel. Nobody wanted to be apart from the miracle and finally even Senior Franklin came creeping from the rafters to stand like a ghost at the door, wrapped in his dead father's dressing gown and nursing his precious pencil pot. It was terrible. And while Mr Romance shivered, abandoned in a corner, struggling to cover his shame with an apron, they stood there shouting, heads thrown back, staring amazed, as Dorothy flew in circles above them.

37

SHE DIDN'T STAY for lunch. She had packed and left for the station before we'd had time to clean up the kitchen. Her departure was swift and silent. She left nothing behind but the smell of Pandemonium and a few stray Jesus comic books.

We did our best to explain away her knack of defying gravity – except father who simply refused to believe his eyes and, despite the fact that he'd raised the alarm, could not be persuaded that he'd seen anything more than his only begotten son flagrante delicto on the table.

Mother blamed Dorothy for everything that had happened, convinced that we'd been attacked by ghosts summoned through the power of prayer, and a flight around the kitchen cupboards was suitable punishment for meddling in the spirit world. For a long time afterwards she expressed the desire to have the house vacuum-cleaned by a team of psychic investigators.

Janet held me entirely responsible and seemed to think that I'd waited until she had reached the kitchen before I'd exposed myself.

'He exposed himself!' she kept complaining. 'He deliberately exposed himself!' She said it so often over the course of the next few days that it was difficult to know if she expressed disgust or delight.

Franklin was fully prepared to believe that he'd witnessed the work of angels. But his head was already stuffed with griffin, goblin and cockatrice. A floating woman left him unimpressed and he saw no cause for comment.

It was Marvel, alone, who offered his sympathies. While I shuffled around the house in disgrace, shunned by polite society, he did his best to befriend me. He couldn't explain Dorothy's powers of levitation, but was glad enough to have seen her only public performance. He would close his eyes and grin whenever he thought of her hanging suspended on sunlight. He was more impressed by her physical charms than her supernatural abilities.

'She was a big, fine, handsome woman!' he sighed, when we discussed the incident. 'Who would have guessed she was such a fine figure of a woman!' He wagged his head and smiled. Having seen her in full flight, it was plain that he now had his own regrets about spurning her early advances.

'I didn't mean any harm,' I said, anxious to secure my position of injured innocence. We were hidden away in China while, downstairs, they scoured the kitchen table and flooded the floor with buckets of bleach.

'No harm done,' Marvel assured me, from the comfort of his old armchair. 'She came off the ceiling neat enough.'

'How did she do it?'

'Who knows!' he said. 'I can't begin to fathom it. What was happening at the time?'

'I think it was a test of faith.'

'She was testing your faith by floating naked around the kitchen?' he asked, and his eyes shone again at the thought of it.

'She has very modern views,' I said, as I hobbled up and down the room. My knees were bruised and one of my elbows looked angry and swollen. During the scuffles my neck had been scratched from shoulder to shoulder.

'And did she succeed?' He couldn't resist the question. 'How did she manage to test your faith by hanging from the ceiling?'

'No. You don't understand. She thought I'd been sent to test *her* faith. She called it a scheme of divine inspiration. And now I'm feeling guilty,' I said. 'I shouldn't have taken advantage.'

'Don't take it so hard.'

'I feel wicked'.

'It was only a game of saints and sinners.'

'And I'm the sinner.'

'You should never play with saints, no matter how tempting the challenge. They mark the cards. They load the dice. They always have angels for referees.'

'But if the saints always win the game, why should anyone play with them? Who wants to take a thrashing?

'Well, it depends very much on the game and what the saints can find as reward. They like to offer some very big prizes. Freedom. Understanding. Opportunity. Clemency. Love…'

'It was love,' I said. 'It was love…'

He smiled and shrugged and watched me pacing the carpet. 'If it's any comfort,' he said, 'she must have taken a fancy to you.'

'Is that what it means?'

'Certainly. She wouldn't have taken that much trouble

if she hadn't found you attractive. You're the perfect victim. Simple. Trusting. Anxious to please. The trick was to make you carry the weight of responsibility.'

'Well, if she liked me, she didn't make it very obvious!' I complained, sitting gently down on the bed and nursing my injured elbow.

'How's that?'

'She cursed me with the botch of Egypt.'

'Nasty.'

'And the itch and the scab and the emerods.'

'The emerods?'

'Yes.'

He puffed out his cheeks in a little pantomime of distress, as if the mere mention of emerods were enough to provoke their pain and discomfort. 'Do you think we'll ever see her again?' he said presently.

'Doubtful,' I said.

'Pity,' he said.

We sat together and felt forlorn. Life without Dorothy suddenly seemed a dismal prospect. Her relentless good humour and her absolute certainty that she held the keys to Heaven's gate had filled the house with a sweet confusion. She had teased and threatened, seduced and scolded in equal measure. We felt lost without her disapproval.

'Wherefore I say unto thee, her sins, which are many, are forgiven; for she loved much...' I declared wistfully. 'Luke something something.'

Marvel gave me a worried glance, as if he feared I might break into song and lead him through Ancient & Modern.

'I've an idea!' he said suddenly. 'Why don't you come to lunch tomorrow?'

'Lunch?' He ate so seldom and with such a lack of enthusiasm that it was hard for me to imagine him out in the world with a napkin tucked beneath his chin and a knife and fork in his hands.

'Yes.'

'Tomorrow?' The invitation puzzled me. If my calculations were correct it should have been the day he slipped away to confront his tormentors. What had happened to change the arrangement? 'Will there be others?' I asked him suspiciously.

'No.' He sounded surprised, cocked his head and frowned. 'I trust we'll be dining alone.'

I hesitated. 'Well, I don't know,' I said. 'I think I should stay and work. I'm supposed to be on kitchen duty.' Washing and boiling. Scratching and scrubbing. There would be no end to it. I'd be sentenced to months of drudgery before my trespasses were forgotten.

'I leave it to you,' he said, with a little wave of his hand. 'Entirely your decision. But I thought you might appreciate escaping the present circumstance…'

'I suppose I could spare a few hours.'

'That's the spirit!' he grinned. 'You need a rest. Your nerves are shreds. And I'd be glad of your company. I find myself obliged to dine at the Snooty Artichoke…'

38

MARVEL POLISHED HIS cracked, brown brogues and wore his best waistcoat for the occasion. We took the bus to the outskirts of North Street Market and then walked the length of Trinidad Square until we had reached the restaurant quarter. The Snooty Artichoke was small and expensive, set apart from the street by a cordon of dusty, potted palms. Marvel looked distinctly nervous as we approached and paused to check his buttons before he pulled on the heavy steel door.

We found ourselves trapped in a narrow chamber, lit by a beam of silver light, where the major-domo stood at a lectern guarding an open, leather-bound ledger. He was dressed in black with a blue carnation for decoration. He was tall and thin as a cut-throat razor, his skin deathly pale and his dark hair slapped and slicked into shape. He raised his head to the draught from the street and stared at us in surprise. The door gave a hiss and clicked smartly shut at our heels.

There was silence.

Marvel opened his mouth to speak but no sound came from his throat. He looked so scared that I thought, for a moment, he might turn tail and take flight.

'Marvel,' Marvel said, at last. 'A table for two.'

The major-domo flinched as if he'd been goosed, jerked back his head and looked at the ceiling. Then he sighed deeply, raised a bony finger and dragged his fingernail down the open page of the ledger. He studied the page for a long time. He consulted the watch on his wrist. He stared at the ledger again. Finally, and with great reluctance, he stepped from behind the lectern, adjusted his shoulders, puffed out his chest and walked us through to the dining room where he offered the comforts of a small table obscured from the general view by a clump of exotic shrubbery.

'Une table pour deux, monsieur,' he said. He thrust a menu into my hand, tossed his head and minced away.

'Thank you,' Marvel whispered and smiled meekly.

The Snooty Artichoke had been planted to look like an overblown garden. There were flame nettles and creeping figs and ferns of every description. Ivy struggled across the ceiling and hung in festoons above the tables. A salvaged wood-nymph, carved from stone, her face half-eaten by frost and rain, stood on a pedestal in one corner. The walls were darkly varnished and masked with antique trellis-work decorated at intervals by autographed pictures of actors and politicians, as if their endorsement of the food made it fit for human consumption.

I sat in silence and stared at the table. I had never encountered such rich surroundings. There were damask napkins the size of bath towels, folded into the shapes of swans. There were orchids floating in black, glass bowls. The silver flashed. The crystal sparkled and shimmered with rainbows. The menu was written in brown ink on parchment, bound in morocco with a scarlet silk cord.

'What do you fancy?' Marvel inquired as we peered at the menu through the artificial twilight.

'It's in French!' I whispered indignantly.

'Ignore it!' Marvel said, with a little wag of his hand. 'Merely designed to intimidate and irritate the gastric juices.'

'But I can't understand a word of it.'

'Allow me to translate.'

The menu, once it had been unscrambled, was daunting and dangerous. There were boars' brains with skunkweed pickle. Poached sweetbreads. Rolled tongue. Stewed lungs. Pigs' ears stuffed with truffle.

'What do you suggest?' I said.

'I suppose you might chance the fish...' he said without enthusiasm. It was curious that he seemed to have lost all appetite for lunch but he was, it must be confessed, a very curious man.

'The mackerel wrapped in salt cod with lobster giblet sauce?'

'Yes. Or the sturgeons' stomach salad with fermented apricots.'

I glanced nervously at the prices – no attempt here at Frenchification. They were printed bold and black in the local currency. 'Isn't this rather expensive?' I whispered across the table.

'Perfectly obscene,' Marvel said. 'For the price of an omelette in this hell hole you could buy enough chickens to start your own poultry farm.'

The Snooty Artichoke was not the most fashionable restaurant in town. The most desirable address at that time was Curly Colon's Hamburger Bash. It was a restaurant that dealt exclusively with celebrity food. Hamburgers, hotdogs, ribs and milk shakes. Anything that didn't require the skills of a knife and fork. It was a place of pilgrimage for film stars, sports stars, singers and TV hosts who needed to be seen clutching their hotdogs and laughing. Curly Colon had been a big rock-and-roll star until rheumatism had forced his retirement. His Hamburger Bash was a three-ring circus, a photo opportunity, a popular tourist attraction. The Snooty Artichoke, by contrast, was a strictly traditional temple to food, retaining all the old customs and rituals, where grave men in dark suits made appointments to eat their money.

'Shall we try somewhere else?' I suggested. I knew that he wasn't a wealthy man and I didn't want to embarrass him.

'Courage!' he whispered. 'You may rest assured that we're not required to pay for this folly in anything but risk of injury to our stomachs.'

I blinked and waited hopefully for some kind of explanation. But Marvel said nothing. He must have felt that the circumstances were obvious. 'Perhaps you should explain,' I said at last.

He stared at the ceiling. He glanced around him. 'Think of me as a kind of agent,' he murmured, leaning towards me.

'Secret agent?'

'Confidential. More of a confidential agent.'

'You mean, like a private detective?' I said. The mystery was solved! I was meeting Marvel the gumshoe. A man in pursuit of Nazi diamonds, hidden hoards of dangerous drugs, smuggled babies, stolen children; tormented by gangsters and tattooed hoodlums.

He shook his head. 'We can't talk here,' he whispered.

I looked again at the menu. 'What are you having?' I asked him.

He sucked a tooth and frowned. 'I suppose I'll attempt the stags' liver in oak apple sauce,' he said finally, casting the menu aside, and then shook his head as if he already regretted it.

'I'll have the mackerel,' I said cheerfully. A light lunch. Something simple. Cheap and cheerful.

'And for an hors d'oeuvre?'

'Is it required?'

'Yes.'

'What's cervilles de veau au beurre noir?'

'Boiled brains.'

'Oursin?'

'Sea urchin.'

'Knobbards avec garniture Anglaise?'

'Knobbards?' Marvel said suspiciously. He scowled again at the menu. 'They're whelks! Plain and simple. Whelks with brown bread and butter.'

'I'll have 'em!' I said, much relieved.

The sommelier appeared at Marvel's shoulder. He was old and crumpled and gave off the sour smells of the cellar. His eyes were no more than clouded glass buttons. His lips were blue and his nose very bulbous, the nostrils packed with tufts of hair. He wore a heavy silver chain about his neck and a row of medals at his chest. His chain of office seemed to weigh on him, forcing him forward, directing his gaze towards the floor, which he viewed with a bored contempt.

'Might I recommend our Cabernet Sauvignon, monsieur?' he murmured confidentially, tapping a finger against his nose. He might have been trying to rent out his sister. 'A wine of great and noble vintage, aged in wood and shipped directly from the Krikova Winery on the far shores of rugged Moldova exclusively for the Artichoke. Voluptuous and bold by nature yet without a hint of vulgarity. Inquisitive yet never intrusive. Devoted yet barely dependent. Trusting yet far from innocent. Pungent yet hardly pugnacious. Confusing yet rarely confounding. In short, the perfect lunchtime companion.'

'We'll have a bottle,' Marvel said and slapped the wine list shut. 'And your largest bottle of Vichy water.'

The sommelier smirked and crept away through the undergrowth.

It seemed to take a very long time to be served with any morsel of food. The wine was presented, opened and tasted. Marvel nodded mournfully and watched the sommelier fill our glasses. I'd hoped to talk about Dorothy but the mood at the table discouraged me from trying to start a conversation. The atmosphere was stifling. The restaurant was filled by a hushed and whispering congregation, full-grown men and women, heads bowed to their plates in prayer.

We sipped at the wine in silence. I knew, from watching TV shows, that wine should taste of apricots, geraniums, walnuts, rhubarb, figs, nettles, raspberries, blackcurrants, gooseberries and vanilla. A glass of wine was the promise of summer, the flame of winter, a kiss of sunlight, the hint of twilight, a rumour of laughter, a rush of passion. But perhaps you had to be dangerously drunk before these allusions came to mind. The wine in my mouth was terrible! Sharp as vinegar. Dark as ink. It skinned my tongue, scorched my throat and quickly started to burn my brain.

'I don't drink a lot of wine,' I said, hoping I might be spared the misery of a second glass.

'Count your blessings,' he said.

The knobbards were finally served with ornate tongs and a slender snailing fork. They didn't taste too bad. The narrow slices of bread and butter helped soften the sound of the sand crunching between my teeth.

When I had finished I picked at the crumbs on my plate and watched Marvel still working at a little bowl of soft-boiled brains.

'How do they taste?' I asked him.

He shook his head and belched. He lay down his fork, wiped his face and greedily rinsed his mouth with water.

The mackerel was delivered with much pomp and circumstance beneath a polished silver dome. When the dome was raised I was left with a grey and gelatinous sausage in a pool of pink sauce on a large white plate. The plate had been further embellished with burnished cockle shells, strands of peppered bladderwrack, gull feathers, lobster whiskers in nautical knots, kelp curlicues, octopus eyes and the claw from an unknown Dublin Bay prawn.

'How do you find the mackerel?' Marvel inquired, as he watched me slicing into the sausage.

'It's very artistic,' I said.

'And how does it taste?'

'Strong,' I said, to please him. 'A strong taste of mackerel.'

'And the salt-cod wrapping?'

'Salty.'

'And the lobster-giblet sauce?'

'Pink,' I said. 'Unusually pink.'

'Conclusion?'

'I don't know.'

'Well, for example, would you describe it as appealingly simple with charming rustic overtones/ deeply defined/ dramatically balanced/ broadly amusing/ an embarrassment of astonishments?'

'It's more like a mouthful of bones!' I confessed, picking the needles from my tongue.

'Good,' he said. 'An honest opinion!'

'How do you like the liver?'

'It's strange but it seems to have acquired the smell of an army latrine,' he declared. 'And squirts blood at the prod of a fork.'

'And the gravy?'

'A dark and loathsome puddle,' he said, with slightly more enthusiasm. 'A spread of filth. A pestilence. A concentration of misery.' He set down his knife and fork and paused to wash out his mouth with wine.

I picked at my mackerel skeleton. The meal was clearly not a success but to my surprise he didn't seem in the least concerned. He wasn't disappointed. He looked as if he'd expected it. And then, from the far corner of the restaurant, the owner of the Snooty Artichoke appeared with an anxious waiter pulling frantically on his sleeve. There was no mistaking him! It was Chester Chumley-Blight. His face was everywhere. He twinkled from cookery columns. He sparkled on game shows. He was a newspaper personality. He was a TV celebrity. He served seafood to stars. He tossed pancakes for charity. The waiter pointed in our direction and whispered urgently into Chumley-Blight's ear.

'What's wrong?' Marvel said, sensing my alarm.

There wasn't time to answer him. Chumley-Blight had reached the table and was prodding Marvel in the fat of the neck with a long and beautifully manicured finger.

'What's your game?' he growled. He plucked away Marvel's napkin and threw it angrily to the floor.

'I beg your pardon?' Marvel said, twisting around to confront him. He sounded most indignant but I caught a glimmer of fear in his eyes.

'We don't take kindly to your sort of riffraff in this establishment! We don't want it! We don't need it! We're in the Michelin Guide! Do I make myself understood, sunshine?' Chumley-Blight shouted. He looked furious. He was trembling with rage. A fan of the famous black hair fell about his ears.

'Are you asking me to leave?'

'No! I'm telling you to piss off and don't come back!' Chumley-Blight shrieked, shaking the back of Marvel's chair. A fat woman yelped and clasped her necklace. A brace of young businessmen grunted in protest. Waiters came running from every direction.

'Now, wait a moment!' I said, banging my fist against the table and making the cutlery jangle. 'What's the problem?'

'Don't get smart with me, Sunny Jim!' Chumley-Blight sneered as he shook Marvel from his chair. 'I've launched my own range of pasta sauces!'

'But we haven't done anything…' I protested. A waiter wrapped my head in his arm and pulled me to the floor.

'Shut your gob!' Chumley-Blight shouted.

'I'm warning you!' I blustered, as I found myself carried across the restaurant. 'We shall want a written apology!'

'Enough!' Marvel spluttered, breaking away from his captors. 'Enough!' But he was quickly overwhelmed. Chumley-Blight had grabbed him by the scruff of the neck and yanked him savagely from the table. A waiter took hold of his arms and another took charge of his feet. He pleaded and struggled in vain as they carried him away and tossed him into the street.

39

WE TOOK A taxi home. Marvel was in a poor condition. His stomach bubbled and churned, his knuckles were bruised and one of his old, brown brogues had been split from stem to stern. He sat in the back of the taxi cab, clutching his paunch and breathing hard.

'What went wrong?' I said, bewildered. 'Why did they throw us out?' I hadn't been hurt in the scuffle but the wine had damaged my brain and was spreading a pain that drilled my teeth and smouldered behind my eyes.

Marvel merely rolled his head, nursed his stomach and stared vacantly through the window. 'I'm too old for this game,' he muttered sadly.

We staggered into the house and tried to creep to our rooms but mother came squelching from the kitchen, demanding an explanation. She might have been prepared to hold Dorothy responsible for my earlier mischief but I was to take the blame for bringing Marvel home sweating and seasick. I struggled with my apologies and took to my bed for the rest of the afternoon. She scolded me at supper and refused to believe my account of our rumpus at The Snooty Artichoke.

But the next day something so peculiar happened that even mother was forced to agree that Mr Marvel was a marked man.

It was a dismal morning with a mountain of cloud rolling over the city and a threat of rain from the east. The house felt unusually gloomy. Dorothy had abandoned Belgium. Franklin had been on a drinking spree with one or two faithful cronies and was languishing still in a room at Grouchers. Marvel was sleeping. I was loitering in the kitchen. Janet, sweet Janet, honest and reliable, went off to work as usual, busy as a clockwork mouse.

I fed her Shreddies and cups of black coffee and followed her through to the hall where she stopped to rummage in her bulging handbag. Lipstick, mascara, address book, manicure set, tampon, Kleenex, house keys, loose change, attack whistle, discount card, department-store identity badge.

'I've forgotten my Katie Pphart!' she complained.

'Where is it?'

'I must have left it in my room.'

'Shall I fetch it for you?' I said, wanting to be helpful, anxious to win her trust again.

She glanced at her wristwatch. 'No time!' She was flustered, impatient, three minutes late. She rushed across the hall but as soon as she was through the front door she stumbled and shouted.

'What is it?' I said, running at once to her rescue. I found her standing on one leg, surprised and angry, rubbing an ankle.

'There!' She hopped from foot to foot and scowled down at a large paper parcel left abandoned on the doorstep.

'It's for Mr Marvel!' I said, lifting the parcel into my hands and peering at the scratchy, hand-written label. I gave it a shake. 'It's heavy!' But Janet had already gone, running away down the street.

I took the parcel into the front parlour and left it on the table beneath the window. It was the shape of a shoe box, wrapped around with brown paper and fastened with a mess of adhesive tape.

It was nearly lunchtime when Marvel emerged from his room and painfully plodded downstairs. He appeared in his dressing gown and red felt slippers. His eyes were bloodshot and he needed a shave. He shuffled into the kitchen and begged for a pot of hot, strong tea.

'It's too late,' father grumbled. He'd been ordered into the kitchen to repair the glass shade on the ceiling light, cracked during Dorothy's flight. He was balanced on a pair of stepladders with a toolbox in his hand. He was having some trouble unthreading the broken plastic collar that held the shade to the socket.

'It's no trouble to make him a pot of tea,' mother said gently, smiling, nodding Marvel towards the table.

'I'm much obliged,' Marvel murmured and sank thankfully into a chair.

'There's a parcel for you this morning,' I said, as I filled the kettle and searched the cupboard for cups.

'A parcel?' He looked startled.

'It was left on the doorstep. I've taken it into the front parlour.'

'No!' he cried fiercely. 'No!' He jumped from his chair with such violence that father nearly fell from his ladder.

'Steady!' father shouted. 'Steady!'

'But it's not possible! No, there must be some mistake,' Marvel said, trying to compose himself again.

'There's no mistake,' I said cheerfully. 'It's clearly addressed to you.'

He gave a little cry of despair and hurried from the kitchen with such an expression of horror on his crumpled face that we thought it best to follow him.

'Aren't you going to open it?' mother inquired, as we gathered around the table and peered at the packet.

'No!' He shook his head. 'Take it away. Take it away and bury it!'

'Why? What is it?' father demanded.

'I've no idea!' poor Marvel confessed. He clutched at his dressing gown and tottered in circles about the room.

'Well, shall I open it for you?' I suggested helpfully. I was burning with curiosity. Whatever the parcel contained, I felt sure it was something that might throw some light on Marvel's curious circumstance.

'Don't touch it!' he barked. 'It could explode!'

'Damned nonsense!' shouted father, the seasoned pyromaniac. 'Pull yourself together, man!'

But Marvel could not be pacified. 'I've been discovered!' he muttered, as he staggered up and down the carpet. 'Quick, Skipper, lock the doors! The devils are upon us again!' It was terrible to watch. All his old suspicions and fears seemed to come flooding back again.

'What are you talking about?' father snapped. He was wasting his time. He wanted to fix the kitchen light and hurry away to the cellar. He didn't have patience for Marvel's dramatic performances. So he rushed forward, forced his fingers beneath the bandages of tape and quickly broke the parcel apart.

'Oh, filthy!' he gasped. 'Filthy! Disgusting and filthy!' He jerked back his hands in disgust and wiped his fingers against his apron.

We gathered around to peer into the wrappings and there, at the bottom of the box, resting in scraps of shining, wet paper, skinned and bloody, grotesque and grinning, was a peeled sheep's head.

'Horrible!' mother shuddered, clasping a hand against her mouth. She sat down hard in a chair, went very pale and fingered her cardigan buttons.

'What does it mean?' father whispered. He stood trans-fixed. He couldn't believe it was happening. He stared down at the glistening muzzle, the mad, bulging eyes, the flared and blood-caked nostrils.

'Throw it away!' Marvel cried in despair.

'Wait!' I said. 'Look, there's something caught between its teeth...'

'He's right!' father said, but he made no move to inves-tigate. So I summoned all my courage and using no more than a finger and thumb, plucked a damp wad of paper from the clutch of the animal's jaws.

It looked very much like a newspaper cutting. I gently unfolded the scrap and tried to decipher its message. The newsprint was damp and flecked with blood but I saw enough to confirm my suspicions.

'It's a restaurant review,' I said, 'by Belcher of the *Sunday Leviathan*.' I glanced at Marvel but he looked away.

'Well, read it!' father demanded.

'*The Stuffed Owl. 159 Theobald Street,*' I began. '*Since suffering a refurbishment at the hands of its owner, the barmy Bertie Bollinger, this deplorable restaurant with its cold, chrome fittings and walls of porcelain tiles now conveys all the atmosphere of an empty public urinal. The intolerable Italianate menu of past days has been swept away in favour of full-blown Frenchification…*' And here the print was so badly soaked with blood that I couldn't follow it. '*…the waiter served my Toulouse sausage,*' I continued, '*with all the reluctance of a man who has just been forced to butcher and sell his own daughter… the offending article looked like a turd and smelt like the rump of a wet dog toasting before an open fire… secures the award as the most expensive restaurant carrot… a madhouse designed by a man who drags his knuckles when he walks…*'

'Enough!' Marvel cried, snatching the paper from my hand. 'Enough!' He thrust the scrap into his dressing-gown pocket and threw himself at the sofa where he sat with his shoulders hunched and his hands between his knees.

'But why did they send it to this address?' father asked. He glared at Marvel. He scowled at me. He thought he might be the victim of some elaborate hoax.

'Mr Marvel is Belcher,' I explained. 'The famous restaurant critic. He writes for the *Sunday Leviathan*!' Everyone knew Belcher although no picture had ever been published. The man was a legend. The scourge of chefs and scullions. A plague on preening restaurateurs and unctuous oenologists. A thorn that never failed to catch in the throats of gullible gastronomes. He was feared and revered in equal measure. A paramour. A philistine. An enemy of the connoisseur. The stomach's gallant saviour. A man who made other restaurant critics look like snivelling syco-phants.

'That's all very well and good,' mother remarked soberly. 'But that doesn't allow him to receive bodily parts through the post.'

'How did they find you? How did they know you were here?' I said, turning to Marvel again.

'Someone must have recognised me. A waiter most likely. Waiters are a cruel and cunning breed.'

'That waiter from The Snooty Artichoke…?'

'One of a kind from a thousand hell holes,' he said, wagging his head. 'I must have been followed. They must have been watching the house.'

'They went to all this trouble just because you didn't like the look of a sausage?' mother said. She was very impressed. She had never imagined that cooking could provoke such passion.

'That's nothing!' Marvel grumbled, waving a hand at the butchered head. 'It's merely to serve as a warning. At the Royal Chutney they came at me from the kitchen with knives and poultry scissors. At the Pampered Plaice they tried to set my table on fire with a blasted flambé pan.'

'You must have said some terrible things,' father said, peering again at the dreadful parcel of flesh and bone.

'I merely expressed an opinion. No more than an honest opinion.'

'What are we going to do with him?' I asked.

Father shook his head. The situation was quite beyond him.

But Marvel understood the terrible consequences. 'I must leave at once!' He moaned. 'I shall have to disappear again. The devils won't rest until they've done me a serious mischief.'

40

'BUT WHERE ARE you going?' we demanded. We had crowded into his little room to watch him packing his cardboard suitcase. He shrugged as he folded another frayed shirt.

'Do you have any family?' mother asked from the arm-chair.

'None to my knowledge.'

'You can't walk the streets,' I said.

'I can't stay here!'

Danger everywhere! His enemies prowling the streets, watching the house, waiting for him to show his face. Flog him with cheese wires. Gouge him with graters. The man who dared pour scorn on the soufflé.

'I still don't understand,' father grumbled. 'If you hate dining to such an extent, what made you become a restaurant critic?'

'I love food!' Marvel protested. 'And there's the tragedy in a nutshell. It's the restaurants that I can't tolerate. It's the wretched restaurants with their bogus butlers and unwashed waiters and their poisonous pâtés and over-blown wine lists and burnt coffee and gateaux trolleys. I've had enough of their sauce Provençal and their broccoli spears and their wet spinach and cockroach-infested candlelight. I've had a bellyful of radishes carved into roses and dung heaps made from profiteroles. I'm finished with their celery tassels and vandyked tomatoes and anything called a mousse or croquette!'

'Dorothy!' mother shouted, flushed with triumph, snapping her fingers at the air. 'We should send him down to Dorothy!'

'No, no!' Marvel said, busy clearing his bedside table. 'I wouldn't dream of it.'

He wrapped his alarm clock into the folds of a badly darned vest and tucked it beneath his shirts.

'Why Dorothy?' I said. I couldn't decide if she wanted Marvel to escape or merely wished Dorothy to find herself in receipt of assorted animal parts. She wasn't an easy woman to fathom. It was possible, I suppose, that she merely saw in this twist of fate the chance to throw them together again.

'It's the perfect arrangement,' father agreed. 'She lives alone in the back end of nowhere. It's a big cottage. It's quiet and peaceful. Nothing happens. Who would think to follow him there?'

'Do you really think it would work?' I said reluctantly. It felt wrong. I was pierced with jealousy. They were asking me to balance my love for Dorothy against my love for the mighty Marvel. But unless I devised a superior scheme I could think of nothing to keep them apart.

'I can't see any problem,' mother said, pulling herself from the chair and helping Marvel to stuff his suitcase.

'She might find it rather difficult...'

'Why?'

'The neighbours,' I said, search vainly for obstacles. 'Think how the neighbours are likely to gossip.'

'Nonsense! She's a poor, respectable, Christian woman,' mother said, as if she really believed it. I was lost for words. What had become of the Devil's daughter, Beelzebub's bride, the sister of Satan?

'But shouldn't we give her some warning?'

'She'll be glad to help,' mother said confidently. 'She'll welcome him with open arms.'

'How do you know?'

'Because you're going to phone and explain it to her.'

No! I was scandalised. How could she even dare to suggest it? 'I can't do that!' I protested.

'She's *your* friend,' father said darkly.

'What do you think?' I said, appealing to Marvel for mercy.

'In the light of a dangerous predicament, all things weighed and fully considered, I find myself most obliged to you,' he said. He paused in his work, glanced up and smiled at me. The old rascal looked distinctly pleased by the prospect of running to Dorothy. Perhaps the memory of her floating, unfrocked and fancy-free, had some influence on his decision. A big, fine, handsome woman. Whatever he thought, he didn't seem in the least concerned that, in giving himself to Dorothy, he might be required to give himself to the arms of Jesus.

'That's settled!' mother said happily, plucking his tangle of shirts from the case and neatly refolding them.

Supper was finished before I found the courage to pick up the phone. I felt doubtful and confused. How could I explain the situation? What would happen if she simply refused to speak to me? It was a bad business. I dialled the number and Dorothy answered before I'd had time to gather my thoughts.

'Dorothy?'

'Yes.'

'It's Skipper.'

There was a long silence. Was she still there? The line began to fizzle and fill with the distant murmur of other voices lost in that vast electric night.

'Dorothy?'

'What do you want?' she said at last. A bad beginning. She sounded frosty.

'I'm sorry.'

'Have you told Jesus?'

'Yes,' I lied.

'Then ask Him to forgive you,' she snapped.

'Wait!' I shouted, fearing that she might cut me dead. My breath blasted into the mouthpiece. I had to make myself understood.

'Well?'

'I love you!' I blurted. 'I love you and whatever you think, I didn't mean you any harm.'

'Is that it?'

'No. Something happened to Mr Marvel.'

She hadn't expected such a sudden swerve in the conversation. 'Is he hurt? Has there been an accident?' Her voice changed and she seemed concerned.

'Well, no,' I confessed. 'But we honestly fear for his life.' And then I told her the strange, sad story. I told her everything. I told her about his mysterious arrival at the house and my early suspicions and how I had befriended him and his little kindnesses to me and the way we had been evicted from the Snooty Artichoke and the sheep's head in a box. I told her about his secret life as Belcher of the Leviathan. I dwelt on the dangers. I counted the insults and injuries. 'They're attacking him because they're afraid of what he might say about them!' I concluded with a dramatic flourish.

'But, that's terrible!' she said, with a genuine measure of sympathy. 'The poor man! Why, they can't be allowed to persecute him! They mustn't torment him for telling the truth.'

'And he was strong and of good courage,' I said. 'But they rose up against him and he hath escaped with the skin of his teeth. For he is despised and rejected of men; a man of sorrows, and acquainted with grief.'

'Isaiah,' she said.

'Yes,' I said. 'And we thought you might look after him.'

She paused for a moment, sensing the trap. 'How?'

'We could send him down to you on the train. Special delivery. He needs to get away from here. He needs to escape.'

'I don't know...'

'He has a lot of respect for you,' I said. 'He often used to tell me how much he admires you.'

'You discussed me!' she said, in a hurt tone of voice.

'I disgust myself,' I said, feeling wretched. 'But Mr Marvel is not a young man. The sea air would be good for his liver. He's no trouble. He keeps himself clean. He'd make himself useful around the house,' I said quickly.

'Does he know how to prune an apple tree?'

'He'd make an excellent gardener!' I said with confidence. You didn't need to be a genius to hack a few limbs from an apple tree. He might even have the knack for it. A very satisfactory arrangement. Marvel in moleskin and gaiters, growing his own spuds and cabbages while Dorothy bottled fruit and made Swiss-cheese novelties for her favourite good causes.

'But I barely know him.'

'He's a gentleman,' I said.

'I thought *you* were a gentleman until you took advantage of me…'

'I gave him my bible,' I said, in a moment of pure inspiration, hoping to cast away her doubts and soothe any fears she might have for her safety.

'You did?'

'For the comfort of it.'

'That was a very kind thought, Skipper, ' she said gently. Ah, but she was flattered! She was melting. She was mine.

'And I think he needs a friend in Jesus,' I whispered.

'Send him down and Godspeed,' she said. 'I'll be waiting for him.'

41

AFTER BREAKFAST THE following morning I took Marvel down to the railway station. He'd been ready and waiting to leave since dawn. He was dressed in his very best waistcoat and wearing a pair of father's shoes. He had shaved and managed to comb his hair and he rather looked like an anxious suitor, waiting to be introduced to his partner in some arranged marriage. I hadn't told him that Dorothy was expecting her guest to be radiant with the love of God, but I'd found it easy enough to slip the bible into his suitcase. He was certainly going to need it.

We gathered in the hall to say goodbye. Father, in very formal mood, accepted the return of the keys, shook his hand, gripped his shoulder and wished him health and good fortune.

'I'll return your footwear at the earliest opportunity,' Marvel assured him.

'There's no need to trouble yourself,' father said briskly, fearing another unwholesome parcel appearing on the doorstep. He'd donated a pair of ginger suede loafers he hadn't worn for twenty years.

Then mother rushed forward and squeezed him and pecked him and tried to force a slice of fruit cake into his overcoat pocket.

'Something for the journey,' she whispered.

Janet, sensing that something was wrong but knowing nothing of the sheep's head or having the slightest notion of the dangers that surrounded him, now threw her arms around his neck and bravely attempted to plant a kiss. He staggered beneath her embrace and emerged frightened and stained with lipstick.

'I hope you'll come back and visit sometimes,' she said and blushed beautifully. 'I shall miss our game of dominoes.'

At the same moment Senior Franklin came stamping downstairs, small-eyed, sour and late for breakfast.

'Ah, my comical cockroach, what's this?' he demanded, cocking his head and directing his inquiries at me. 'Can it be that the Marvellous One departeth? I smell mischief! His Venerable Ventosity hath plans afoot to leave our little company.'

He stood before Marvel, puffed out and grinning, flaring his nostrils, sensing some kind of victory. He didn't have the faintest idea what was happening. And he didn't much care to be informed of the circumstances. It was quite enough for him that Marvel appeared to be in retreat. He was happy to see the back of him.

The two men glared at each other for a few moments. Franklin snorted like a stallion and made several circles of his opponent. Marvel growled and held his ground. They were natural enemies. The one cavorting and convoluted, the other square and pragmatic. They threatened each other in equal measure.

'And so to breakfast!' Franklin shouted suddenly,

breaking away from the contest. 'Hounds stout, horses healthy, earths well stopped and foxes plenty!' And he turned on his heel and disappeared into the empty dining room.

We took a taxi cab to the station. The city was already startled awake, the streets filled with thousands of marching people, young men shouting, truck horns blaring, buses smoking, steel shutters rolling on shabby shop windows. Marvel seemed very agitated, crouching low in his seat, watching the faces in the street as if he expected to be molested, dragged from the cab and beaten senseless.

At the entrance to the station we struggled to force a passage through the rushing flood of commuters pouring through the high, stone arches. Trotting bank clerks, galloping salesmen, swaggering executives and scissoring secretaries. A fast and relentless tide of silent men and women, grey-faced and hopeless, draining into the streets of the city.

I helped Marvel to purchase a ticket, checked the departure board and carried his creaking suitcase towards the appropriate gate. He paused then, wincing with the effort of walking, while he shifted his weight from leg to leg, trying to ease the pain of his feet trapped in the ginger loafers.

'Do you want a newspaper for the journey?' I asked him, nodding towards a kiosk, but he shuddered at the thought of it.

'I'm happy enough with a slice of fruit cake,' he said, as we slowly shuffled forward.

There were still a few minutes until the departure of his train. I kept a watch on the ticket hall, half-expecting to see a shouting sommelier or a pale and demented pastry chef come charging towards us through the crowd. Marvel's fear was infectious although I knew that we hadn't been followed.

And then he gave out a startled cry, stopped short in his tracks, staggered and stared about him with a wild look in his eyes.

'What is it?' I hissed, searching the crowd for some sign of danger.

'Flowers!' he exclaimed, slapping his overcoat pockets. 'I need flowers. I can't arrive without a big, bright bunch of something.'

'Wait here,' I instructed and dashed away in search of baskets, bouquets and arrangements. I wanted roses and fragrant lilies. I found nothing but stems of stale carnations, red and yellow, wrapped in funnels of wilting plastic. I picked the biggest bunch in the bucket and hurried back to him.

'She'll like carnations,' I promised, pressing the packet into his hand.

'I'm much obliged. How much do I owe you?'

'Nothing.'

He stared at the flowers and gave them a little shake, hoping to revive their spirits. 'You've been a good friend to me, Skipper, and I feel that this strange occasion demands an attempt to offer you some short but practical advice,' he said, peering up at the great glass canopy of the station as if the words he were searching for might be written there in fire. 'But I'm damned if I can think of it,' he added sadly, wagging his head.

'You could always write to me,' I said, as we continued to push forward, but he didn't look enthusiastic.

'Politics!' he shouted, suddenly inspired. 'Never forget that the Left and Right are two wings flapping the same fat turkey. Religion! Choose a god with a sense of humour. Food! Never put anything into your mouth that you can't pronounce or spell for a doctor.'

'Romance?' I prompted.

He shrugged and shook his head. 'I can't help you in that department. A man will always make a fool of himself in pursuit of a beautiful woman.'

The early morning express was already waiting at the platform. The carriages were empty, seats smeared with food, floors strewn with trampled cans and bottles, windows fogged and doors flung open. He hobbled towards the front of the train, clambered aboard with his suitcase and flowers and battled to pull down one of the windows. He suddenly looked very small and lonely. His oiled hair had sprung loose and his shirt collar was starting to curl.

'Farewell!' he called softly. 'Farewell!'

'Good luck!' I shouted back at him.

And then, as the engine began grinding forward, I realised there was something wrong. There was something missing from his luggage. The typewriter! Yes! How could we have forgotten it? He'd abandoned his ancient mischief-maker.

'Wait!' I bellowed, chasing along the platform as the clanking train curved away from the station. 'Your type-writer!'

He smiled, shook his head and gave a little wave of his hand. 'No matter!' he shouted from the window. 'I trust you'll learn to master it. A small token. A modest gift. You'll find it waiting beneath my bed. Goodbye! Goodbye!'

I stood there and watched him shrinking from view, rushing forward into the daylight. I never saw him again.

42

I STILL HAVE his typewriter. It hasn't been easy to find replacements for those old-fashioned spools of ribbon and the roller is worn and the clattering keys are prone to stick, but I wouldn't trade it for a king's ransom of computer hardware. The machine stands on a little table beneath my window where I like to sit through the long afternoons, gazing down at the yard.

The house was bleak without Marvel. We went into China with polish and dusters, stripped the bed and bullied the carpet. We wiped away his fingerprints and picked stray hairs from the armchair cushions. We left no evidence in the room to suggest that he'd ever existed.

For two or three days we waited for the promised procession of angry restaurateurs. But nothing happened. No one called at the house. The most sinister object that came through the post was a miniature free-sample box of Kellogg's Frosties. We soon began to suspect that Marvel's fears had been nothing more than the rambling thoughts of a lonely man.

We were wrong.

It happened late in the afternoon. It was raining. Father had left the house in search of a haircut. Mother was working in the kitchen, turning chicken scraps into supper.

I was in the front parlour with Senior Franklin, who had stretched himself out in the sofa to shout and swear at the daily papers. He peered at the arts sections with particular contempt. There were rumours that the Dwarf had been nominated once again for the Stanley Butler Prize for Fiction. The rumours had goaded Franklin to new extremes of indignation. Whenever he found an offending snippet, he would tear it from the page, screw it into a soft, grey ball and stuff it into his pencil pot.

'Laurels for the alexic!' he barked. 'His arrogance astonishes. His gulosity astounds!'

The Dwarf's name had also started appearing on Lists. And this marked a new phase in his long and relentless campaign for universal recognition. His latest book had appeared on Big Bertha Mapplethorpe's Fifty Most Important Novels of the Century list compiled for the *Sunday Superior*. He was mentioned in the list of Sexiest Scowlers in the *Wonder Woman* magazine popular readers' poll. He was listed as Man About Town by the *Trumpet Society Supplement* for most appearances at literary cocktail parties in any single calendar month. He was listed in *Scribbler Quarterly* as having produced The Longest Sentence, written in English, in any Modern Work of Fiction. He'd been appointed to the list of the World's Most Dazzling Dentalwork in a vote by the Hollywood Dental School. He'd even been given his own special entry in *The Modern Dictionary of Expletives* as the author of sixteen novel terms of abuse.

These fresh accolades, no matter how trivial, wounded Franklin and served to sharpen his misery. 'I cannot breathe!' he complained. 'I cannot breathe for the stench of him!'

I was sitting in my own armchair, flicking through *Grappler* as rain crackled on the windows. There was a special feature on the Great Kabuki, the lion-faced brawler from Singapore. But it was difficult to concentrate. I kept thinking of Marvel, delivered into Dorothy's arms, and the pair of them walking together along the cliff paths surrounding the cottage. Dorothy taking a sketch book on their rambles through mouldering village churches. Marvel the amateur naturalist, keeping wild flowers in an album. Blackberries in the garden. Cats asleep on the hearth. A romance for Katie Pphart. In my jealous heart I hoped that it might be different. Marvel trapped in his room, defiant and sulking, while Dorothy vainly prayed for him and pushed bible stories under the door. She might be levitating! Floating helpless under the ceiling while Marvel sat on the floor and played with her mooring ropes. It was a crime! She shouldn't be left alone with him. I knew how he felt about Dorothy. I knew that he couldn't be trusted.

My speculations were interrupted by a violent banging on the front door.

Franklin looked startled, gathered up his papers and tried to bury them under the cushions. 'Who is it?' he shouted, as if he expected a sensible answer.

We were constantly under siege from roaming gangs of gaunt strangers selling combs and safety matches, dusters, pens and cleaning fluids. But even they would shrink away from working the streets in such bad weather. So I clambered from my chair and hurried into the hall.

He was large and pale and furious. A pot-bellied brute of a man with incandescent eyes and a bristling ginger moustache. He was wearing a ruined black suit with a satin collar and a drooping bow tie. The rain sprayed from his head and shoulders, splashed from his ears and the tip of his nose. His jacket pockets were flooded and his shoes were waterlogged. He was clutching a frying pan in his fist.

'Bring me Belcher!' he bellowed. 'Bring me Belcher's head on a plate!' He raised his fist and shook the frying pan in my face.

'He doesn't live here!' I shouted, trying to force the door closed again.

'Liar! Pig! Stand aside for justice!'

'Are you the Stuffed Owl?'

'Guilty!' he roared. He swung back his arm and smacked me full in the chest with the edge of the cast-iron pan.

I snapped forward, blinded with pain, and fell to the floor on my knees. I tried to crawl as far as the umbrella stand in some feeble attempt to find a weapon, but the Owl had splashed into the house and now stood over me, wheezing, triumphant, swinging the pan like a pendulum. His shoes puddled the carpet. His glossy black jacket began to steam.

'Where is he hiding? Show me his carcass!'

'He's gone!' I croaked. 'It's the truth!' I was choking so much that I couldn't breathe. My chest was on fire. There were cinders and sparks in my eyes.

'You miserable bowl of tripe! I'll find him for myself!' the Owl said in disgust and made directly for the front parlour.

He found Franklin standing beneath a stained-glass window with his head wrapped up in the curtains.

'Belcher!' he roared. 'Is it Belcher the Scribbler?'

'No!' Franklin shrieked. 'You're mistaken! A moment's weakness. No more than a little foolishness. Forgive a wretched writer's malaise. I meant no harm. I meant no serious injury.'

'You bastard!' the Stuffed Owl bellowed. 'You miserable bullshit bastard!'

Franklin whinnied in terror, broke loose from the curtains and ran to shelter behind an armchair. 'Is this a dagger which I see before me?' he demanded, staring wild-eyed at his assailant. He dashed from one armchair to another. 'Nay, 'tis but a frying pan!' He looked perplexed, frowning at the weapon, as if he'd expected his murderer to carry a sharpened fountain pen.

The Owl stood square in the centre of the room and watched his victim rushing around the walls in search of a nook or cranny, a bolt hole in the chimney, an escape hatch in the floor. 'We've had enough of you and your cheesy comments!' he shouted as Franklin came within range of him. He raised the skull-splitting frying pan and twirled the handle between his fists.

'Don't hit me! I'm dyslexic! I have a suspected heart condition!' Franklin cried, as the Owl took a sudden lunge at him. For a brief moment he made a gallant effort at combat, flapping his hands in a queer sort of paddling movement that only served to annoy his opponent.

'I'll have your blasted head on a plate!' the Owl shouted, whisking the air with the pan. He lashed out and caught the back of Franklin's head, sending him sprawling over the carpet.

Franklin went down and came up again, staggered in circles, clutching his scalp. 'Come, my friable friend, set down your weapon,' he babbled. 'We'll say no more about it. No damage done that can't be mended. Anger is a noble infirmity.'

'Death is too good for you! They should skin you alive and make you suffer! They should pickle your eyes in vinegar! They should push your tongue through a bacon slicer! They should boil down your bollocks for glue!'

'Go, poor devil; get thee gone!' Franklin ranted as he ran about the room. 'Why should I hurt thee?'

The Stuffed Owl grew so enraged by his victim's conceit that he swung the frying pan again and this time chopped with such force that he nearly hacked Franklin's head from his shoulders.

Franklin gasped and dropped to his hands and knees, head hanging loose, exposing his neck for the executioner's blade. He tried to speak but his voice was reduced to a whistle.

'You fancy ball of shit! You disgust me! You turn my stomach! You curdle my guts! You make me heave! You make me want to vomit!'

Franklin's face was scuffed and swollen, an eyebrow had burst and one of his ears looked badly torn. Despite these injuries he managed to drag himself away and propped his shoulders against the wall.

'Wounded, Horatio?' he muttered, dabbing at the blood on his face. 'Ay, past all surgery...' he declared, wiping his fingers against his shirt. 'Thou hast dealt me a mortal blow!' he shouted. 'Enough! Death pays all debts...!'

For some reason these words infuriated his fat tormentor, who began to batter him with increased vigour. 'You dung ball! You badger bait! You boil-in-the-bag! You big girl's blouse!'

Franklin came back to life, shrieking, scrambled away, leapt across tables and chairs and vaulted into the sofa. But his feet broke through the threadbare covers so that he became entangled about the ankles with exploding springs and found himself trapped, buried to the knees in horsehair and rusty wire, and remained there struggling like some tragic monster, half man and half sofa, a doomed creature trapped in a treacherous briar patch.

'Don't hit me!' he bleated, holding his face in his hands. 'I'm an artist! I'm not responsible for my actions. I'm a registered simpleton. A poor buffoon. I'm tuppence short of a tanner!'

The Owl wiped his moustache with a thumb as if the sweet taste of revenge were clinging to its bristles. The sight of so much blood didn't trouble him. His kitchen must have been washed with blood. He had spent half his life gutting and draining animals. He raised the pan for another attack.

'Stop it!' I shouted. 'Leave him alone!' I threw myself at the fat assassin and tried to wrench the pan from his hands.

But he was large and he was terrible. He threw down his buckled weapon, slapped me aside and sent me spinning against a chair. The moment I'd picked myself up he came charging at me, seized me from behind, wrapped a huge arm around my neck and started to throttle me. I twisted. I choked. My throat snapped shut and the blood began to boil in my brain.

And here the tide of battle was turned. He had made a mistake. He was choking a serious wrestling student. I dropped forward, grabbed at his wrist with both hands and by kicking my heel against his ankle, upset his balance to such an extent that his own weight carried him forward over my shoulder and sent him crashing into the floor. It was crude but effective. He hit the ground with such force that he left a dark, damp shadow of himself stamped into the carpet.

He sat up and snorted in surprise. His bow tie sprang from his collar. 'You snivelling snot-shit-shat-ball!' he ranted. 'You snit-snat-shit-shot! You snat-snivel! You shit-shovel! You shittering-snit-snotter!' He seemed more insulted than injured. He sneezed, shook his head, climbed to his feet and flung himself forward.

This time I was prepared for him. I waited until I felt his full weight against my shoulder and then snatched his arm and part of his jacket to bring him around in a perfect cross-buttock counterattack. He turned a somersault and hit a chair, making it jump back in surprise, overturn and throw its legs in the air. He landed with a great shout of rage, thrashed out and rolled beneath the table.

But nothing could stop him. He appeared to be indestructible. 'You snaffling shit-snogger!' he wheezed as he hauled himself upright again. 'You slit-slickering slot slubber!' His shirt had been torn from his ruined pants, revealing a monstrous, dimpled belly.

He staggered to his feet and came towards me for a third time when mother, who had been watching the action from the safety of the door, came squelching into the room, picked up the bloodied frying pan and whacked him smartly over the head. It was simple. She smacked his head and he toppled face-down into the carpet. His legs collapsed. His belly capsized. He let out a small, sad sigh of surrender.

There was silence.

'Are you all right?'

'Yes,' I managed to gasp. 'Nothing broken that can't be mended.'

'What happened?'

'He was trying to kill me!'

She looked at me and frowned. 'You let him have the advantage. You should have taken him out with a belly-to-back suplex and followed him down with a hammerlock,' she complained as she wiped the frying pan with her apron. 'You're hopeless. I've never seen such a clumsy throw!'

'I'm not the Great Muta,' I said.

'And he's not Abdullah the Turk,' she said scornfully, prodding him with her foot.

It was then we remembered Franklin, still sitting knee-deep in sofa, with his eyes closed and bubbles of blood on his chin. His face was a bitter shade of green. His tattered ear was blistered and black.

'He doesn't look quite right,' mother said anxiously.

'It's a miracle he's alive.'

'Do you think it's safe to move him? He's made a nasty mess in these cushions.'

While we stood there gawping, transfixed, father came home, soaked to the bone, stepped into the parlour, stared around him in amazement, groaned, turned about and went back to walk in the rain. We didn't see him again until midnight and by that time we'd restored law and order and scrubbed the blood from the curtains and carpet.

The Owl, once persuaded of his mistake, was a man driven mad by remorse. He wept and gnashed his teeth, he fell on the floor and howled. Despite his own cuts and bruises, he insisted on helping me pull Franklin free from his torture and take him down to the hospital.

43

FRANKLIN WAS UNCONSCIOUS for three days. He lay in an iron bed with his broken head wrapped in bandages. Who can imagine his wonderful dreams? Did he stroll arm in arm with Laurence Sterne or stray farther afield to seek the advice of Tristram Shandy? Did he share a carriage with Daniel Defoe or walk in the sand with Robinson Crusoe? His brain must have bulged with the booming of voices, complaints of Johnson and chatter of Goldsmith. For three days he was lost in the golden city of his own enormous imagination; roaming through another, happier world where George Bernard Shaw had never been born, where John Bunyan wrote bawdy ballads and Smollet was free to send Peregrine Pickle to interfere with Jane Austen, leaving Darcy time to escape and run to the arms of Moll Flanders.

For three long days Franklin slept without stirring. The Owl sent ridiculous hampers of food that were carried away and shared by the nurses. Fresh salmon and smoked oysters. Onion tarts and venison pies. Janet went to visit each evening, forgetting Yoga and Pottery, sitting by Franklin's bed, holding his hand and whispering prayers, begging God to spare his life. She thought he was going to die. She thought she had lost him. When he finally came to his senses he looked at Janet and smiled. He squeezed her hand. Tears of happiness filled his eyes. But it took several days to learn the full extent of the damage.

He was changed. He had been transformed. The bellowing literary giant was slain and Franklin came back to the land of the living in the form of a friendly, half-witted child. Here was a full-blown miracle! His rage had leaked away with his blood and the poison had drained from his system. Nothing remained of his old obsessions. He was now the lonely and frightened creature that he'd always tried so hard to disguise. He was born again and everything was new to him. He appeared astonished by the world, delighted with the universe. He was fascinated by drinking straws, amazed by screwcap bottles and hoarded the plastic knives and forks that came each day with his supper tray.

He stayed in hospital for a month. The surgeons had managed to save his ears and stitch his eyebrows back into place. He didn't look too bad. Towards the end of his treatment I went to visit him with Janet. It was a big city hospital with all the charm of an old Victorian factory. An entrance that would have graced a cathedral plunged the innocent visitor into a maze of gloomy chambers, tunnels and narrow corridors. A world of noise and heat and sorrow, yellow light and stale air. We found the patient sitting in bed with a copy of *Chit-Chat* in his hand. He was wearing a shawl and his father's pyjamas.

'Don't let him know that you're frightened of him,' Janet whispered. 'It seems to upset him…'

'Hello!' I shouted, grinning, as we approached his bed. The room was small and painted green with a cracked handbasin in one corner. The air was charged with the smells of urine and boiled food. The top of his bedside cabinet was littered with plastic bottles, old magazines and half-chewed polystyrene cups.

'Booga!' he burbled at me. 'Booglie bob-jobbah!' And he waved his magazine in greeting. His eyebrows looked enormous, painted with antiseptic and darned with a thick, black thread.

I smiled and nodded encouragement.

'He's happy to see you,' Janet explained, as we settled ourselves into small metal chairs.

'How are you getting along?' I shouted at him. It was a bad habit. I was always shouting at invalids, as if their dis-abilities had driven them deeper into their bodies. 'Is there anything you need?'

'Chooka,' he said. 'Chooka.'

'That's good!' I shouted. 'Let me know if you change your mind.'

'Dim bam blabba!' he protested, rocking himself back and forth in frustration. 'Me chooka!'

'More magazines,' Janet whispered.

'How do you know?'

She shrugged and combed at her hair with her fingers. She looked lovely enough to bite. She was wearing her beauty counter make-up and a new pair of wine-dark high-heeled shoes. Her eyes were shining. Her mouth was wet and swollen. She was radiant with love. 'We just seem to understand each other,' she blushed.

'Hello!' he said, and grinned at me as if he'd seen me for the first time. He beckoned me forward, glanced quickly around the room and then pressed a plastic spoon in my hand.

'Hello!' I said.

'Hello!' he said.

'He says he wants *Hello!* magazine,' Janet said patiently. 'He seems to like looking at pictures of film stars.'

'I'll bring some the next time I visit,' I promised, slipping the spoon in my jacket pocket.

'Bigga job-job!' he burbled. He grew very excited, trampled the pillows with his fists and bounced up and down on the mattress. 'Bugga whiddle! Jim-jam bugga whiddle.'

'You bet!' I said, grinning. 'What did he say?' I whispered to Janet.

'He says he wants to come home.'

44

WE STRIPPED HIS rooms and carefully moved his effects down to China for fear that he'd fall on the attic staircase. He was still very weak and his legs weren't working. China was crowded with towers of books and bundles of papers but Franklin was happy with the confinement. It gave him a sense of security. When we brought him back from the hospital and introduced him to his new quarters he laughed in delight and clapped his hands. He wrapped mother in his arms and covered her face in drooling kisses until she spluttered and pushed him away.

'Oh, lubberly!' he snuffled, wiping his nose in his hand. 'Lubberly lubberly!'

'He likes it,' Janet translated.

'Welcome home!' father shouted at him. 'Do you think he wants a rubber sheet?' he whispered.

'He's perfectly safe,' Janet said, reaching out and squeezing his hand. Franklin beamed and slobbered.

That first night, while he slept secure in his bed, we spent hours in the kitchen, discussing his fate. We didn't know what to do with him. We couldn't cast him into the street but we knew that we couldn't support him.

'It's hopeless,' mother concluded, after reviewing the household budget. She slapped shut the battered exercise book and threw down her pencil in despair. 'We can't afford to feed him.'

'I could look for work,' I volunteered.

'You can't do anything!' father protested. 'You're useless. You big lace hankie. You can't even rewire a radial circuit!'

'I'm a qualified skivvy!' I said indignantly. 'There's always work for a skivvy!' I could cook, clean, wash and wipe. I could scrub, scour and polish. They were fine skills. I was proud of them. There were captains of giant corporations who couldn't tie their own shoelaces. There were stars of stage and screen who couldn't wash their own underwear. Without its army of skivvies the world would quickly be buried beneath a deep crust of dirty laundry.

But we need not have worried. Despite his disability Franklin continued to pay his share of expenses because, as we should have guessed, he had never earned a penny from writing but depended on a generous monthly allowance provided by his absent mother. He now gave his entire allowance to Janet who bought everything he required, paid his rent and kept him supplied with a little regular pocket money that he squandered on biscuits and raspberry sherbet.

Janet became his nurse and companion. She would feed him and wash him and take him for walks. He remained entirely at her mercy. He was alone. His literary friends had deserted him. His enemies had forgotten him. For a long time she was the only person who could understand his bubbling stream of gibberish.

They grew devoted. She would help him to dress in the morning, feed him breakfast, kiss him goodbye and leave him to sit and wait patiently for her return and the pleasure of the evening when, after supper, she would guide him to the best armchair in the front parlour and read aloud from her Katie Pphart romance library. How he loved Katie Pphart! He couldn't get enough of it. He wept at *The Cornflower Chronicle*, whimpered at *Secret Throb of Desire* and became so upset at *The Sultan's Embrace* that Janet never finished the story.

'*Estelle staggered and fell against the glass doors of the fine French bookcase,*' Janet read to him. '*Her intricate white, silk gown had been roughly torn from her perfect shoulders, revealing her pert and trembling breasts. 'I would rather die!' she gasped, her delicate rose-pink nips catching fire, as she watched Farouk the perfumed Arab unbutton his riding breeches. 'That can be arranged,' he said with a throaty chuckle, while he fondled his haughty engorgement…*'

And when he heard these words, Franklin shouted with terror and became so agitated that he had to be taken up to his room and steeped in hot milk and brandy from his favourite pink, plastic, piglet mug.

'Poogle,' he sobbed. 'Nobbly bah-da.'

'It's just a story,' Janet told him, pulling a Kleenex from her sleeve and tenderly wiping the tears from his face.

But Franklin proved too delicate for this mixture of romance and high adventure. He preferred the sentimental tales of true-love lost and love denied. So Janet returned to the more tranquil world where princes fall for waitresses and blind girls marry gifted mutants.

For a time I tried to teach him to read for himself with a pile of *Photo Romance* comics. '*I missed you, Brad darling! What a fool I was to stay with Kent!*' But he stubbornly refused to learn, ignored the captions and speech balloons and started to colour the pictures with crayons.

He developed a passion for biscuits, ice cream and sugar in all its disguises. Pineapple poppers, strawberry bloomers and soft, sticky, liquorice laces.

He lost interest in wearing his dead father's clothes and chose instead to shuffle around the house in yellow pyjamas, red sweaters, green woollen gloves and a knitted hat in a jolly pattern of contrasting stripes. He looked like an orphan from Little Nemo. He didn't care. He was happy to remain a child for the pleasures he found in Janet's arms.

45

WHEN MARVEL FINALLY heard of Franklin's encounter with the Stuffed Owl he wrote a letter of apology to father and sent mother a brand new three-seater sofa in two-tone fake leather. It was delivered by men in uniform from a big department store. The sofa was sealed in a polythene wrapper to protect against damage in transit, and mother never unwrapped it.

'It's brand new!' she declared proudly, whenever she passed through the front parlour. 'It's brand spanking new!' And she'd pause to fondle its heavy flanks. Here was something far beyond her experience. An article in show-room condition, so fresh and clean that it still had attached its printed fire-hazard warning label. It dominated the room like some queer sarcophagus, a gift from a distant galaxy.

'Should we sit on it?' Janet inquired nervously, when the novelty wore thin. We were tired of treating it as a large and delicate obstacle.

'I don't know,' mother said.

'Perhaps we should stay with our chairs,' Janet said quickly, blushing at her own audacity.

'I suppose you can sit if you're careful,' mother announced. 'But try not to wriggle or spoil the cushions.'

'And don't let Franklin piddle on it!' father warned me, convinced that I could control his plumbing in some maleficent manner.

So we sat squirming on the polythene as we tried to make ourselves comfortable. It chilled the backs of our legs in winter and made our buttocks burn in the summer. It gave little farting sounds whenever we left its sticky embrace. But we endured the discomforts because the wrapper was vital evidence that the sofa was new and although the polythene envelope grew brittle and yellow with age, the sofa beneath retained its promise of eternal youth.

A little later mother found heavy plastic runners, which we laid from room to room to protect the carpets from footprints. This worked well enough for the first two or three months but then she noticed that the plastic runners themselves had grown soiled by the work of our shoes. She overcame this difficulty by sewing pairs of soft felt slippers and making us wear them whenever we returned from walking the streets. And so we became skaters, gliding through the house as if the floors had been cut from ice, spinning and turning in loops and circles.

Franklin went skidding from room to room, shrieking and laughing and bruising himself. He never grew tired of this knockabout game. It was wonderful to watch him bouncing from furniture.

Father surprised everyone by proving himself a champion and learning to speedskate from the front door to the back of the kitchen with his arms loaded with groceries. But life was easier for him. When he grew tired of the exercise he could always abandon his slippers and creep downstairs to the filth of the cellar.

Mother, her Reeboks wrapped up in dusters, found her feet grown so huge and heavy that she couldn't lift them from the floor and had to be content to push herself around the room in a sort of soft shoe shuffle.

Janet took the changes in her stride. At the earliest opportunity she enrolled for Dancing at night class and soon perfected her pirouettes on the ice sheet that once had been Wilton.

Tradesmen and neighbours, unfamiliar with the slippery nature of felt slippers, were prone to hair-raising accidents and refused to enter the house. But mother had no regrets – visitors were an unwelcome source of dirt and disease. They raised the dust. They shed hair and skin on the furnishings. They were dangerous. They were held in quarantine at the front door where I was made to interview them through a transparent plastic curtain.

And so we continued.

Mother retired to the back parlour where she settled each day to watch the wrestling tournaments. Once the house had been sealed there were fewer and fewer excuses for housework. She seemed content. I began to notice, for the first time, how quickly she was growing old. Her dark eyes were cloudy and faded. She was shrinking beneath her cardigans. But she could still summon the energy to bellow at referees. Wrestling retained its magic by constantly renewing itself. Old favourites were replaced by fresh champions. Heroes were disgraced and villains turned into deities with comforting regularity.

Father returned to the cellar where, after many experiments, he found himself on the brink of inventing the all-purpose household cleaner, disinfectant and stain digester. Another revolution in modern home comforts. It was a long and difficult task. The fluid he brewed proved so virulent that it melted his plastic mixing bowls and, even diluted one part to a thousand, retained the strength to damage brickwork and kill small animals with its fumes.

Janet grew fat with confidence. She was swelling softly into a matron. A plump and freckled beauty with framed qualifications in the art of make up and pedicures. Franklin remained in her perfumed arms and seemed to enjoy being mauled. He grew to resemble a large rag doll. He finally learned to dress himself, despite having trouble with hooks and buttons, and even mastered a spoon and fork. But Janet alone understands his language.

I've managed a few rudimentary phrases. When Janet goes to work in the mornings, Franklin will trail me around the house with his chin shiny with slobber and his slippers slapping against his heels. I do nothing to encourage him but he seems to enjoy my company.

'Lubberly ouja!' he says, pointing at his mouth. 'Lubberly ouja!'

And I know enough to feed him chocolate milk and biscuits.

The year after the sofa, Marvel wrote to announce his marriage to Dorothy. He sent back the bible. We were astounded. No one believed that he had the power to shake her faith and yet his corrupting influence had proved so strong that she'd lost her interest in marching for Jesus. She'd also lost the power to levitate with her sudden fall from grace and one night had asked Marvel to toss her Glad Tidings catalogue into the sea. They'd stood holding hands on the harbour wall to watch the catalogue tossed on the tide and her guilt was washed away with its pages. Here finally was something to celebrate. God, in His mercy, had set her free.

I've given a lot of thought to my time in her bible classes. And looking back at those events, I've come to believe I was badly treated. It's not my guilt that I question but, rather, her protests of innocence. We were equally matched in our passion and, in the bold quest for martyrdom, the saint is required to choose a tormentor. Saint and sinner. There's nothing between them.

She loved Mr Marvel. No doubt about it. She loved his simple, blunt honesty. Whatever faith she felt she had lost, it was more than returned by the faith that Marvel had found in himself. And I think he loved Dorothy for her energy and enthusiasm. Whatever she had given to the New York Bible Tract Company, she now gave to the pleasures of life. They had plans to open a seaside restaurant. Boiled crabs and lobsters. Shrimps, whelks and winkles. Everything served with brown bread and butter. Good, plain food and plenty of it.

Their wedding photographs show Marvel grinning in a rented suit with his bride, bashful in taffeta, standing tall beside him. Dorothy wears her most ravishing smile as the sunlight sparks on her spectacles. They are standing in a little country churchyard on a bright, cold, winter's day.

They are holding hands. Behind their heads the sun hangs like a halo in the branches of the empty trees. They look so pleased with themselves. They look foolish with happiness.

And what became of Mr Romance?

He became Sophie Appleyard, aka Patricia Pavan. In the solitude of his room he began tapping out romantic novels on the abandoned mischief-maker. It was difficult in the beginning but the long, slow-burning years of smothered desires, fumbling advance and tumbling retreat, have proved the perfect apprenticeship for writing tales of true love lost and love denied. The agony of fascination, anticipation and swift rejection have seasoned me for the task of weaving a world of sweet deceit. A world where nothing exists but the struggle to love and be loved. A comforting world where women are wonderful, warm and wise and all the men are strong but stupid.

The books have been a great success. They are sold in stations and supermarkets, hospitals, hotels and distant airports. You'll find them everywhere. They are regular Cupid Book Club specials, recommended for holidays, short excursions and wet weekends. The names may be unfamiliar but you'd recognise the lurid covers of brave and struggling beauties trapped in the arms of dangerous men.

The Appleyard books are lit by gaslight, packed with bustles and powdered bosoms. Women swoon in royal ballrooms, men ride to hound in high boots and ribbons, and gypsies gather to copulate in all the surrounding barns and orchards. The heroines are easily named Emma, Jane and Elizabeth. They have wonderfully clear complexions, dancing smiles and bright, intelligent eyes. They play the piano beautifully and make clever conversation.

Patricia Pavan takes the modern approach, preferring to write the big, brawling bra-busters. Her women are high-flown executives haunted by terrible family secrets, childhood sweethearts and pinhead fathers. They have names like Cordie, Monsoon and Mercedes. They wear lavish amounts of jewellery and French silk underwear and make love to men with unlikely names in ridiculous situations. Bank vaults, pyramids and nuclear submarines. Novelty is everything. And it's as Patricia Pavan that my true identity has been most jealously guarded, since if it were known that these 'highly polished erotic tales for the modern, independent woman' were written by a brute of a man they'd be seized and condemned as pornography.

It's a peculiar occupation. A solitary life. Sophie Appleyard and Patricia Pavan will never be nominated for the Stanley Butler Prize for Fiction. They are never invited to festivals, writers' suppers or literary lunches. They're never seen at Grouchers. Their books escape the attention of the mighty Polenta Hartebeest. But we're happy enough. We have no complaints. I'm not ashamed of our work.

Mother collects the books without bothering to read them. I think she likes the bright foil jackets. Father, for reasons I've never entirely fathomed, is convinced that I write adventure yarns and brags about me constantly to his cronies at the back of North Street Market.

Janet reads my work for the thrill of knowing that she shares the house with their authors. She seems to enjoy in particular the stories of Sophie Appleyard. I suppose she likes her passions stirred beneath the shelter of petticoats. She reads the books to Franklin who listens to them with something approaching his Katie Pphart rapture.

'Bimberly poojah!' he burbles. 'Dubberly pinjam!'

I confess that I've grown to dislike Katie Pphart in the way that Franklin despised the Dwarf, but I won't let myself feel smothered by hatred. I try to ignore her photograph twinkling from posters in bookshop windows. The powder-puff hair and ridiculous earrings. I do my best to forget that she never fails to win the annual Crystal Rose for services to women's fiction. I am not daunted by her reputation. I will not be dismayed that her prose must now be endured in thirty different languages, including Pacific Pidgin and Hebrew. Whenever vanity threatens to strike, I take care to remember Marvel's crusade against humbug and bumfoolery.

My books are romantic entertainments. They provide the money we need to take care of our security. It's not a fortune but more than enough to keep the roof above our heads and grant me some small indulgences. A new silk blouse. A cashmere skirt. A pair of fancy, red, satin shoes. And sometimes, when the afternoons are dark and the house is quiet and rain comes down to lash at the windows, I sit in my room with my elbows propped on the polythene-covered writing desk and try to imagine what might have happened if our lives had been different.

But that's another story.

Also by Miles Gibson, published by THE DO-NOT PRESS

The Sandman

'I am the Sandman. I am the butcher in soft rubber gloves. I am the acrobat called death. I am the fear in the dark. I am the gift of sleep....'

Growing up in a small hotel in a shabby seaside town, Mackerel Burton has no idea that he is to grow up to become a slick and ruthless serial killer. A lonely boy, he amuses himself by perfecting his conjuring tricks, but slowly the magic turns to a darker kind, and soon he finds himself stalking the streets of London in search of random and innocent victims. He has become The Sandman.

'A splendidly macabre achievement. As an account of a descent into homicidal mania, it has seldom been bettered'
Time Out

'Confounds received notions of good taste – unspeakable acts are reported with an unwavering reasonableness essential to the comic impact and attesting to the deftness of Gibson's control'
Times Literary Supplement

Dancing With Mermaids

'Murder and mayhem decked out in fantastic
and erotic prose'
The Times

Strange things are afoot in the Dorset fishing town of
Rams Horn.

Set close to the poisonous swamps at the mouth of the
River Sheep, the town has been isolated from its neighbours for centuries.

But mysterious events are unfolding... A seer who has
waited for years for her drowned husband to reappear is
haunted by demons, an African sailor arrives from the sea
and takes refuge with a widow and her idiot daughter.
Young boys plot sexual crimes and the doctor, unhinged by
his desire for a woman he cannot have, turns to a medicine
older than his own.

'An imaginative tour de force and a considerable stylistic achievement. When it comes to
pulling one into a world of his own making,
Gibson has few equals among his contempo-
raries.'
Time Out

'A wild, poetic exhalation that sparkles and
hoots and flies.'
The New Yorker

Kingdom Swann

'Wonderful fun. Read this delightfully comic book'

The Daily Mail

Kingdom Swann is a delicious fantasy by one of our most exuberantly imaginative novelists, a comic foray into the sub-world of Victorian and Edwardian pornography and the double standards that marked art and life. Rumbustuous and bawdy, it imagines the red-hot reality behind the coy sepia nudes of ninety years ago.

'With enormous relish Gibson presents a memorable and hugely enjoyable portrait of… a world in which the double standard abounded.'

Daily Mail

Kingdom Swann, Victorian master of the epic nude painting turns to photography and finds himself recording the erotic fantasies of a generation through the eye of the camera.

A disgraceful tale of murky morals and unbridled matrons in a world of Suffragettes, flying machines and the shadow of war.

Art has come to life and all hell is breaking loose…

'As in Daniel Defoe's Roxanna, a voyeuristic fascination plays games with high morality

The Times

Also by Miles Gibson, published by THE DO-NOT PRESS

Vinegar Soup

'Savagely black comedy along Evelyn Waugh
lines with its merriments even kinkier'
The Observer

Gilbert Firestone, fat and fifty, works in the kitchen of the
Hercules Café and dreams of travel and adventure. When
his wife drowns in a pan of soup he abandons the kitchen
and takes his family to start a new life in a jungle hotel in
Africa. But rain, pygmies and crazy chickens start to turn
his dreams into nightmares. And then the enormous
Charlotte arrives with her brothel on wheels.
An epic romance of true love, travel and food...

'As though Martin Amis had been written by
Henry Green and David Cook'
The Times Literary Supplement

'Gibson writes with a nervous versatility that
is often very funny and never lacks a life of its
own, speaking the language of our times as
convincingly as aerosol graffiti'
The Guardian

Also published by THE DO-NOT PRESS

First of the True Believers
by Paul Charles

'The Autobiography of Theodore Hennessy'

ISBN 1899344 78 0 paperback (£7.50)
ISBN 1899344 79 9 hardcover (£15.00)

THE BEATLES formed in 1959 and became the biggest group in the world. Among other less celebrated Merseybeat groups of the time were The Nighttime Passengers, led by Theo Hennessy, who almost replaced Pete Best as drummer of the 'Fab Four'.

First of The True Believers tells of a decade in the life of Theodore Hennessy, intertwined with the story of The Beatles. It begins in 1959 with his first meeting with the beautiful and elusive Marianne Burgess and follows their subsequent on-off love affair and his rise as a musician.

The Beatles provided the definitive soundtrack to the '60s, and here novelist and musicologist Paul Charles combines their phenomenal story with a tender-hearted tale of sex, love and rock 'n' roll in '60s Liverpool.

Kiss Me Sadly
by Maxim Jakubowski

A daring new novel from the 'King of the erotic thriller'
Time Out

ISBN 1899344 87 X   paperback (£6.99)
ISBN 1899344 88 8   hardcover (£15.00)

Two parallel lives: He is a man who loves women too much, but still seeks to fill the puzzling emptiness that eats away at his insides

She grows up in an Eastern European backwater, in a culture where sex is a commodity and surviving is the name of the game.

They travel down separate roads, both hunting for thrills and emotions. Coincidence brings them together. The encounter between their respective brands of loneliness is passionate, heartbreaking, tender and also desolate. Sparks fly and lives are changed forever, until a final, shocking, epiphany.

Also published by THE DO-NOT PRESS

Double Take
by Mike Ripley

Double Take: The novel and the screenplay (the funniest caper movie never made) in a single added-value volume.

ISBN 1899344 81 0 paperback (£6.99)
ISBN 1899344 82 9 hardcover (£15.00)

Double Take tells how to rob Heathrow and get away with it (enlist the help of the police). An 'Italian Job' for the 21st century, with bad language – some of it translated – chillis as offensive weapons, but no Minis. It also deconstructs one of Agatha Christie's most audacious plots.

The first hilarious stand-alone novel from the creator of the best-selling Angel series.

Pick Any Title
by Russell James

RUSSELL JAMES is Chairman of the CRIME WRITERS' ASSOCIATION 2001-2002

PICK ANY TITLE is a magnificent new crime caper involving sex, humour sudden death and double-cross.

ISBN 1899344 83 7 paperback (£6.99)
ISBN 1899344 84 5 hardcover (£15.00)

'Lord Clive' bought his lordship at a 'Lord of the Manor' sale where titles fetch anything from two to two hundred thousand pounds. Why not buy another cheap and sell it high? Why stop at only one customer? Clive leaves the beautiful Jane Strachey to handle his American buyers, each of whom imagines himself a lord.

But Clive was careless who he sold to, and among his victims are a shrewd businessman, a hell-fire preacher and a vicious New York gangster. When lawyers pounce and guns slide from their holsters Strachey finds she needs more than good looks and a silver tongue to save her life.

A brilliant page-turner from 'the best of Britain's darker crime writers'
The Times

The Do-Not Press

Fiercely Independent Publishing

Keep in touch with what's happening at the cutting edge of independent British publishing.

Simply send your name and address to:
The Do-Not Press (Dept. MR)
16 The Woodlands, London SE13 6TY (UK)

or email us: mr@thedonotpress.co.uk

There is no obligation to purchase
(although we'd certainly like you to!)
and no salesman will call.

Visit our regularly-updated web site:

http://www.thedonotpress.co.uk

Mail Order

All our titles are available from good bookshops, or (in case of difficulty) direct from The Do-Not Press at the address above. There is no charge for post and packing for orders to the UK and EU.

(NB: A post-person may call.)